FINLAY DONOVAN
DIGS HER OWN GRAVE

ALSO BY ELLE COSIMANO

Finlay Donovan Is Killing It

Finlay Donovan Knocks 'Em Dead

Finlay Donovan Jumps the Gun

Finlay Donovan Rolls the Dice

"Veronica Ruiz Breaks the Bank" (e-short story)

YOUNG ADULT NOVELS

Nearly Gone

Holding Smoke

The Suffering Tree

Seasons of the Storm

FINLAY DONOVAN DIGS HER OWN GRAVE

ELLE COSIMANO

MINOTAUR
BOOKS
NEW YORK

First published in the United States by Minotaur Books, an imprint of St. Martin's Publishing Group.

www.minotaurbooks.com

Designed by Omar Chapa

The Library of Congress Cataloging-in-Publication Data is available upon request.

ISBN 978-1-250-33734-4 (hardcover)
ISBN 978-1-250-38997-8 (international edition, sold outside the U.S., subject to rights availability)
ISBN 978-1-250-33735-1 (ebook)

First U.S. Edition: 2025
First International Edition: 2025

10 9 8 7 6 5 4 3 2 1

To the booksellers and librarians,
for all you do

FINLAY DONOVAN DIGS HER OWN GRAVE

PROLOGUE

The stern-faced woman stared down her nose at me, her solid black smock dress and crisp white collar framed by the regal arms of her leather chair. The fingers of her left hand closed around a fancy Montblanc pen. Her right fist rested on my open file like a gavel, each letter of my last name printed sideways on the tab. "Do you have anything to say, Ms. Donovan?" Her narrowed eyes pinned me to my seat, reading me like a rap sheet across her wide mahogany desk.

He had it coming was probably not the answer she was looking for. "This entire situation has been blown out of proportion," I said as she took notes with harsh strokes of her pen. It was impossible to come off like a badass while I was down here and she was up there.

"The evidence speaks for itself."

"What evidence?" I inched higher in my chair, trying to read her terse scribbles from my disadvantaged position.

"We have two witnesses to the assault."

"Assault?" I held up a finger (not the one I wanted to raise), cutting her off. If she was going to conduct a trial and lay down a sentence, I'd be damned if I'd let her do it without putting on a defense. "That's a very serious accusation to level at a person."

"The victim suffered injuries that required treatment by a physician."

"It was only a few stitches."

"And two bruised ribs," she added without looking up.

"I already said I'd be willing to cover his medical costs."

"You can't just buy your way out of this, Ms. Donovan. You said it yourself, assault is a serious accusation. If I were to let this go with a warning, I'd be setting a dangerous precedent."

"But this wasn't an assault! It was self-defense," I insisted, fighting the urge to demonstrate the difference. "Whatever the outcome, Cooper provoked it. The situation clearly called for a response, and he got one. Unwanted touching is *also* an assault," I pointed out.

Her eyes lifted from the file, meeting mine over the rims of her glasses. "*That* would be blowing the situation out of proportion."

I put my hands on my hips. Or rather I would have, if the arms of my chair had allowed me to. "If you were in the same shoes, what would you have done?"

"I would have reported it to someone with the authority to handle the situation."

"Handle it how? With another slap on the wrist? He's a repeat offender!"

"Violence is never the answer, Ms. Donovan. Please sit down." She pointed a sharp finger at the small wooden chair I'd been relegated to.

I glanced down at myself, surprised to find I was indeed standing up.

I folded myself back into my seat.

The woman took off her glasses. She set them on her desk with an aggrieved sigh. Her weary lids made slow blinks, as if she hoped I might disappear between them. "Rules are rules, Ms. Donovan, and it's my job to enforce them. I've spoken with Cooper's mother about his behavior on the playground, and she has assured me the hair pulling will not continue."

I glanced sideways at Delia. Her head hung between her hunched shoulders, the short, downy ends of her blond pigtails still noticeably uneven after she'd cut her own hair a few short months ago, mussed where Cooper had, according to Delia, repeatedly grabbed them. Her hands were tucked shamefully under her thighs, her tiny legs dangling from the edge of the chair she'd been perched on while she'd waited for me to pick her up after the principal had called me.

"Fine," I said, ready to put the entire ordeal behind us. "I'll have a similar talk with Delia about her behavior when we get home."

Mrs. Carmichael, the preschool principal, gave a stern nod. "I expect you will. Cooper's mother has filed a formal complaint. Given the extent of her son's injuries, she's expecting the school to take a hard stance. I'm going to have to ask you to keep Delia home for the next two weeks."

I leapt up again, the child-size chair clinging stubbornly to my hips. "You're suspending her!"

"Would you rather she be expelled?"

We both turned as her office door flew open behind me. My children's nanny burst in, her lungs heaving as if she'd run the full five miles from my house to get here. Her hair was wild where it had come loose from her long ponytail, and her cheeks were red with exertion. She clutched my naked two-year-old son to her side, his dimpled butt hanging over her arm. "Thank god," she said when she spotted Delia sitting penitently beside me.

The principal scowled at Vero. "Who are you?"

"This is Veronica Ruiz, my nanny," I explained.

"I came as soon as I got the message," Vero said, ignoring the principal's disapproving look. "Is Delia okay? I was in the bathroom with Zach when the school called. All they said is that someone was hurt." She rushed to Delia's side and sank down on her haunches until she was eye level with both of us, checking my daughter for injuries.

"Delia's fine," I said, taking Zach from her and resting him in my lap. The pint-size seat didn't leave room for his pudgy legs, so I turned him around and propped him on my knees. He beamed at the principal. She grimaced as every part of him wiggled in his relentless effort to get down. I set him on the floor to keep him from pitching a fit. He stood obediently beside my chair, momentarily content, beaming at the principal as he tugged on his tiny penis.

Vero threw her arms around Delia, prodding every inch of her, just to be sure she wasn't injured. "What happened?"

"Cooper was pulling Delia's hair on the playground. She asked him to stop, and he didn't, so she defended herself." I threw a pointed look at her principal. The school might be holding Delia responsible, but I knew exactly where the blame for this fell, and it wasn't on my daughter.

Vero glowed with pride. "That's my girl!" She held up a hand for a high five. I pulled it down before Delia could slap it. She might be the victim of a miscarriage of justice, but we didn't need to invite any more punishment.

I covered my eyes, swearing quietly as my ex-husband's voice boomed in the lobby. "Delia! Where's my daughter? Is she back there? Back off, lady," Steven shouted. "If my daughter's in there, I'm going in and you can't stop me!" He rushed past the front desk and through the open office door, blue eyes blazing and mud flaking from his work boots.

"Great," Vero muttered. "What the H-E-double pumpers is he doing here?"

"What's a double pumper?" Delia asked.

"Never mind," I said.

"We'll discuss it when we get home," Vero added helpfully.

"What's going on?" Steven asked, as breathless and red-faced as Vero had been when she'd burst in. "Why'd the school call my office? And why is Zach naked?"

"Potty training," I said. Steven looked confused. "Vero saw some boot camp on the internet that's supposed to guarantee success in three days. You take off their clothes and keep them close to the toilet."

"Is it working?"

We all turned as Zach began peeing on the carpet. The principal gasped. I gritted my teeth.

"Guess that answers that," Steven said.

Vero flashed a middle finger at him behind Delia's back.

The principal stared sternly at all of us. "Need I remind you that you are in a school? We are models for young minds here. I'll ask you both to show some decorum!"

Steven frowned at his mud-spattered flannel and the dirt-caked toes of his work boots.

Vero tossed a fresh diaper over the puddle on the floor and used the toe of her shoe to blot up the wet spot.

The principal closed her eyes, lips pressed between her teeth as if it was all she could do to hold back a retort. She reached inside her desk drawer for a bottle of ibuprofen and shook two tablets into the palm of her hand as Steven helped me out of my pint-sized chair and pulled me aside. "I was walking lots with a developer when the school called," he said in a low voice. "I got here as soon as I got the message. They said they needed someone to come down to the school right away. What's going on? Is Delia okay?"

Steven's forehead crumpled as I explained. "A boy named Cooper has been harassing Delia on the playground. She gave him six stitches and a couple of bruised ribs."

Zach giggled when Steven's eyebrows shot up.

"And then I kicked him in the tentacles," Delia said, "just like Vero showed me."

Steven's chest swelled like a Little League coach whose star player just took home a trophy. He offered Vero a tentative salute. She answered it with an almost conciliatory nod as she tossed the wet diaper in the trash can. My god, were they actually agreeing on something?

"What?" they asked in unison as I looked back and forth between them.

"Delia's been suspended from school," I said sharply.

Steven swore the equivalent of a double pumper, and Vero covered Delia's ears.

Mrs. Carmichael nearly gouged out her own eye in her hurry to put her glasses back on. She signed her name to the bottom of a disciplinary action report and pushed it across the desk toward me. "I see now where Delia has learned to model this kind of behavior. I'll ask Cooper's mother to send you a copy of the medical bills. You can collect Delia's belongings from her cubby before you leave."

Delia's lower lip began to wobble. I picked up Zach and settled him on my hip, then took my daughter's hand and helped her down from her seat. Steven snatched the report off the principal's desk, crumpled it up, and tossed it in the trash. Vero gave the principal a heavy dose of side-eye as I led our entourage out the door.

There was no way this day could get any worse, but I knew how to make it tolerable. "Come on, everyone," I said. "We're going out for ice cream."

CHAPTER 1

Vero and I herded the children upstairs for baths right after dinner, hoping to get the kids down for an early bedtime. Then Vero took Zach to his room, singing silly songs to hold his attention and keep him still while she wrangled him into his pajamas. I drew back Delia's comforter and tucked her into bed. Her eyelids were heavy, still swollen from her crying jag hours ago, after we had left her principal's office and emptied her cubby at school.

"Mommy," she said, playing with a loose lock of hair that had slipped free of my elastic band, "do you still love me?"

I kissed the thoughtful wrinkle in her brow. "I'll always love you, Delia. More than anything in this world."

"Even when I do something bad?"

I tucked her stuffed unicorn under her arm and pulled the blanket over both of them. "Making a mistake doesn't make you a bad person, sweetie. There is nothing you could do that would make me love you any less."

"But Daddy did something bad, and you don't love *him* anymore."

Vero stopped singing in the next room.

"Who told you that?" I asked.

"Cooper. He said Daddy is a cheater. I told Cooper my daddy *never* cheats when we play board games. But Cooper said he heard his mommy talking to Dylan's mommy at the bus stop, and they called Daddy a cheating bag of dirt." The crinkles in Delia's tiny forehead deepened. "I tried to ignore him, like you told me to, but he just pulled my hair and kept saying it."

"Cooper shouldn't have said that. And neither should his mother." The women in our neighborhood loved to gossip, but discussing Steven's infidelities at the bus stop took gossiping a step too far. "Your father is a good man and a wonderful daddy."

"But Daddy said it, too. He said he did something bad and that's why you don't want to be married to him anymore."

A lump formed in my throat. I settled down onto the edge of Delia's bed beside her, struggling to come up with the right way to explain the nature of my evolving relationship with her philandering father to my five-year-old without saying more than she was ready to hear. "Just because your dad and I aren't married anymore doesn't mean I don't love him. I love your daddy very much—"

A muffled cough that sounded suspiciously like *bullshit* permeated the wall of Zach's room.

I bit down hard and forced myself to smile. "—even if he made some very . . . very big mistakes."

"Then why can't Daddy live with us?" She picked at a thread in her frayed unicorn as I looked around her room at the frilly, pink curtains and watercolor rainbows and hanging kitten posters, searching for an answer.

"You love your brother, right?" I asked. Delia nodded. "You still love him even when he does things that make you angry, but you get along better with him when you each have your own room."

"Like when he pooped in the bathtub and it made me cry, and now I don't have to take baths with him anymore?"

"Exactly like that."

"So now you take baths with Nick?"

Vero stifled a cackle. I resisted the urge to smack the wall.

"Yes . . . I mean *no*!" Detective Nicholas Anthony and I had only started dating a few weeks ago. We'd shared a bed (several times) but never a bathtub. "What I mean to say, Delia, is that just because your brother did something that made you angry doesn't mean you love him any less. Because when you love someone, you love them no matter what."

"Even when they poop in the tub?"

I fought back a grin. "Even when they poop in the tub."

"Do grown-ups get in trouble?" she asked after a thoughtful pause.

A laugh broke free. Steven had made far worse mistakes in far bigger bathtubs. For that matter, so had I. "Grown-ups get in the most trouble of all," I said through a heavy sigh. "The important thing is we say we're sorry and learn from our mistakes. And we try to do better the next time." One day, maybe I'd start following my own advice.

I smoothed the comforter around her and stood to go.

"If I say sorry, can I go back to school tomorrow?" she asked as I switched off the light.

"Not tomorrow, sweetie."

"Then what will we do?"

"I don't know." That was a problem for future me. Present me had laundry to do, bills to pay, a house to clean, and a new book to write. Tomorrow, we would do what we always did. "We'll figure something out."

When the kids had both finally drifted off to sleep, I slumped onto the sofa beside Vero with a pile of take-out menus, too exhausted from the events of the last few hours to even think about cooking. We'd taken the kids out for ice cream after our meeting with Delia's principal, then Steven had gone back to work and we had spent the rest of the day at the park. The kids had been exhausted by the time we got home. We'd fed them an early dinner of frozen chicken nuggets and instant mashed potatoes and given them both a bath; neither one of them had the energy to protest when we'd tucked them in for an early bedtime.

"What do you want for dinner?" I asked, thumbing through the menus.

"Chocolate," Vero said.

"We had ice cream for lunch. We can't have chocolate for dinner."

"Then booze."

I was about to object to that choice, too, but on second thought, it wasn't the worst idea she'd ever had. It was Thursday night, which meant the week was almost over. Steven would pick up the kids for the weekend after work tomorrow, and I could look forward to a quiet weekend at home, watching TV in my pajamas. And we definitely deserved a few indulgences after the day we'd had.

There was a knock at the door.

"I'll get it!" Vero looked a little too eager when she jumped up from the couch to see who it was.

Curious, I set down my take-out menu and followed her to the door. Stacey Pickens stood on my front stoop. Stacey lived two streets down from us and had three kids at the local elementary school. She was active in the PTA, the HOA, the BSA, and all the other A's, which were mostly dominated by the same moms who churned the community rumor mill.

"Delivery!" she sang. She held a brown paper bag over the threshold. Vero took it with greedy hands, peeked inside, and crushed the top closed again as I came into the foyer.

"How much do I owe you?" she whispered to Stacey.

"Twenty even," Stacey said, not bothering to lower her voice. "I wasn't sure how much stimulation you were looking for, so I went with something with a little extra *oomph*." I raised an eyebrow, wondering what Vero and Javi were up to. Stacey had a home-based business selling marital aids out of the back of her station wagon. Her products came in inconspicuous boxes and bags, but while Stacey's packaging was discreet, Stacey was not. Vero slapped my hand away when I tried to get a look. "Need anything for yourself, Finlay? I'm running a special this month on lube. I've got a few new flavors if you want to try some samples."

"Thanks," I said politely, "but I'm all set."

"You sure? The ladies at the bus stop were all buzzing about some hot cop they saw leaving your house the other morning."

I bit my tongue, hoping they hadn't been so loose-lipped in front of their kids. "I'm sure."

"Speaking of cops, does your new boyfriend have any idea when they're going to take down the police tape across the street? I know it's only been a week since they found the body at Mrs. Haggerty's place, but the Patels are getting ready to put their house on the market and they're worried the whole crime-scene vibe will make it harder to sell. I told them I'd ask you and see if you knew anything."

"I don't," I said, not only because I refused to contribute to the gossip in the neighborhood, but because I honestly had no idea. "Vero and I were out of town for a while. We missed the whole ordeal," I explained. We had returned from Atlantic City just in time to see the police arrest my elderly neighbor after human remains had been discovered in her yard. Mrs. Haggerty was president of the neighborhood watch and our community's biggest busybody. Since I wasn't Mrs. Haggerty's biggest fan, I hadn't troubled myself with the details of the crime. All I knew is that the body had been taken away and so had Mrs. Haggerty. Truthfully, I didn't mind the yellow police tape if it meant I no longer had to worry about living across the street from the woman who had nothing better to do than binge-watch my dumpster fire of a life and document it all in her neighborhood watch diary for her own entertainment.

If Mrs. Haggerty had murdered someone, she was exactly where she belonged—in jail.

"Poor Arlene was traumatized," Stacey said. "She saw the whole thing from her bedroom window after that ice storm we had. Mrs. Haggerty must have forgotten to winterize her sprinkler system in her garden and a pipe burst. Arlene noticed the pooling in her yard and knocked on the door, but no one was home, so she called an emergency plumber to stop the flooding. He came with a digger to find the broken pipe, and that's when he found the body." Stacey shuddered.

According to Nick and my sister, Georgia, who were both cops in the next county over, the body had been badly decomposed and had been carted off to the crime lab for identification.

"Have they figured out who he was yet?" Vero asked.

Stacey nodded. "From his dental records. His name was Gilford Dupree."

"Why does that name sound familiar?" I asked. "Did he live here in South Riding?"

Stacey shook her head. "Remember that news story about the forty-five-year-old mortgage broker who went missing from Ashburn five years ago? The one who left for work one morning and they found his abandoned car at Ashburn Park? It was him."

Ashburn Village was less than thirty minutes away, but as far as I knew, Mrs. Haggerty didn't get out much. "How did he know Mrs. Haggerty?" I asked.

"That's the weird thing," Stacey said. "He didn't."

Vero looked confused. "If they didn't know each other, why'd she kill him?"

Stacey blinked at us. "Haven't you heard the news?"

"What news?" Vero asked.

"It's been all over the TV. The prosecutors dropped the charges today and told her she was free to go. Every network has been reporting it since they released her this afternoon."

A horn honked in the driveway. "I've got to go," Stacey said. "David's a little on edge and he's waiting in the car. He insisted on driving me to my deliveries. Says he doesn't want me walking alone in the neighborhood after dark with some unknown killer on the loose. I mean, for all we know it could be one of the other neighbors! Can you imagine?" She waggled her fingers in farewell. "You two ladies be safe, and keep that handsome detective of yours close, Finlay. If you change your mind about placing an order, you know where to find me." With a wink, she was gone.

I closed the door and locked the dead bolt, feeling a little creeped out.

"I need a drink," Vero said, carrying her brown bag with her to the kitchen.

I gathered up the take-out menus and put them back in the drawer. On second thought, chocolate and booze didn't sound like such a terrible idea. I poured a glass of bourbon for each of us and broke open a package of Oreos while Vero rummaged in the freezer and came back with a tub of Cool Whip. We carried it all to the living room. Vero turned on the TV and changed the channel to the evening news.

"Look," she said, "there she is."

The ticker scrolled across the bottom of the screen: *Suspect in Loudoun County homicide case released from custody.*

The news camera panned to a reporter, the Loudoun County Police Department building forming the backdrop behind her. *"According to the Commonwealth's Attorney's Office, all charges against the suspect have been dismissed in light of new evidence, which was discovered by investigators over the last twenty-four hours. Eighty-one-year-old Margaret Haggerty, the owner of the home where the body of Gilford Dupree was discovered a week ago, was released from jail earlier this evening after police confirmed she had no known connection to the victim. A spokesperson for the Loudoun County Police Department says investigators are already pursuing a promising new lead . . ."*

The camera cut away to a prerecorded clip of my elderly neighbor being escorted from the police station under the arm of her grandson, Brendan. A reporter thrust a microphone in his face. Brendan's smile was polite but tight as he shuffled his grandmother to his waiting car. "My grandmother has been through a terrible ordeal," he said. "We're grateful to put this injustice behind us, and we wish the Commonwealth's Attorney and the investigators a speedy resolution to this complicated case. Thank you. No further questions."

Vero frowned and turned the TV off. "They found a dead guy buried in her backyard, and they're just letting her go?"

"Whatever new evidence they have must be pretty compelling."

"Do you think she'll come home?"

"Would you?" The woman was an eighty-one-year-old widow who lived alone and she'd just spent a week in jail because someone had buried a body in her rose garden. "I wouldn't blame her if she never wanted to come back."

"Maybe we'll get lucky and she won't," Vero grumbled. "Living across the street from that woman creeps me out. She's seen too much. I don't trust her."

I had harbored a strong dislike for Mrs. Haggerty since she blew the whistle on my ex-husband, after documenting his extramarital relationships with our real estate agent more than a year ago, but it was what my neighbor might have witnessed in the last five months that disturbed me most of all. Vero and I couldn't be sure how much Mrs. Haggerty had seen the night Harris Mickler was murdered in my garage. I'd never intended to get involved when his wife tried to hire me to kill him, but when someone else left me holding the body, Vero and I had panicked. We'd buried Harris on my ex-husband's farm and pinned the whole thing on the Russian mob, but that hadn't been the end of it. Harris Mickler's murder had set off a chain reaction of unthinkable events. Vero and I had spent the last five months finding bodies, hiding bodies, and trying to figure out who had murdered those bodies. Somehow, the two of us had survived it all unscathed, but I wasn't foolish enough to assume we were in the clear for good.

Vero dunked an Oreo in the Cool Whip. "What if Stacey's husband is right and the killer is someone who lives here in South Riding?"

I sucked crumbs from my teeth as I considered some of my

neighbors. "The Patels don't exactly give off serial-killer vibes. What about Frank Dwyer, the computer analyst? He's a little weird."

Vero shook her head. "All computer analysts are weird. My money's on that big, muscle-y guy who's always picking fights at the homeowners association meetings."

"Don Weber? The car salesman?"

"Stacey thinks he's a little crazy from all the steroids."

"Stacey would know," I said drily. She'd probably heard it at the bus stop from the other gossipy moms. "Sounds like the police already have a suspect in mind. I'm sure we'll all hear who it is soon enough." If the TV reporters didn't tell us, the rumor mill would.

The doorbell rang. We both paused our chewing.

"You expecting someone else?" Vero asked around her cookie.

I shook my head. "Nick's working late again tonight." My boyfriend had been working late nearly every night since we'd returned from Atlantic City a week ago. I was pretty sure Commander Ortega was punishing him, reminding him that Fairfax County cops who sneak off on renegade investigations outside their jurisdiction wouldn't do so without repercussions—in Nick's case, a mountain of paperwork. But a niggling doubt had taken root in my mind that he was pulling away, putting distance between us. That he couldn't keep turning a blind eye to the secrets I'd been keeping from him. I had texted him a few hours ago to remind him the children would be staying with their father this weekend. I also let him know I'd leave a key under the downspout beside my front stoop. His reply had been quick but short, promising he would try to come by on his way home from work on Friday night *if* he made it home at all.

"Maybe it's your husband," I teased.

Vero flipped me off. She and Javi weren't actually married. Their tequila-induced trip to a neon-lit Atlantic City chapel last week hadn't been legally binding, but there was no use trying to convince Javi of that. Vero's childhood crush was hopelessly in love with her, and he'd taken it as a personal challenge to win back her affections after they'd spent the last three years apart. "You've got Oreos in your teeth. You should probably go brush them just in case."

She called me a name under her breath as she sprinted to the bathroom. I took the liberty of finishing her drink for her on my way to answer the door.

I opened it, expecting to see a long-haired, tattooed Latino hunk on the other side.

Instead, I blinked at the conservatively dressed white man standing on my stoop. Mrs. Haggerty's grandson smiled uncertainly and adjusted his tie. His sour-faced grandmother stood beside him. She glowered at me over the handle of her purple American Tourister carry-on bag.

"Mrs. Haggerty! This is . . . a surprise," I said, fumbling over my greeting. Was there a polite way to greet your neighbor after she'd been released from custody on murder charges?

She pushed her way past me into my foyer, her bony elbow catching me in my bladder as the wheel of her luggage ran over my toe. Brendan gave me an apologetic smile, shifting the huge suitcase he held to his opposite hand so he could reach to shake mine. "It's good to see you again, Ms. Donovan. Brendan. Brendan Haggerty?" His smile grew pained as he waited for me to respond.

The last time I had spoken to Brendan had been two weeks ago, during our last morning at our local citizens' police academy. He'd been toting that same piece of luggage for his grandmother as he'd helped her into the bus that would take them both home. Our farewells had been cordial, but that was before any of us had known about the dead man in her backyard.

I glanced past him, to his grandmother's empty driveway across the street. Mrs. Haggerty's windows were still dark. Yellow police tape drooped from the corners of her fence, and the muddy tracks of a backhoe still trailed down her frost-covered lawn.

Brendan's shiny white Volvo idled at the curb in front of my house. Steam billowed from its exhaust pipe and ghosted across my sidewalk. He sagged with relief as I stepped aside and held the door open, making an opening wide enough for him to wedge the giant suitcase past me into the foyer.

Vero ran a hand through her hair, primping as she hurried down the stairs. She skidded to a stop on the bottom step, frowning at Mrs. Haggerty. "What the hell is she doing here? And why does our foyer look like the baggage claim at Dulles?"

I shot Vero a look. "What Vero means is that we didn't expect you back so soon, Mrs. Haggerty."

"Why wouldn't I come back?" the woman quipped. "Just because a body turned up in my yard doesn't give anyone the right to assume I'm guilty of anything. I never met that man before in my life. I told the police as much, but I guess they had to figure that out for themselves. Took them long enough," she muttered, unbuttoning her coat. "Those brutes had no business putting me in handcuffs. They're lucky I didn't sue the police department for unnecessary roughness."

"I think you mean unnecessary force, Grandma," Brendan gently corrected her. He set down the suitcase he was holding and rushed to help her out of her coat. When I didn't offer to take it from him, he folded it awkwardly over his arm. "I apologize for barging in. It's just that the power is still off in my grandmother's house, and it's freezing over there." He rubbed warmth back into his hands. The tips of his ears and nose were red under the lights of my foyer, and

I could practically feel the cold February air from outside radiating from them both. I could only imagine the state of Mrs. Haggerty's home. It had been sitting vacant, without power, since the whole ordeal started a week ago.

Brendan continued in a low voice, "The Commonwealth's Attorney dropped all charges and released Maggie tonight. She insisted on going straight home, but the place is a wreck. There was a lot of damage from the flood, and there's no way I'll be able to get someone out to fix it over the weekend—"

"Which is why I'm staying here," Mrs. Haggerty finished.

"Here?" Vero shrieked.

"I'd let her come home with me, but my condo is only one bedroom, on the third floor," Brendan explained.

"Isn't there *anyone* else who can take her?" Vero asked.

Brendan shook his head. "We don't have any other family in the area, and she insisted on staying close to home."

"I'm sure she'd be more comfortable in a hotel," I suggested.

"Hotels are expensive," Mrs. Haggerty snapped.

Vero thrust my purse at me. "Finlay would be more than happy to pay for it."

"Don't bother. I'll be just fine here," Mrs. Haggerty said, dragging her carry-on toward the stairs.

Vero leapt into her path. "You can't stay here! We have bedbugs. And lice. And a kid in preschool! This place is a Petri dish of child-borne diseases. You'd probably get cooties."

Mrs. Haggerty pushed her aside. "I'll take my chances."

Brendan offered an apologetic smile as his grandmother helped herself up my staircase. One age-spotted hand gripped the banister as she lugged her tiny bag behind her, grunting like Yoda with every step and grumbling to herself when she finally reached the top. Vero gritted her teeth when the woman moved down the hall, poking her head in each of our bedrooms, giving herself the grand tour of my home.

I turned sharply to her grandson. There were limits to neighborly obligations, and I was pretty sure harboring a murder suspect was one of them. I lowered my voice to a harsh whisper. “My children are sleeping upstairs, and you’re asking me to take in a woman who is being investigated for murder!”

“A murder she clearly didn’t commit,” he argued. “The police never would have released her if they thought she was guilty. Does she look like someone who could bury a grown man and get away with it?”

I refrained from answering that. I probably didn’t look like one either, and I’d moved more bodies over the last four and a half months than I cared to admit.

He raised his hands in supplication. “My grandmother didn’t even know the man. All she wants to do is go home.”

“I know you’re in a bind, but there must be someone else your grandmother can stay with.”

“Preferably someone on another coast,” Vero muttered.

“She specifically asked to stay here,” Brendan said.

“Why would she do that? She doesn’t even like me!”

“Don’t be silly. She’s very fond of you.”

Vero snorted.

Brendan put a hand to his heart. “I promise, she won’t be any trouble at all. And I’d be happy to contribute toward whatever you feel is a fair charge for her meals and rent. At her age, she doesn’t eat much. All she needs is a bed and a TV to keep her happy. Please,” he begged. “She’s eighty-one years old, she lives alone, and I don’t know what else to do for her. All I’m asking for is a few days. Just until we can get her power and water turned back on.”

I sighed, already hearing my mother's lecture, which would inevitably contain an abundance of Bible passages and guilt. "I suppose she can stay for a few days."

Relief washed over Brendan's face as he handed me her coat. He shook my hand fervently before I could change my mind. "These are her house keys," he said, handing me a key ring. "I'll call her insurance company first thing tomorrow and try to get some repairmen out to look at the place. And this is my cell number," he said, scribbling a number on the back of a business card. "Call me if either of you need anything. The name and number of the detective in charge of her case is on the front. I left Detective Tran a voice message earlier, letting him know she'd be staying with you."

"Presumptuous much?" Vero mumbled.

Brendan continued as if he hadn't heard her. "Everything Maggie needs is in her suitcase. If there's anything she's missing, this should cover it." He opened his wallet and handed me several twenties. Vero plucked them away from me as Brendan gushed out a flurry of emphatic thanks and showed himself out the door. A moment later, he disappeared into his Volvo and it peeled off down the street.

"She's not sleeping in my room," Vero said.

"She can sleep on the rollaway in my office." I hurried up the stairs, hoping Mrs. Haggerty hadn't woken the children, but she was standing in my bedroom, rummaging in my drawers. She handed me a pile of my jeans and sweaters, then placed her own nightgown and a stack of granny panties in the drawer she had just emptied. My window blinds were open, even though it was well past dark, affording her a clear view of her deserted house across the street.

"Mrs. Haggerty, this is my room," I said, plucking her panties out of my drawer. I slammed it closed with my hip before she could put anything else inside it.

"I suppose it will have to do."

"There's a rollaway bed in my office," I said, taking a stack of clothes from her arms so I could return them to her suitcase. "You're welcome to sleep in there."

Mrs. Haggerty stole her clothes out of my hands. "I prefer this one. It's on the right side." She poked me in the ribs, nudging me away from the dresser.

"Right side of what?"

"The right side of the house. You know, facing the street. How else am I supposed to keep watch?"

"Over what?"

"My home! How else will I know if the killer comes back?"

I bit my lip, holding on to my temper by a thread. She had, after all, spent a week in jail after discovering a body in her backyard. I suppose I couldn't fault her for being anxious. "I'm sure there's nothing to worry about, Mrs. Haggerty. I seriously doubt we're in any danger here."

"All the more reason to stay vigilant. Anything can happen in the middle of the night. Burglaries, vandalism, human trafficking, *fires* . . ." She pierced me with a look, pointedly reminding me of a night only a few short weeks ago, when Vero and I had been trapped atop a burning building at the police academy training grounds and Mrs. Haggerty had been the only one to answer our desperate calls for help. Whatever favor she felt she was owed, she was apparently cashing in now.

"Fine," I conceded. "You can stay in my room. But is it really necessary to unpack? You're only going to be here until—"

"Where's my other suitcase? It's late, and I'd like to get some sleep." She stared at me impatiently over the rims of her glasses, though we both knew she was more than capable of carrying her suitcase herself. Not more than two weeks ago, she had tackled me, handcuffed me, and nearly beat me and Vero in a police academy obstacle course, but I also knew from experience there was little point in arguing with her about it.

"I'll bring it up," I offered grudgingly.

"I'll need a fresh set of sheets, too. Yours smell funny."

My hands clenched at my sides. Mrs. Haggerty might not have been guilty of murder, but I wasn't sure I would be able to say the same for myself by the time the weekend was over. Surely this situation justified a homicide.

I negotiated with myself as I retreated down the hall to get her bag. One weekend. I would give the woman one weekend in my bed, if only to repay her for saving our lives. I would call Brendan Haggerty first thing on Sunday and have him fetch his nosy, overbearing, pain-in-the-ass grandmother and find somewhere else for her to stay, or I would load the woman into my minivan and relocate her body myself.

CHAPTER 2

"Hold still," I told Zach as he tried to wriggle out of his pants while I hiked them over his Pull-Up.

"No pants!" he screeched. He'd been in a foul mood all day since Delia had decided that she was going to start her own school and Zach would be her pupil. She'd spent hours trying to force him to keep his clothes on and learn to write the alphabet. Zach had rebelled by streaking through the house, shredding her notepad, and throwing her crayons in the toilet.

"I don't like wearing pants either, buddy, but Daddy's going to be here any minute to pick you up. If you keep your clothes on like a good boy, maybe he'll take you someplace fun for dinner."

Zach's tiny mouth pursed, holding stubbornly to the promise of a tantrum as I fed his feet into his overalls. The quiet was nothing more than a temporary victory. The rest of the evening would hinge on a game of toddler roulette; he was either going to lose it the minute I put him in his car seat or he'd conk out in the truck, sleep the whole way to Steven's house, and then remain awake for the rest of the night.

"Delia!" I called up the stairs as I wrestled him into his coat. "Are you ready to go?"

She thumped down the steps wearing a plaid romper and a pout that was giving off teen-angst-grunge-band vibes. "I want to wear my Barbie pants."

"Those aren't pants, they're pajamas."

"So?"

"You can't wear pajamas out to dinner. You can put them on when you get to Daddy's house."

The doorbell rang. I passed Delia her coat, hoping Zach didn't manage to strip himself naked while my back was turned as I answered the door.

"Whoa!" Javi said, dodging a flying sneaker as he came inside. I turned in time to see Zach strip off his other one, the lights in their soles blinking as he tossed it over his head and sprinted behind the couch. I pinched the bridge of my nose as a pair of overalls flew over the back of the sofa and landed on the floor. Zach darted out of his hiding place and streaked past both of us, his bare butt on full display. His turtleneck was stuck around his head, the empty arms flapping behind him as he tore wildly through the house. I caught him around the waist before he could run face-first into the wall.

"Vero!" I called out. "Javi's here!"

She was still putting in her earrings as she came down the stairs. "Naked time?"

Javi's brows shot up. "Absolutely."

She rolled her eyes as he kissed her on the cheek. "I was talking about the kids."

Zach wailed and attempted to rip off the rest of his shirt. There was a familiar rap on the door. Steven cracked it open and peeped inside. "Everyone ready to go?"

"Almost," I said, struggling to get Zach back into his Pull-Up.

Vero handed her purse to Javi. "Hold this."

Steven and Javi watched with matching expressions of fascination and horror as Vero and I re-dressed my screaming toddler in a rehearsed coordinated effort in which one of us held him in a bear hug while the other worked him back into his clothes. I slung him over my hip when we finished. He writhed for a moment before finally giving up, leaving a trail of tears and snot on my shirt as he collapsed against my shoulder.

"What's going on?" Steven asked me.

"The boot camp didn't work. We're back to Pull-Ups, but Zach refuses to keep his clothes on. Everything I've read says it's just a phase."

"How long will it last?"

Vero gave Steven a pointed look. "I hear some children never grow out of it."

I passed Zach to his father before he could flip her off. "Let's go," I said, putting the straps of the diaper bag over Steven's free shoulder. I gave each of the kids a kiss. "Have a fun weekend. Be good for your dad."

"Better hurry," Vero told Steven when Zach started squirming. "It's only a matter of time before Mount Vesuvius erupts."

"We're definitely going to the pharmacy for condoms on the way home," Javi said to Vero.

"What's a condom?" Delia asked her father as he shooed her out the door.

The house fell blissfully quiet once the children were gone. The only sound was the game show Mrs. Haggerty was watching on the TV in the next room.

"Who's that?" Javi asked, tipping his head toward the sofa.

"A displaced neighbor," I said before Vero could supply an adjective of her own. "Her heat's not working and she needed a place to stay."

Javi leaned down to give Vero a proper kiss hello. She smiled as his raven-black hair fell over both of their eyes. The plastic ring on the fourth finger of his left hand caught in the strands as he raked them back, and he gently pried it free. He'd acquired it during their drunken late-night trip to a cheesy hotel wedding chapel in Atlantic City. Judging by how often he'd been showing up here lately, I didn't imagine he'd be taking it off anytime soon.

The purple glow-in-the-dark bat ring was barely visible under the layer of glittery violet spray paint on his fingers, suggesting he'd come straight from Vero's cousin's garage. Javi did salvage and bodywork in exchange for free rent and a place to sleep on Ramón's sofa, and since Vero's cousin and Javi had been best friends since elementary school, the arrangement had been working out fine. That is, until Javi had told Ramón that he and Vero had (sort of) gotten married. Javi's cheek still carried the ghost of a bruise.

Vero caught his hand and smirked. "That's a pretty bold choice," she said, raising an eyebrow at the purple paint on his knuckles.

"Tell me about it," Javi said irritably. "I told Ramón's customer the same thing when he picked out the color. I didn't even finish spraying the front end of his truck before the asshole changed his mind. Now I've got an open bucket of Eggplant Ecstasy sitting on a shelf in the garage."

Vero laughed. "You'd better go wash that mess off your hands before you take me out to dinner."

"I was kind of hoping we could stay in." He dangled a set of keys between them.

"What's this?" she asked, snatching them from his fingers.

"You know that storage room over your cousin's garage? I talked your cousin into renting it out to me. It's not a storage room anymore." He wagged his eyebrows at her. "Want to help me move in?"

"Do I have to carry anything?" she asked.

"Only the bed and whatever we pick up for dinner."

"I'll get my things." Vero turned and hightailed it up the stairs. Two minutes later, she shuffled back down with her overnight bag slung over one shoulder. She turned to me as she dragged her boyfriend out of the house by way of the garage. "Text me when the old bat is out of here. You can sleep in my room. Don't let her snoop," she said, slamming the door behind them.

I pulled back the curtain in the foyer, watching through the window as Javi's Camaro pulled out of the driveway. Vero's Charger rolled out behind him, and I sighed, wishing I had the house to myself.

Mrs. Haggerty was staring out the living room window, ignoring whatever game show was playing on the TV when I came in to join her. She was unusually quiet, maybe a little melancholic. I wondered if she was watching her house, waiting for her porch light to turn on, or if she was hoping her grandson would come back and pick her up.

"Looks like it's just the two of us for dinner," I said over the television. "I have some leftover meatloaf if you'd like something to eat."

She didn't bother to acknowledge me.

"Suit yourself," I said, turning back to the kitchen. I had been caring for two cranky children all day. I had no plans to dress, change, coddle, or feed anybody else.

"Children need discipline. And rules." Mrs. Haggerty's stern tone made me pause at the threshold. I turned around slowly, biting my tongue as she went on. "When I was your age, children knew what was expected of them. They knew the consequences. If you let those kids think they're in charge, they'll have no reason to listen to you."

My doorbell rang and I was grateful for the excuse to discontinue the conversation. Mrs. Haggerty was the last person I would go to for parenting advice.

I opened the front door to find Cam standing on my porch. His close-cropped hair was just beginning to grow out, the soft brown edges peeking from under his beanie.

"Hey, Mrs. D," he said, grinning like a fool.

I held the door open for him. Any company was better than being alone in the house with a glowering Mrs. Haggerty. "This is a nice surprise. What are you doing here?"

"I was just in the neighborhood." Cam was unusually chipper for an eighteen-year-old high school dropout who lived with his grandmother and had recently quit being gainfully employed as a hacker for the Russian mob. I had first met Cameron four months ago, when I'd hired him to do some online sleuthing for me on the dark web. I'd been attempting to suss out the identity of a contract killer who was soliciting clients through a popular local women's forum. It was in part thanks to Cam that Vero and I had been able to thwart the killer and shut the forum down. Call me crazy, but despite Cam's faults he had a good heart, and I was pretty sure all he needed to straighten himself out was for someone to give him a chance. I was also pretty sure he was hungry.

He sniffed the air as he came inside and set down his heavy backpack. A tiny Chihuahua in a matching leather jacket trailed in behind him.

"Who's this?" I asked.

"Arnold Schwarzenegger." Cam handed me the dog's leash so he could strip off his jacket and hang it on the coatrack. He left the dog's jacket on, which was probably for the best. The tiny thing hardly had enough body fat to keep warm. For that matter, neither did Cam. He had the rangy frame of a growing boy who was accustomed to having to scrape for his meals, and while Cam adored his grandmother, I got the sense he was more her caretaker than she was his guardian. Sometimes, I think he wasn't so much hungry as he just needed someone to treat him like the kid he hadn't had the luxury of being.

Cam patted the Chihuahua's head. "I found the little guy at the shelter last week. He isn't as cool as Kevin Bacon . . . yet," he added, picking up the dog before it could lift its leg on my foot. "He just needs a little training. Right, Arnold? Don't piss on the nice lady's leg or she won't let us stay for dinner." Kevin Bacon had been a lost, long-haired wiener dog that we'd been temporarily stuck caring for during our stay in Atlantic City. Cam had grown attached to Kevin, and he'd been reluctant to return the dachshund to its owner before we left. She had paid Cam a generous reward, and I wasn't surprised to see he'd used some of that money to adopt a furry friend of his own.

Cam followed his nose to the kitchen and set Arnold down to wander. "Something smells good."

"Meatloaf and mac 'n' cheese. You're welcome to join me. Help yourself to a drink."

Cam rubbed his hands together and opened the fridge.

"Absolutely not," I said as he reached for a beer. He heaved a sigh and settled for a Coke. Contrary to Mrs. Haggerty's opinion of me, I was perfectly capable of setting boundaries and enforcing rules. Cam's stomach growled. He peeked over my shoulder as I gave the pot of macaroni a final stir. "How's your grandmother?" I asked him.

"Good, I guess. She'll be back in a week."

"A week? Where is she?"

"Remember the reward money I got for returning Kevin Bacon to that rich lady? I used it to send my grandma on one of those singles cruises for old people. I found a killer last-minute deal online."

I turned from the stove, catching him as he blushed. "That was sweet of you, Cameron. But I thought that money was supposed to be for school."

He shrugged. "I can go back to school anytime. Besides, my grandma always wanted to see all those fancy places in Europe, and I think she's been kind of lonely lately."

I got the sense that his grandmother wasn't the only one. "Who's taking care of you while she's gone?"

He scoffed. "I'm eighteen. I don't need a babysitter." I raised an eyebrow as I sliced the meatloaf. He answered that with a dramatic roll of his eyes. "I'm crashing with my uncle Joey," he admitted. Cam's uncle was Detective Joey Balafonte, Nick's most recent partner. While Cam's relationship with his uncle was contentious at times, Joey's heart seemed to be in the right place. "But the guy's a shitty cook."

"Well, you're always welcome here." I handed Cam a heaping plate of meatloaf, macaroni, and green beans.

"Thanks, Mrs. D." He sat down at my kitchen table and pulled Arnold Schwarzenegger onto his lap. Blowing the steam off a corner of his meatloaf, he offered the dog a taste. Then he tucked into his meal as if he hadn't eaten in a week.

"Who's that in the other room?" he asked, using his finger to scrape the last of the cheese sauce from his plate.

"My neighbor. Her heat's not working and she needed a place to stay for a few days." I figured the less Cam knew about Mrs. Haggerty's situation, the better.

"What's the matter with her? Not a fan of meatloaf?"

"I think she might be a little homesick."

"Huh," he said thoughtfully. "Do you mind?" he asked, reaching for the untouched plate of food I'd prepared for her.

"Help yourself."

Cam stood and carried Mrs. Haggerty's plate to the living room. He set it on the coffee table in front of her with a set of utensils, a napkin, and a Coke. Mrs. Haggerty blinked at him as he sat down beside her on the sofa and took the remote.

"You like video games?" he asked her as he changed the channel.

Two hours later, I had washed the dishes, tidied the playroom, taken a shower, and run a load of laundry, all to the sound of screeching wheels, sirens, and shouting from the living room. Cam and Mrs. Haggerty were still sitting in front of the television when I came back downstairs. Mrs. Haggerty's hunched, frail shoulders were side by side with Cam's taller ones. Arnold Schwarzenegger was curled at their feet, an empty dinner plate on the coffee table in front of them.

"That's it! You've got him! Take the shot!" Cam said.

Mrs. Haggerty gripped the controller in her lap, her knobby fingers haphazardly pressing all the buttons at once. Gunfire erupted on the screen. Blood spattered on brick.

Cam whooped. "Get it, Mrs. H!" He perched on the edge of his seat as he watched Mrs. Haggerty's avatar break through a window. She shimmied down a fire escape and dove into a car.

"Everything okay in here?" I asked.

"I taught Mrs. H how to play *GTA*. Look at her go. She's a natural!"

A target appeared on the screen and the man's head exploded, brains and gore spraying everywhere. "Take that, you hooligans!" Mrs. Haggerty cried.

I winced. "Wouldn't she rather watch TV?"

"Studies have shown video games are very beneficial to seniors," he said sagely. "Something about all that cognitive shit and hand-eye coordination and whatnot. I play *Call of Duty* with my grandma all the time."

"You couldn't have taught her *Animal Crossing*?"

"She wanted a first-person shooter. What can I say? The woman's a badass." Mrs. Haggerty's character whipped a gun out of her car window, releasing a hellscape of bullets and taking down a few innocent bystanders along with the bad guy. Satisfied, she rose stiffly from the couch while holding her lower back.

"Thank you, young man. That was very exciting." She passed Cam her controller and patted his shoulder.

"Remember the rules we talked about, Mrs. H." He held up his index finger, preparing to count them off.

"Always use two-factor authentication," she said dutifully.

"Number two?"

"Rich Nigerian princes don't need any money." He held up a third finger. "The IRS does not take payments over the phone." He held up a fourth and fifth finger. "Don't believe everything you see on the internet, and never post photos of yourself without clothes."

"Good job." He gave her a thumbs-up.

"I'm heading to bed," she announced. "I have a long day tomorrow."

"What's happening tomorrow?" I asked.

"I have a meeting, and I'll need a ride. The police impounded my vehicle after they detained me, and now they refuse to give it back . . . some nonsense about how my license has expired and I'm too old to drive. My book club is expecting me and it's my turn to bring lunch."

Cam's hand shot up. "I can drive you!"

"You don't have a car," I reminded him.

"No problem, Mrs. D. I'll just take yours."

I threw him a look. "Mrs. Haggerty, what time do you need to be at your meeting? I'll take you."

She didn't thank me so much as offer me a curt nod. "Eleven o'clock. I'll see you all in the morning," she said, turning for the stairs.

Cam put his game controllers in his backpack, scooped up Arnold, and headed for the door.

"Hold on. I'll give you a ride home," I offered, reaching for my coat. I didn't like the idea of Cam walking to the nearest bus stop alone.

He held up his phone. "I got an Uber."

"How much is it?" I asked, opening my wallet. The least I could do was spring for his ride.

"Don't worry about it. I already Venmo'd myself a hundred from your bank account. Later, Mrs. D," he said on his way out the door.

I shook my head as I watched him duck into the back seat of a rideshare. Not two weeks had passed since Vero and I had caught Cam hacking our mobile devices for his mob-boss employer. I had given him a stern lecture while Vero had purged all the spyware she could find from our phones. Still, the fact that he was being honest about his crimes felt like progress.

CHAPTER 3

I waited for Mrs. Haggerty to retire for the night before I headed to Vero's room. The house was dark and unsettlingly quiet, and I felt a little safer as I closed and locked her door. I changed into a comfy pair of sweatpants I'd found in the dryer and crawled into Vero's bed, pulling the blankets all the way up to my chin before turning off the lamp. I stared at the ceiling in the dark, listening for the sound of breaking glass or a door creaking open.

What if Stacey was right and the real killer was still out there? What if they came back?

I squeezed my eyes shut, frustrated that I had let that thought enter my mind. Gilford Dupree had been murdered five years ago, and whoever killed him probably didn't care one iota about me or my family. If anything, Mrs. Haggerty had far more reasons to be afraid than I did.

That thought didn't make me feel any better.

What if the killer came here looking for her?

I threw an arm over my eyes. I was being ridiculous. No one was going to break into my house tonight. No one except for Nick.

I bolted upright in the bed.

Oh, god. What if Nick did come after work? What if he used the key to let himself into the house? What if he snuck into my bedroom, stripped off his clothes, and accidentally spooned with Mrs. Haggerty?

I threw off the covers and tucked Vero's pillow under my arm, carrying it with me downstairs to the living room. The sofa wasn't as comfortable as Vero's bed, but if I slept within sight of the front door, at least I could prevent any traumatic late-night booty calls.

I fluffed the pillow and arranged the blanket on the couch, but I couldn't seem to settle in. I got up and tested the dead bolt on the front door. Then I headed to the kitchen to check the one in the garage, hoping Vero had remembered to lock up when she'd left.

I opened the service door and turned on the light, relieved to find the bay door shut.

Before I could turn off the light and lock up again, my gaze snagged on my small collection of household tools on the pegboard on the back wall. I entertained the thought of bringing one of them into the house with me for protection, but I didn't have a great selection of pointy garage implements to choose from.

As I closed the door, an idea began to form.

When Steven had moved out, he'd taken everything in the garage with him but my tiny pink garden trowel. He'd argued that I didn't know how to use most of the home-improvement tools anyway, and he'd promised to come back to fix anything that broke.

I reached for my phone, my anxiety yielding to hope as I sent a quick text to Steven, telling him I needed a favor and asking him if he could drop by my house with his tool kit tomorrow. He replied almost immediately with a thumbs-up emoji and said he and the kids would be there around noon. I had told Brendan his grandmother could stay until her power and water were fixed. Steven was handy when it came to repairs, and in his line of work he knew a lot of contractors. If I asked him to take a look at Mrs. Haggerty's house, I'm sure he could figure out what needed to be done. With any luck, I could have her back in her own home before the weekend was over.

I poured myself a glass of wine and turned the TV on at a low volume. Then I flipped past a few police procedural dramas before settling on a Hallmark rom-com. I sipped my wine, waiting for the alcohol to settle my nerves as I burrowed under the throw blanket. My situation could have been worse, I reminded myself. The kids were safe with their father, Vero was safe with Javi, and Mrs. Haggerty was probably fast asleep. With any luck, the only body that would turn up here tonight was toned and perfect and definitely warm. I checked my phone, hoping for a message from Nick.

Instead, a message from my literary agent was waiting on the screen.

Sylvia: *What are you doing this weekend?*

I tapped the edge of my wineglass as I weighed my options. 1) Answer her, a choice that hadn't ended well for me lately. Or 2) Ignore her, text her back on Monday, and suffer her agent wrath.

My phone lit up with a new notification.

Sylvia: *It's Friday night. I know you're not busy. Call me.*

Sylvia: *Unless your hot cop is with you. Then by all means, take whatever time you need and call me when you're done.*

I put my phone down out of spite. I had no intention of working this weekend. I had turned in my last revision less than two weeks ago and my newest book was off to production. I deserved a break, and I was damn well taking one. The screen lit up again.

Sylvia: *If I don't hear from you in ten minutes, I'm calling your next of kin.*

I swore to myself as I muted the television. I had no idea if Sylvia actually had my mother's phone number, but I wasn't willing to test that theory. Georgia and I had both been avoiding our mother's calls about a dinner invitation since we'd returned home from Atlantic City, and the last thing I needed was for Sylvia to ping my mother's radar.

I dialed Sylvia's number.

She answered on the first ring. "Is he there?"

"Who?"

"You know who! Your hot cop. How was it? Tell me everything."

"All ten minutes of it?" I asked, pointing out the ridiculousness of her last text message.

"I saw your hot cop on those TV interviews, Finlay. He's exactly how you described him in your books. If it takes you more than ten minutes to climax with that man, there's definitely something wrong with you."

"You can call off the search party. And no, he isn't here."

"Good, then there's nothing to distract you."

"From what?"

"Work. Something urgent has come up, and I need you to meet me in the city on Monday."

"That's three days from now! I can't go to New York."

"Not New York. I'm coming to you."

I sat up, my wineglass nearly tumbling onto my lap. "You're coming here?" Last time my agent had splurged on a train ticket to meet me, it had been to tell me my career was in the toilet and I was about to lose a book deal. That otherwise normal morning had then spiraled into disaster. "Why?" My next book proposal wasn't due to my editor for at least another month.

"Remember that Hollywood executive I told you about? The one who wants to turn your novels into a TV series? He'll be in DC next week filming some hot new FBI drama. I told him you live just outside the Beltway. He wants you to come into the city and have lunch with him on Monday. But don't worry, I'm coming, too."

My stomach bottomed out. "I can't!" I sputtered.

"Get your ex to take the kids. Or better yet, let your accountant do it. I've seen your royalty statements, Finlay. It's not like she has anything better to do."

"I have company," I argued, grasping on to Mrs. Haggerty for an excuse.

"Unless your houseguest is Reese Witherspoon, you're going to this meeting. I'm leaving on the first train Monday morning. I'll need you to pick me up at the station in time for lunch."

"Sylvia, please, it's not a good time—"

She growled in frustration. "We've discussed this, Finlay! We both know exactly what your problem is."

"I don't have a problem! I just . . ." I *what*? There wasn't a single legitimate reason I couldn't make that meeting. This was exactly what Sylvia had diagnosed me with in Atlantic City—*impostor syndrome*, she'd called it. She and Nick were right. I was terrified of my own success. Of what it could lead to. But I'd be crazy to pass up an opportunity like this, wouldn't I? "What time does your train get in?" I asked, pinching the bridge of my nose.

"I'll text you the details," Sylvia said in a rush. "I need to book my ticket. I'll see you Monday."

I stared at the screen when she disconnected, wondering exactly how I was supposed to prepare for a meeting with a TV producer. Was I supposed to come up with answers to questions like: What inspired you to write this story? What kind of research did you do for the book? Are any of the situations you write about based on real people or events? *Well, I'm so glad you asked, Mr. Fancy TV Producer. Actually, yes, I do have a lot of experience with organized crime. I also own the highest-rated garden shovel money can buy. I could tell you exactly how many hours it takes for a frozen body part to thaw, how many bath bombs it would take to cover the smell, and in a pinch, I could probably figure out how to operate a backhoe.* My research on the topic of murder was extensively (and disturbingly) thorough. My knowledge of Hollywood, on the other hand, was not.

Downing the last gulp of my wine, I traded my cell phone for the TV remote and turned up the volume. I switched from the Hallmark Channel to a cop drama, chalking it up to preparation for my meeting as I settled back under my blanket to watch.

I stirred some time later, roused from a deep sleep. I blinked, barely awake as the TV suddenly turned off.

A man-shaped shadow hovered over me. With an ear-splitting shriek, I bolted upright. My skull smacked against something hard and Nick barked out a curse. I slapped a palm over my throbbing forehead, squinting as he slowly came into focus. I could barely make out his dress shirt and tie in the dim moonlight sifting through the blinds. He massaged his forehead and sat down beside me.

"Hello to you, too," he whispered.

"I thought you were still at work. Why didn't you tell me you were coming?"

"I did." He pushed my cell phone across the coffee table toward me. An unread notification waited on the screen. "I would have knocked when I got here, but you told me to use the key." He sank into the cushions of the old sofa, took off his holster, and loosened his tie as I read his message. I set my phone down and knelt on the cushion beside him.

"How was your day?" I asked, pressing a soft kiss to the spot where our foreheads had smacked together.

He dropped his head back against the sofa and threw an arm over his eyes. "I don't want to talk about it. How about yours?"

Aside from Delia being suspended from preschool, Mrs. Haggerty moving in, and a possible killer on the loose? "I don't want to talk about mine either. I'm just glad you're here." I slid one leg over him and sat on his lap. He peeped out from under his arm as I ran my fingers through the short, dark waves of his hair and stole a kiss.

His brown eyes twinkled in the dark. "How glad?"

"Very glad," I said as I loosened the top button of his shirt.

His hands moved to my waist and pulled me closer. He'd only used the key under the downspout twice since we'd come back from Atlantic City, but we were already good at these stealthy middle-of-the-night visits, the near-silent sex, and sneaking him out of my bedroom before the children woke up. Mostly, we were good at not talking about all the delicate and dangerous topics we'd been avoiding, namely my involvement with several unsavory culprits in a few criminal cases Nick had been tasked with solving.

"Want to go upstairs?" he asked, his body responding as I untucked his shirt from his slacks.

"No." I definitely did not want to go upstairs.

"What about Vero?"

"Gone for the night—" He took my whole mouth with a savage, hungry kiss. I felt his arm loop around my waist, and I was a little dizzy as he slid me off his lap and set me down onto the couch. We were both breathing hard as we fumbled with my elastic waistband and his belt buckle. I hoped I had remembered to wear cute underwear—or at least, not old and hole-y underwear—as we took turns stripping each other of our pants, too impatient to waste time taking off anything else.

I took him by his tie and dragged his body down onto mine, arching against him as his hand slid under my T-shirt. I grabbed the ends of his boxer briefs and started to pull them down.

"Finn?" His entire body had gone rigid above me—every part but the one I had been hoping for. His Adam's apple bobbed with a slow, hard swallow as he stared over the back of my sofa. "Why is Mrs. Haggerty in your house? And why is she pointing a gun at me?"

"*Oh, god!*" I said, scrambling out from under him.

"Put your hands where I can see them, home invader, or I'll shoot!" Mrs. Haggerty cried.

Nick sat up very slowly and put his hands in the air.

"Stand down, Mrs. Haggerty!" I lunged for the lamp switch, tripping on our pants, certain Mrs. Haggerty wouldn't be able to see Nick's raised hands if he'd been waving them right in front of her face. I turned on the light, momentarily blinding all three of us. "It's only Nick!"

Mrs. Haggerty squinted in his direction. "Detective Anthony?" He shielded his head, tucking me behind him as she waved her gun at the wall clock. "It's past eleven o'clock, young man. What in heaven's name are you doing here?"

He raised his hands higher, the half-buttoned shirt and loose ends of his tie lifting to reveal the fire-engine red boxer briefs I thankfully hadn't had the chance to strip off him.

"I just came to see Finlay." His voice was hoarse, his eyes locked on her weapon. It looked old and solid, like something Dirty Harry might have carried. If I hadn't seen her handle a .357 Magnum revolver during our police academy firearms class, I might have doubted her ability to shoot it. "She invited me," Nick said. "You can put the gun down. Please," he added with another tight swallow.

Mrs. Haggerty threw me a scandalized look as she lowered her weapon.

Nick dropped his hands. "I'm assuming you have a permit for that?"

"This old thing?" she asked as she waved it again. "It's not mine. It's my late husband's."

I refrained from pointing out the fact that it was, by default, now hers.

"What is it doing in my house?" I snapped, tugging my T-shirt down to cover myself. Apparently, I had not worn proper underwear for a make-out session *or* a holdup at gunpoint.

Nick flinched as Mrs. Haggerty gesticulated wildly with her gun. "I have a right to defend myself. There could be a murderer in the neighborhood! A dead man was buried behind my house and the killer is still at large."

"Which is one of many reasons it's a bad idea for you to have this," Nick said, taking a cautious step toward her. "May I?" He reached out a hand for the gun. She looked put-upon as he deftly and gently relieved her of the weapon. "I promise, you and Finlay aren't in any danger while I'm here. Are there any other firearms in the house?" he asked her.

Mrs. Haggerty crossed her arms. "Of course not. Who do you think I am? A felon?"

Nick's jaw tensed as he refrained from answering that.

I clutched a hand to my racing heart. "Please, Mrs. Haggerty. We're all safe. You can go back to . . ." I narrowed my eyes at the winter coat zipped securely around her. A flashlight handle stuck out from one of the pockets, and the ends of her nightgown protruded from the hem. Her legs were clad in a pair of my black yoga pants, the long ends of which were tucked into a mismatched pair of my socks. I raised a suspicious eyebrow at her orthopedic sneakers. "I thought you had gone to bed?"

"I did," she said defensively. "I wanted to be fresh for my Friday night watch. Weekends are busy in South Riding. All those hoodlums and teenagers running around making mischief," she griped, "toilet-papering houses and vandalizing mailboxes . . . I was in my room getting dressed when I heard a kerfuffle down here and decided to investigate. Your gentleman caller is lucky I see so well in the dark. Otherwise, he might have been shot."

I didn't bother pointing out that it was in fact *my* room she was occupying. And that if her night vision was so exceptional, she would have chosen matching socks.

"Still, I think it would be best if I hold on to this," Nick said, unloading her gun.

"Fine, but I expect my personal property to be returned to me in the morning. I'll just be going," she said as she headed for the door.

Nick called after her, "Mrs. Haggerty, I don't think it's a good idea for you to go out by yourself so late at—"

She either didn't hear him or didn't care to let him finish as she slammed the door behind her.

Nick hastily pulled on his pants. "Why is Mrs. Haggerty sleeping in your house?" A sheen of nervous sweat still glistened in the hollow of his throat as he shrugged on his holster and tucked her empty gun in his belt.

"Because her house has no power or water and she needed a place to stay. Her grandson dropped her off a few hours ago. He didn't know what else to do with her."

"So you agreed to let her stay here?" he asked, struggling to keep his voice low. "She's a suspect in a murder investigation, Finlay."

"*Was* a suspect," I clarified as I picked my pants off the floor and turned them right side out. "What was I supposed to do, Nick? She had nowhere else to go."

"She had a *gun*. In your *home*."

"Don't remind me," I said, dragging on my clothes. "I had no idea she had that thing in her suitcase. I'm sure Brendan didn't either. He promised to have her out of here as soon as her heat's back on."

Nick took my chin in his hand. "Tomorrow," he said, his stare unrelenting. "Promise me you'll call her grandson first thing in the morning and tell him to pick her up."

Normally, I would have objected to being told what to do in my own home. But after what she had just put us through, no one was more ready to be rid of Mrs. Haggerty than me. "I'll call him tomorrow."

Nick seemed to relax at that. He pulled me against him, his heart still quick in his chest as he pressed his lips to the top of my head. "You okay?"

I nodded. "I should probably go with her." I peeled myself from his arms to put on my sneakers.

"Wait for me. I'll go with you in a minute." He cast a glance toward the stairs. His eyes had taken on that sharp, focused look. I had known enough cops in my life to recognize it. "Give me permission to search your room first."

"You can't do that! You don't have a warrant to go through her things."

"I'm not searching her room. I'm searching yours. She brought a gun into your house, Finn. I'm not leaving you alone here tonight without making sure she's not a threat to you."

"But—"

"Do you trust me?" His eyes bored into mine. There was only one right answer.

"I can't believe I'm letting you do this," I said as I put on my coat, "but don't go poking around in my drawers." There was a dangerous glint in his eyes as he started up the steps. "Two minutes, Detective," I called up after him. "I'll wait for you outside."

I waited for Nick on my front stoop, looking both ways down the street for signs of Mrs. Haggerty. I caught the flash of her bright white sneakers as they passed under the streetlamp at the end of the block. She turned left at the stop sign and disappeared from sight.

"Shit," I muttered, venturing out into my front yard to keep an eye on her. I turned back to my house, but Nick's shadow was still moving behind the curtains in my bedroom. I couldn't very well let an eighty-one-year-old woman wander the neighborhood alone at night. He would just have to catch up.

I zipped my jacket and started after her, not bothering to call out to ask her to wait. There was no sense in waking everyone on the street. Besides, if I lagged a little, Nick would have an easier time finding us.

When I made it to the end of the block, I spotted Mrs. Haggerty ahead of me. She carried her flashlight in her hand but hadn't bothered turning it on. She walked with a purpose, pausing only once to scowl at a car full of teenagers as it zipped by. They rolled through a stop sign, nearly running her over, their music blaring loud enough to rattle the windows of their car. I expected her to whip out her neighborhood watch diary and write down their license plate number—some scathing documentation she could present at the next meeting of the homeowners association in an attempt to flush out the names of the guilty kids' parents. I was sure I wasn't the only person in South Riding who had fantasized about burning those diaries in a bonfire. Mrs. Haggerty only shook her head at the car and kept walking.

I followed, watching her from a distance between glances over my shoulder for Nick. At the next corner, she paused to turn on her flashlight. She fiddled with the switch and shook the handle until the beam finally flickered on. She held it in front of her, clicking it on and off several times before finally giving up and turning it off.

A curtain in the upstairs window of the nearest house parted. I cringed as I wondered who Mrs. Haggerty might have disturbed as she'd been carelessly waving her flashlight about. Mrs. Haggerty, however, didn't seem concerned. She shambled to the mailbox at the foot of the driveway and tucked a folded piece of paper inside it.

This house probably belonged to the teenager who had almost mowed her down just now. Of course, she hadn't needed to write down his license plate number when he'd zipped past her, because he had probably done it countless times before. She probably already knew who the kid was, had already documented his infractions in some neighborhood watch grievance report, and had come here prepared to deliver it straight to his parents' mailbox.

When I glanced up at the house again, the curtain was closed. I lingered there a moment as Mrs. Haggerty resumed her walk. A niggling suspicion burrowed in the back of my mind when no one inside the house bothered to come out. Weren't they curious about all the flashing lights? Or why someone had visited their mailbox in the middle of the night?

I paused beside it. Curious, I opened the latch and unfolded the paper under the faint glow of the moonlight.

It wasn't an infraction report. In fact, it wasn't a neighborhood watch form at all. The note was handwritten on blue-lined paper in Mrs. Haggerty's shaky, careful penmanship.

Book Club. Saturday. 11am at Vi's.

I folded the note and placed it back in the mailbox, feeling like a nosy fool as I followed Mrs. Haggerty away from the house. Footsteps echoed behind me. I spun around, hand to my chest as Nick jogged to catch up to me.

His breath steamed as he fell in step beside me. "I thought I told you to wait for me."

"I thought I told you two minutes," I whispered. Mrs. Haggerty maintained her steady pace ahead of us, apparently none the wiser that either of us were there. Clearly her hearing was as good as her vision. "Did you find anything noteworthy in my room?" I asked him.

"Your nightstand was particularly interesting. So was the second drawer of your dresser."

"The granny panties belong to Mrs. Haggerty."

"I was talking about the second drawer down."

My face flushed at his smoldering sideways glance. Vero and I had been at the mall a few days ago when I'd spotted the slinky red negligee in a Valentine's Day clearance bin. Vero had insisted I buy it, but after I'd brought it home, it had seemed a frivolous, impractical purchase. I was pretty sure my kids would be grown and moved out before I'd ever have an occasion to wear it.

"I might have some follow-up questions about the contents of that drawer when your houseguest is gone."

"Anything else?"

He shrugged. "Nothing dangerous. Just her clothes, some medications, a few books."

"No manifesto of a criminal mastermind?"

"Not unless you count her neighborhood watch diary."

I choked on a wry laugh. "I wouldn't exactly call her diaries harmless." Mrs. Haggerty had documented more than just rule violations in those diaries. As far as I could tell she had recorded plenty of private dramas as well, including Steven's and mine. And yet, for all the times she'd shoved her nose into my personal business over the last few years, I still felt guilty for reading the note she'd left in her friend's mailbox just now.

Mrs. Haggerty turned at the next corner and retraced her steps to my home. I glanced at the time on my phone. We had been patrolling for less than thirty minutes. For someone who had been so concerned with the state of the community, her watch rotation seemed awfully short.

"Looks like she's heading back to bed." Nick slipped his hand in mine as we followed her up the driveway. "About that negligee . . . Is Mrs. Haggerty a sound sleeper?"

I laughed. "Don't take this the wrong way, Detective, but I'm not really in the mood to try after our last encounter."

His smile was wicked as he pulled me closer to his side. "Promise me you'll get rid of her tomorrow."

CHAPTER 4

I awoke at daybreak to the scent of coffee. The pot sputtered and dripped in the kitchen. I blinked my eyes open, bleary and disoriented, my bare legs tangled in the throw blanket on the couch. Nick's shoes and tie had been lying on the floor beside my sweatpants when I'd finally lost the battle against sleep last night. I rolled over to look for his clothes, but they were gone.

I got dressed and padded to the kitchen as the coffeepot gave one final hiss. A sticky note hung from an empty mug beside the pot, written in Nick's familiar block letters.

Today. No excuses.

A door opened in the upstairs hall. I braced myself, expecting Mrs. Haggerty, but it was Vero who came down the stairs. She paused in the entry to the kitchen and frowned at me, her heavy eyelids blinking slowly as I handed her a mug from the cabinet.

"When did you get home?" I asked as she shuffled to the coffeepot and poured herself a cup.

"Couple hours ago."

"Why didn't you spend the night with Javi? Trouble in paradise?"

"Far from it." Her mascara-streaked eyes took on a faraway look as she pulled a carton of milk from the fridge. "We had one of those amazing nights, if you must know. The kind when you stay up for hours and talk about everything. All the things we dream about and the stuff we're afraid of. All the little things we never told each other before."

My mouth went dry. I plucked the carton from her hand. "What do you mean, you told him everything? Like *everything* everything?"

Vero pulled a face. "Of course not! I'm not an idiot. Don't worry," she said at my dubious look. "I left all your personal shit out of it." I wasn't sure exactly what that meant since all of her personal shit had been tangled with my personal shit since the night we buried Harris Mickler together. She waved away my unease. "Relax. I didn't tell him about any of *that*," she whispered.

I released a held breath as I sat down at the table and poured myself some cereal. "If it was such a perfect night, then why'd you come home?"

"Apparently, my husband snores. Why'd you sleep on the couch? I told you to use my room."

"Nick came by after work and we fell asleep before we made it upstairs. Is Mrs. Haggerty awake yet?" I asked quietly between bites.

"Don't think so. Your bedroom door is still closed."

"Figures," I muttered. "The woman was up half the night."

"That makes two of us." Vero blew steam from her mug, swallowing her first sip of caffeine with a rapturous expression. "Your boyfriend is a saint."

I was struck by a sharp stab of guilt as I glanced at the sticky note he'd left beside the coffeepot. Vero was right. Nick was a saint. And after putting up with Mrs. Haggerty's nonsense and sleeping on my couch last night, he had only asked one thing from me.

Today. No excuses.

I took the card with Brendan's number from the counter and reached for my phone.

"What are you doing?" Vero asked.

"I'm calling Brendan to pick up his grandmother."

"You told him she could stay until her heat was back on."

"She pulled a gun on Nick last night—"

Coffee shot out of Vero's nose.

I patted her back as she choked and handed her a napkin. "She thought he was a home invader when he let himself in, so she came downstairs waving her late husband's pistol around, threatening to shoot." A laugh bubbled out of Vero. It turned into a full-blown cackle as I tried to shush her. "Would you be quiet! You're going to wake her up!"

She waved me off. "Mrs. Haggerty's hearing is as bad as her eyesight, Finn. I'm surprised she even heard Nick come in last night."

"I doubt she would have if she hadn't been on her way out of the house. Apparently, she takes her neighborhood watch duties very seriously. She insisted on patrolling the neighborhood last night."

Vero frowned. "That's weird. According to the whisper network at the playground, Mrs. Haggerty got voted out of the neighborhood watch right after she was arrested. Stacey's been acting as interim president since."

I covered the receiver in case Brendan picked up. "Stacey? The same Stacey who sells sex toys out of her hatchback?"

"Among other things. She's running a special on edibles this month, and not just the panties. The moms at the playground say her brownies are pretty good. I'm saving mine for a special occasion."

I gasped. "That's what Stacey brought you the other night?"

"Don't look at me like that. They're hidden in the freezer. The kids don't even know they're there."

I hadn't had enough coffee for this conversation.

"Brendan's not answering," I said as the phone continued to ring.

"He's probably still sleeping. Leave him a voice mail."

"It's not rolling over."

Vero shrugged. "We'll try him again later. He can pick up Granny Oakley when he wakes up."

Later that morning, I eased my van to the curb in front of a two-story Colonial in Broadlands. The homes in Broadlands didn't look much different from most of the homes in South Riding, all of them having been constructed around the same time from a handful of cookie-cutter shapes. Some had orange or redbrick façades, all with an alternating color palette of neutral vinyl siding and two-car garages either on the left or the right. Vero climbed out of the back seat of my minivan and opened the passenger door for Mrs. Haggerty to get out. Letting Mrs. Haggerty ride up front with me had seemed preferable to listening to her complain about the children's sticky, crumb-speckled seats in the back, but she'd only managed to find other things to fuss about on the short drive to her book club meeting. She did not, she said, want a reputation for being late. Punctuality was not a virtue she was willing to compromise, regardless of the heavy traffic on Route 7 or the length of the take-out line at Panera Bread when we'd stopped to pick up lunch on the way.

I reached for a platter of sandwiches. Mrs. Haggerty took it from me. "Wait here," she said when it occurred to her she didn't have enough hands to carry both the platter and a tray of cookies into the house by herself. "I'll come back for the rest."

"Please," I insisted when she nearly dropped the plastic dome. "Vero and I are happy to help." Vero was all too willing to take the tray of cookies. I took the sandwiches and handed Mrs. Haggerty the paper bag full of sides and condiments so she wouldn't object to being left with nothing to do.

"Very well," she harrumphed, "but there's no need to come inside. We don't read your kinds of stories."

"What kind of stories?" I asked.

"The kind with shirtless hunks on the covers."

"I think you mean under the covers," Vero clarified. "They don't put hunks on the covers of those books anymore. Nowadays, they put lots of flowers on the front, so you can read them on an airplane and the person next to you won't know you're reading smut. Like those Georgia O'Keeffes," Vero explained. "You can hang one of those in your living room and everyone will say, oh it's so sophisticated and lovely, but we all know that sophisticated orchid is just a painting of some lady's twa—"

"Those paintings have plenty of artistic merit," I said, slamming my van door shut. "And I do read other kinds of books, you know."

Mrs. Haggerty rolled her eyes, and Vero smirked. I wondered if this is what it would feel like to drop Delia off at a sleepover once she became a teenager. *Thanks for the ride and the snacks, Mom, but could you please stay in the car so none of my friends see how uncool you are?* I didn't know many senior citizens—my parents were barely sixty—but I'd made some observations after all the time I'd spent with my mother and Mrs. Haggerty over the last few weeks, and getting old seemed a little like going through adolescence backward. Between my mother's romantic drama with my father, his brooding one-word answers to just about everything, Cam's constant demands for food and money, and Mrs. Haggerty's petulant know-it-all attitude, I had amassed enough research material to write a YA novel.

We followed Mrs. Haggerty toward the house. The other cars parked along the street were an odd mix of luxury brands and more price-sensitive models. Some had stick-figure decals of mothers with children. Others had parking stickers for government offices or hospitals. Several had bumper stickers about coexisting with nature, fucking the patriarchy, and loving Jesus.

The front door of the home opened as we approached. Women's voices and laughter spilled from inside it. A middle-aged woman in a smart pantsuit stepped outside to greet us. The warm umber skin around her eyes creased with her smile.

"Maggie, it's good to see you! We're all so glad you're back." She glanced at Vero and me over Mrs. Haggerty's shoulder as she took the older woman into a wide, enveloping hug. The voices inside seemed to quiet at Mrs. Haggerty's arrival. Several curious faces appeared beyond the doorway inside. "We've all been watching the news," the woman said, taking Mrs. Haggerty's bag for her. "We've been so concerned about you. Everyone is eager to hear what happened. Who did you bring with you?" she asked brightly, inviting Mrs. Haggerty to introduce us.

"My neighbors," Mrs. Haggerty answered, dismissing us with an impatient wave. "The police took my car and I needed a ride. Don't worry. They're not staying." She let herself into the house, leaving the rest of us standing on the porch.

The woman looked abashed. "Please, come in," she said, realizing she didn't have enough hands to relieve us of all the food. "You can set those trays down inside." Vero and I followed her into the house, where Mrs. Haggerty had already been absorbed by a gaggle of women. They helped her with her coat and purse and ushered her into the living room.

The host showed us to the kitchen, gushing over the assortment of pastries and sandwiches as she took the platter from me and pried off the noisy plastic lid. She set it on the counter with the rest of the food. Someone else had brought vegetable crudités. Others had contributed bowls of fruit salad and chips.

"I'm Viola," the woman said, extending a hand once all the trays had been set down.

"I'm Finlay," I said, "and this is Vero."

A spark of recognition lit in Viola as I shook her hand. "Finlay Donovan? The author?" Her smile faltered when I nodded, but she quickly recovered. "Maggie's mentioned you. It was so kind of you to take her in."

"Yes, Finlay," Vero deadpanned. "So kind of you."

"Why don't you fix yourselves some plates?" Viola offered. "Our book club discussion won't start until we've all visited for a bit. You can go after you've had a bite to eat. I'm happy to drive Maggie home after our meeting."

Viola left us in the kitchen and excused herself to mingle with her guests. I studied the women as Vero and I loaded our plates with sandwiches. It was an oddly diverse group. While they all looked like they'd been cut from the same suburban Virginia cloth, they represented a broad spectrum of age and ethnicities. I had envisioned a handful of elderly ladies discussing *Wuthering Heights* or *The Great Gatsby* as they gossiped about their neighbors over cucumber sandwiches and bragged about their great-grandchildren, but Mrs. Haggerty seemed to be the oldest person there. Viola herself couldn't have been much older than my mother. There were others who looked much younger, like the one who'd arrived carrying a laptop bag and wearing mom jeans; she couldn't have been much older than me. Or the twentysomething who'd arrived in pink Hello Kitty nursing scrubs and a pair of thick-soled, pristine white sneakers, as if she'd just come from work.

A statuesque woman in a coordinated sweater set brought Mrs. Haggerty a heaping plate of food. She set it in the older woman's lap and fluffed a pillow behind her. Another brought her a steaming cup of tea on a saucer. They all hovered close, lobbing questions in concerned low voices about how she was treated in jail and the damage to her home. Vero and I hovered in the kitchen, quietly eating our sandwiches. I felt like the unwanted parent chaperone at a high school dance.

After a few minutes of gossip and small talk, Mrs. Haggerty's friends began clearing their plates. Mrs. Haggerty pulled a well-worn copy of a mystery novel from her handbag and set it in her lap. She uncapped a fountain pen as the women used their chairs and ottomans to form a circle around the sofa, scooting in tightly to close the gaps. Mrs. Haggerty opened her book and threw me a pointed look across the room.

Something Nick had said the other night bobbed to the surface of my mind as Mrs. Haggerty watched me. He said he'd seen books and a diary in her room—in *my* room. I'd always been curious (and more recently, concerned) about Mrs. Haggerty's strange obsession with the daily happenings of my life, but now might be my only chance to know how much of it she'd actually seen. How much had she documented over the last few months, since the night Harris Mickler was murdered in my garage?

I tossed my empty paper plate in the trash can and waved a discreet goodbye to Viola as Vero and I headed to the foyer to show ourselves out. As I slung my purse over my arm, the strap caught the edge of a vase, nearly knocking it off the credenza where it perched. I reached to catch it, surprised to find it wasn't a vase at all, but an urn. The gold plate affixed to the front bore a man's name, presumably Viola's late husband, judging by the engraved set of dates, and I quickly set the urn back in its place, hoping none of the women in the other room had noticed my close call.

"What's wrong?" Vero asked as I took a step away from it.

"I can't imagine putting Steven's ashes in a jar," I whispered.

"Speak for yourself. I think about it all the time."

I nudged her out the door, waiting until it closed behind us to wipe my hands on my pants with a shudder.

"I thought Brendan said his grandma didn't have any friends," Vero mused as we walked back to my van. She gestured to the long line of cars parked along the street in front of Viola's house. "These women all look pretty friendly to me. Why couldn't Mrs. Haggerty have stayed with one of them?"

"She said she wanted to be close to her house."

"I'd rather she be a whole lot closer than she is. In her own damn bed would be preferable. When did Steven say he was coming to look at her place?"

"Soon. We should probably head out." I climbed into the van and checked the time on my phone. There was a text message from Sylvia, informing me she'd be arriving at Union Station on Monday at noon. She'd followed it with a firm reminder not to be late and instructions to "wear something hot." I closed the thread without bothering to read the rest, determined to deal with one crisis at a time. If we hurried home, I might have time to do a little snooping before Steven and the kids arrived.

CHAPTER 5

Vero and I pulled into my driveway a few minutes before noon and found a small green Prius parked in front of Mrs. Haggerty's house. The rear window was laden with stickers about sustainability and social justice. Vero squinted at the peace frog and the tiny dancing bears on the bumper. "I'm betting that's not the plumber."

I was guessing it wasn't a mysterious deranged murderer either. "Maybe it's someone from the insurance company. I'll go see what they want."

Vero hopped out of the van and headed inside while I walked across the street to Mrs. Haggerty's house. Voices carried from her backyard. I ducked under the sagging police tape and opened the fence gate, announcing myself with a quick "Hello?"

Two figures whirled to face me, hands in the air, wearing matching expressions of panic.

"Riley? Max? What are you two doing here?" Their shoulders slumped with relief when they recognized me. I had first met Riley Bernbaum and Max Sievers at the citizen's police academy a month ago. The college journalism students were self-proclaimed true-crime fanatics, and they'd launched an amateur podcast featuring local unsolved murders. Annoyingly persistent (and just sharp enough to be dangerous), Riley and Max had signed up for the citizens' police academy, hoping to glean a few inside scoops. The last time Vero and I had seen them, they'd been hounding Nick for details about a missing person case involving a man from New Jersey named Ike Grindley. Ike had worked as hired muscle for an Atlantic City loan shark and had come to Virginia a month ago to collect a gambling debt from Vero. He'd cornered us in a scrapyard and demanded his boss's money. When we'd explained we didn't have it, he suffered an unfortunate accident while trying to murder us instead. Riley, Max, and the police had no idea what had happened to Ike that night, and if Vero and I had our way, no one ever would.

The two podcasters stood side by side in front of the gaping hole in Mrs. Haggerty's yard. Riley held up his phone. The video indicator light was blinking.

The little shit was recording me.

"Hey!" he shouted as I reached for his phone. His cheeks turned as red as his hair as I played back their podcast footage. The camera had zoomed in on the hole where Gilford Dupree had been buried, then zoomed back out to capture Max. She swatted her windblown curls from her eyes as she somberly recounted the details of the gruesome discovery of Gilford's remains.

I paused the clip when my face filled the screen. My hair was unwashed and I had no makeup on, and as far as I was concerned, that was all the justification I needed. Riley and Max both gasped as I deleted the entire thing. "Did Mrs. Haggerty give you permission to record here?" I asked.

"The police haven't been out here for days," Riley said, trying to steal back his phone.

"No one's here!" Max argued. "We're not bothering anyone."

I powered the phone down before giving it back to them. "This is private property. I'm going to have to ask you to leave."

Riley looked indignant as he took it from me. "This is an unsolved murder! The killer is still out there."

"And there have been new developments in the case!" Max said stubbornly. "Things the police and TV news haven't reported yet. Brendan Haggerty's family owns this property. He's running for public office, and the public deserves to know what happened here before they cast their votes."

"And you know what happened here?" I asked sternly. I was only about ten years their senior, but somehow Riley and Max brought out my mom voice. "I'm ashamed of both of you," I said when neither of them coughed up an answer. "If you know so much about the case, then you know Mrs. Haggerty was released because she's no longer a suspect. And her grandson isn't even a person of interest. You *met* them both, for crying out loud, and you're exploiting them for the sake of your ratings." I wanted to call their mothers and have the entitled brats yanked back to school. "You need to leave," I said, pointing to the gate.

"Fine, we'll go," Riley huffed. "But you're going to want to hear what we have to say. There's more to this story than you realize. Don't say we didn't warn you."

I watched from beside the open grave as they stomped back to their car. A moment later, two doors slammed and the Prius whined down the street.

I stared at the pit of muddy red clay, a wound left to fester, wondering what—if anything—Riley and Max *did* know about it. And, more important, why they'd felt a need to warn me.

I left Mrs. Haggerty's yard and ran back across the street, hoping to take advantage of what little time remained before Steven arrived to do some snooping of my own. I scoured my nightstand, searching for the neighborhood watch diary that Nick had seen last night.

All I found was a collection of prescription medicine bottles and a golden-age mystery novel that still bore sticker residue on its spine. I fanned through the yellowing pages. A thick sheet of aged, lined card stock had been shoved between them like a bookmark. The card contained a list of phone numbers—the makeshift Rolodex of a woman who didn't trust modern technology to remember her contacts for her.

I closed the book and dropped it back on the nightstand. She must have put her neighborhood watch diary in her handbag for safekeeping.

The front door slammed downstairs, followed by the thunder of tiny feet. I looked out the window and saw Steven's truck in the driveway. I left my room just as the children crested the top of the stairs. Delia and Zach plowed into me for hugs. I scooped them up in turn, giving them each a kiss. Zach had his pants on and his Pull-Up felt dry through the fabric. I had just started to wonder how long that would last when I set him on his feet and he gleefully began stripping.

Steven was waiting for me in the kitchen when I came downstairs.

"Thanks for coming," I said.

"Everything okay?" he asked as he turned on the water and checked the garbage disposal.

"Everything's fine . . . here," I clarified. "But I was hoping you could take a look at Mrs. Haggerty's house. The power and water are still turned off since her basement flooded. She's staying with us until the damage can be fixed."

Steven's eyes went wide. "And you didn't think to tell me?"

"She was here when you came over last night."

"My hands were a little full," he said curtly.

"I'm sorry. I probably should have said something."

"You're damn right, you should have said something. I thought the woman was in jail!"

"She didn't do it," I said, lowering my voice so the children wouldn't hear. "She was released last night. It was all over the news."

Worry lines cut into Steven's brow. He crossed his arms and leaned back against the counter. "Do the police have any idea who did it?"

"Not yet."

"Maybe I should stay here with you and the kids, just to be safe."

"Absolutely not. I have too many people sleeping in my house already. The sooner I can get Mrs. Haggerty's power and water back on, the sooner I can get her out of my room."

He sighed. "I guess I can take a quick look at the place."

He grabbed his Maglite from the cab of his truck and followed me across the street. I checked Mrs. Haggerty's mailbox on my way to the front door, tucking the handful of bills and circulars under my arm as I sifted through the keys on her key ring. The door creaked as I unlocked it and pushed it open. The house smelled musty, the air dense with a damp, pervasive chill. Diffuse gray light seeped through the closed curtains. The shadows they cast left a pall over the house. Steven's wary expression suggested he was as uncomfortable here as I was.

"The electrical panel is probably in the basement. I'll go take a look." He flipped on his flashlight. The beam wobbled as his boots thumped through the kitchen and down the basement steps.

While he went to inspect the damage, I checked out the rest of the house. Dried mud and footprints tracked a path through the hallway to the living room. It smelled like old furniture and faintly like damp wool. A pile of knitted throws sat in a basket beside the hearth. The fireplace looked like it hadn't been used in years. The log holder was empty and the firebox was clean, the whole of it probably too much trouble for an elderly widow to bother with. The mantel was crowded with framed photos and keepsakes. A fancy wooden cigar box was engraved with her husband's initials. Every surface in the room was filled with collectible ceramics, candy dishes, and stacks of old golden-age mystery books, some still carrying bright stickers with handwritten prices, as if they'd been purchased from a library clearance sale.

I ran a finger over Mrs. Haggerty's shelves on my way to the kitchen. It came away with a layer of dust. I made a mental note to mention it to Brendan. He'd need to hire a cleaner once the repairs were finished. The house had been sitting without power for nearly two weeks, and the fridge and freezer would need a good scouring, too. The smell would be awful once they were finally opened, and I knew better than to disturb things that had been left in a freezer to rot.

I sorted Mrs. Haggerty's mail into piles on the counter, tossed the junk in the trash can, and sifted through the bills. A thick envelope from State Farm was among them. I skimmed the packet of renewal forms inside it. A declarations page was attached, listing her various policies. Her late husband's 1979 Lincoln Mark V was due for renewal next month, but her homeowner's coverage was (thankfully) up to date. I found a copy of the policy in the packet as well. That would be helpful to have handy if any contractors came.

I was gathering up the pages when I noticed something odd . . .

Two life insurance policies had been listed on the last page—one for Margaret Haggerty and one for her husband, both of them due for their annual renewal.

Which wouldn't have been strange at all if Owen Haggerty hadn't been dead for five years.

Why continue paying seventy-five dollars per month to insure her deceased husband? Mrs. Haggerty's Social Security checks were nowhere near enough to live on, especially in this area. Why hadn't she cashed in Owen's life insurance yet?

Steven's boots thudded back up the steps. I tucked the insurance forms in my coat pocket as he entered the kitchen. He turned off his flashlight and tapped the handle against his palm. "I'm not qualified to handle a job this big, Finn. I made a few calls, but the soonest anyone can get here is Monday—"

A throat cleared behind us. Steven and I both turned to find two plainclothes police officers standing in the living room, their badges displayed on their hips and a uniformed officer behind them.

Steven paled.

"We're not trespassing," I said, holding up the key ring Brendan had given me. "The owner of the house is staying with me. I live right across the—"

"I know who you are, Mrs. Donovan." The plainclothes officer wasn't looking at me. His thumbs were hitched in his belt, his stony gaze locked on Steven. "I'd like to know what your ex-husband is doing here."

My stomach tightened as I caught the flash of blue lights through the front window. Three police cars were parked outside; one blocked Steven's truck in my driveway, the other two blocked both sides of the street. "I asked him to help me with Mrs. Haggerty's repairs. Is there a problem, Officer?"

"My name is Detective Tran. This is my partner, Detective Consuelo," he said, gesturing to the woman beside him. "We'd like a word with Steven, if you'd like to step outside." The detective's name was familiar. Mike Tran was the name on the business card Brendan had given me, the one he'd said was handling Mrs. Haggerty's case.

I thought about reaching for my phone to call my sister, but something in the officers' postures told me that wouldn't be a wise idea.

"What the hell is this about?" Steven asked, glaring at both of them.

"We'd like you to come with us to the station," Detective Tran suggested casually. "We have some questions for you about the victim who was found on this property."

Steven's eyes flashed. "You can ask me right here."

"If that's what you'd prefer."

The detective's indulgent tone set off warning bells inside me. I took Steven's arm to keep him from saying anything else. The number of officers who'd arrived to provide backup for this conversation told me this meeting was far from casual. "Maybe you should call a lawyer," I urged him in a low voice.

"I don't need a lawyer! I don't know anything about the guy."

"Are you sure about that?" Detective Tran asked. He carried himself with the confidence of a seasoned detective, the silver at his temples and crow's feet around his eyes suggesting he had all the time in the world to make this uncomfortable for both of us. "Let me jog your memory," he said, pulling a few photographs from his breast pocket. He held one of them up. "This is Gilford Dupree. His body was found two weeks ago behind this house, under a rose garden that was installed five years ago, the same week Gilford's wife reported him missing." Detective Tran sauntered closer, his eyes never leaving Steven's.

Steven's hands clenched at his sides. A muscle worked in his jaw as he glanced at the photo. "I don't see what any of this has to do with me."

"I've spent the last two weeks trying to find a tie between Mr. Dupree and this house," the detective said. "I investigated all the neighbors. I checked into every possible connection between Dupree and the Haggerty family, and you know what I came up with?" He waited a breath. "Nothing. But I did find something else—a receipt for a landscaping project with your name on it." He wagged a finger at Steven as his temple began to glisten with sweat. "That receipt got me thinking about people who work in the dirt for a living—about how convenient it might be for someone like that to bury a body. Someone strong. Someone with the tools to do it. Like an excavator. Or a landscaper. Or even a farmer," he said, looking Steven dead in the eyes.

My blood went cold. Detective Tran didn't say another word. He didn't have to. The subtext was clear: Steven owned a sod farm—the same farm where five bodies had been exhumed last fall. Steven had been cleared of any suspicion in that case, but Detective Tran didn't appear convinced of that.

"I don't know what the hell you think you're talking about." Steven seethed, pointing a hard finger toward the backyard. "Sure, I installed their damn rose garden. But I never killed anyone. I never even met that Dupree guy."

Detective Tran held up another photo. "Maybe you knew his wife."

I didn't think Steven could get any paler than he was when the detectives first walked through that door, but now he looked ill.

"What is he talking about?" I asked him in a low voice.

Steven and Detective Tran exchanged a look so long it felt like a dare. "You sure you wouldn't prefer to have the rest of this conversation at the station?" the detective asked him.

"Do I have a choice?"

"I'll give you two a minute," Detective Tran said to Steven. "When you're ready to go, we'll be waiting right outside."

The officers filed out, hovering close to the house. Radios squawked in the driveway. I whirled to my ex-husband as they watched us through the windows. "Jesus, Steven! Did you sleep with Gilford Dupree's wife?"

"Of course not!"

"Then why are they taking you in?"

"I don't know!" He dragged a hand through his sweating hairline as he paced. "I might have delivered some mulch to her house a few years ago, but I swear to god I didn't sleep with her, Finn!"

I took a deep breath and let it out slowly, careful to keep my voice down. "Don't say a word to anyone. I'll call a lawyer." I had no idea if Steven was telling the truth, but now wasn't the time to take any chances.

"Call Guy. Tell him to meet me at the station."

Guy had been Steven's fraternity brother in college and, more recently, the ruthless family law attorney who had handled Steven's side of our divorce. He was a shark when it came to custody agreements and weaseling his clients out of child support, but he definitely was not qualified to handle a situation like this. "Guy specializes in divorces, Steven. He doesn't do criminal law."

"Doesn't matter, because I'm not a criminal."

"I'll ask him for a referral."

"I don't want a referral. Guy can represent me."

"He's too close to be objective. I'll find you someone else."

"I don't want someone else! I want Guy to do it!"

Detective Tran opened the door, his gaze sweeping over us as if he'd been drawn by our raised voices. "Time's up. Let's go."

Steven handed me his truck keys as the uniformed officer escorted him out. I followed them to the door, freezing at what I saw waiting on the other side of it. A crowd of neighbors had gathered along the street and in their yards, gaping at the police cars and lights. Stacey was huddled with a group of the neighborhood moms, all of them whispering behind their hands, but I was sure that wouldn't keep the gaggle of kids they'd brought along from hearing them.

Riley and Max stood front and center of the crowd, their phones held up in the air, recording Steven as he was escorted from the house. The words *affair* and *murder* rolled like a wave through the crowd.

The door of my house opened across the street. Vero appeared on my front stoop. She held Zach on her hip, and Delia clutched her leg. One of Delia's friends called out to her in a high child's voice. "Delia, why are the police taking your daddy? Did he do something bad?"

Delia's eyes welled with tears. My heart cracked as her lower lip began to tremble. She buried her face in Vero's sweater as her father was led down the driveway by a procession of cops. Steven clenched his jaw and stared at the pavement, unable to look at our children as the whispers of the crowd grew louder.

Vero must have read the horror on my face. She ushered Zach and Delia quickly into the house.

Detective Tran opened the back door of a police cruiser. A few of the spectators applauded as Steven was escorted inside. Engines started and blue lights swirled as the police cars left Mrs. Haggerty's house, one by one.

CHAPTER 6

Thirty minutes later, my kitchen looked like the receiving line at a funeral. Vero had called my sister in a panic as soon as the police cars had swarmed Mrs. Haggerty's house. My sister had called our mom. My sister's girlfriend, Sam, had called Nick. Nick had called Joey, and just when I thought we couldn't fit one more person in my kitchen, Javi and Ramón had come bursting into my house wielding crowbars, determined to save us from some unspecified danger after they'd heard the police broadcast our street address over the scanner at the garage.

The only people who hadn't yet shown up at my house were Steven's parents and his sister, and I had no intention of calling them. The only call I'd made since Steven had been carted off by police had been to his attorney, and since Guy was practically family to the entire Donovan clan, I didn't imagine it would take long before they all heard the news. My only comfort was that none of them lived within easy driving distance of South Riding.

I scooped up Zach as he raced past me, once again wearing no pants. I handed him to Vero. She passed him to my mother. My mother passed him to my father, who held Zach at arm's length, unsure of what to do with him.

"Why won't he keep his pants on?" my father asked.

"Probably something to do with the apple and the tree. Too soon?" Vero asked when my sister shoved her.

My mother took Delia's hand. "Come on, Paul. Let's take the children to the park so the grown-ups can talk." She kissed my cheek and whispered, "When we get back, I'll have Vero pack their overnight bags. The kids can spend the night with us. I'll keep them as long as you need. You have enough to deal with right now."

"Thank you," I whispered back. She gave my shoulder an encouraging squeeze and led my children and my father out of the kitchen.

"So let me get this straight," Javi said when the kitchen fell quiet. "The dude stepped out on his pregnant wife, messed around with the dead guy's woman, then lied about it when the cops asked him if he knew them?"

Ramón shook his head. "He sounds like a first-class tool."

"You have to admit, it doesn't look good," my sister said to Nick.

"I can't believe he'd do something that stupid," Sam said.

"I can," Vero and Georgia said in unison.

"What now?" Vero asked. Everyone turned to me, as if *I* should know the answer.

I left the room, sick of the gossip and speculation. If they all knew so much about my former husband, let them figure it out.

Joey talked on his cell phone as he paced in the living room. He dropped his voice when he noticed me listening in the foyer. "How long? . . . Are they filing charges? . . . Who's lead on the case? . . . What have they got?"

I grabbed my coat off the rack and walked out the front door, suffocating under the sympathetic looks everyone was giving me.

The crowd had finally cleared from the street. Only a handful of stragglers remained, chatting on a neighbor's porch.

A car stereo thumped in the distance, the bass growing louder as it came into view. I squinted to see who it was as the car rolled slowly toward my house. There was no way Steven's sister could have made it here from Philly this fast. Mrs. Haggerty was due back from her book club any minute, but I didn't imagine any of her friends listened to their music loud enough to wake the dead.

I cringed when the squared-off hood of an ancient-looking sedan cruised toward my driveway. Cam sat proudly behind the wheel. Mrs. Haggerty was riding shotgun. Neither of them looked as nervous about this as they should have as the front tire of her Lincoln Mark V rolled up over the curb and then bounced back down onto the asphalt. Cam put the car in park, reaching around the massive wheel and jamming the lever into place. Grinning like an idiot, he wrenched the stiff turn crank on his door. When his window refused to roll down farther than an inch, he rolled it back up and heaved open his door.

The hinge creaked as he flung it wide and got out. He looked at the car like it was a thing of wonder. "She's a beauty. Am I right?" He ran a loving finger down the length of the rusted hood. "We picked it up from the police impound lot. They said we just needed a licensed driver to sign for the keys. I guess it was leaking some oil. They were so happy to get rid of it, they didn't even charge me for the damage to the fence." He used his sleeve to wipe a few fresh scratches in the paint. "Those gates just aren't wide enough for such a *commanding* turn radius. Right, Mrs. H?" He turned to find she was still sitting in the passenger seat. "Oh, shit, sorry!" He scrambled around the front of the Lincoln and opened her door. He called out to me over the smoking hood as he helped her out of the car. "Mrs. H said if I take her to her meetings and stuff, I can drive it when she's not using it."

A cloud of foul-smelling fumes wafted from the engine, and I waved it from my face. "I'm surprised it still runs."

"Nonsense," Mrs. Haggerty said. "In my day, things were built with sturdier stuff. They don't make cars like they used to. This one will probably outlive you!" At the rate I was going, that wasn't really saying much.

The front door opened. Javi came out of my house with a tire iron in his hand, wearing a dark look. He crossed the lawn toward us with Vero's cousin in tow. They both slowed, raising eyebrows at Cam and his smoking car as they strolled toward it to get a closer look.

Cam eyed Javi cautiously. Their first meeting back in January hadn't been the ideal meet-cute, and I'm pretty sure Cam was still scared shitless of him. He frowned at the tire iron as Javi peeked in the Lincoln's window.

"Seventy-eight?" Javi asked.

"Seventy-nine," Cam said.

"You mind?" Javi asked, reaching for the door handle.

Cam gave the impression of a careless shrug, but his expression was wary. "Be my guest."

Javi opened the door and popped the latch under the dashboard. He settled into the driver's seat, inspecting the car's interior as Ramón looked under the hood. Cam came up beside him, peeking over Ramón's shoulder as he inspected a few connections and checked some of the fluids. They huddled close, talking about the car in low tones as they exchanged contact information on their phones. Javi joined them, the conversation turning to bodywork and paint. I tuned them out, wishing everyone would leave. I had far bigger problems to deal with than book club meetings and automotive repairs, and Mrs. Haggerty's damn hoopty was leaking black and green fluids all over the street. The HOA would probably fine me for that.

Javi and Ramón bumped knuckles with Cam. They called out a goodbye to me and got into Javi's Camaro. The engine roared, and Cam watched them drive off. He snapped Ramón's business card between his fingers, then tucked it in his pocket.

"Why are there so many people here?" he asked me, as if he'd only just noticed the other vehicles. "Looks like one hell of a party. What are we celebrating?"

"We're not celebrating anything," I said irritably.

"I assume refreshments will be provided," Mrs. Haggerty said, scrutinizing me over her glasses.

Cam's face lit up. "You should have been at the party I threw in Atlantic City, Mrs. H. You would have loved it. We had champagne and shrimp . . . the works! I ordered every party favor you could think of," he said smugly. "We even had a few lovely ladies in attendance." I remembered the lovely ladies he was referring to; he'd paid them by the hour. Cam dug his phone from his pocket. "Maybe I should call them and see if they have any friends in the area."

I swiped it away from him before he could dial. "We are not calling any escorts and this is not a party! Steven was taken to the station for questioning about the Dupree murder. That's the only reason these people are all here. And no, I don't plan to feed anyone!"

Cam gave Mrs. Haggerty a playful chuck on the arm. "Did you hear that, Mrs. H? If they arrest someone else, you're probably off the hook. That's something to celebrate, right?"

I shoved his phone back in his hand and stormed off to my minivan, hiding behind it where I could be alone so I wouldn't be tempted to murder anyone myself. I leaned back against the door, taking a deep slow breath as Mrs. Haggerty and Cam retreated to the house. The front door shut behind them, muting the cacophony of voices inside. It was too cold out for the chirps of crickets or the tiny frogs Delia and Zach liked to chase in the spring. The only sound was the quiet *tink* of Mrs. Haggerty's cooling engine and the laughter of children playing in a neighbor's yard. I tipped my head back and shut my eyes, savoring the silence as footsteps approached from my garage. I held my breath, hoping it wasn't my mother or Vero telling me I had to come back inside the house.

"Hey," Nick said softly. I opened my eyes to find him peeping around the side of the van. "I hoped I'd find you out here, but if you'd rather be alone—"

"No." I took his hand, holding it like a lifeline. "I just needed some air."

He brushed a tender kiss to my head. The look on his face told me he wasn't just here to check on me. "What's wrong?" I asked.

"Joey made a few calls," Nick said, tucking my hair behind my ear. He kept his voice low, conscious of the bystanders lingering on my neighbor's porch. "He used to work in Loudoun before Internal Affairs reassigned him. He knows a lot of people in the department over there."

"And?" I pushed when Nick hesitated. "What did he find out?"

"They're looking hard at Steven for this, Finn. They've got means and opportunity. All they need now is proof he had a motive. Given Steven's history with Mrs. Dupree, it won't be hard for Tran to come up with one."

"But what if Steven's telling the truth? What if he doesn't even know that woman?"

Nick clenched his jaw, probably to keep himself from pointing out the glaring fault in my argument. "I'm not saying Steven is guilty. But it might not be a bad idea to distance yourself from him until he's cleared."

"He's my kids' father, Nick! I can't distance myself from that!" The neighbors' chatter quieted at my raised voice, and I threw them a scathing look.

"You're right. I'm sorry." He took me gently by the shoulders, ducking to meet my eyes. "That's not what I was suggesting," he said quietly. "But this investigation is circling too close to you, and I don't like that there's nothing I can do to keep you out of it. Maybe I'd have some sway if it was happening in my own department, but the most I can do is keep an ear to the ground. Joey's feeding me all the news he can, but the cops in Loudoun know he was working with IA, and no one trusts him enough to let him get close. I'm afraid Mike Tran is going to drag you into this investigation before I can get ahead of it."

"This isn't about me!" I cried.

"This has everything to do with you!" he whispered, gesturing for me to keep my voice down. "I know there are things you're not telling me, Finn. About the Mickler investigation and Ike Grindley and the bodies they found on Steven's farm last fall. I know—" He held up a finger as I opened my mouth to protest. "I know you were involved. And I know it wasn't your fault and you probably got mixed up in things you didn't want to be part of, and I don't want you to tell me how or why because once I know, I have a duty to act on that information and I don't want to do that." He pressed the heels of his hands against his eyes, as if speaking those words had cost him something. He shook his head and blew out a breath. "I told myself we could let the truth die with Zhirov's case and we could move on with our lives. But Mike Tran is a bulldog, Finlay.

He knows he can't detain Steven for long. He's found a thread of a motive that connects back to Steven and his farm, and he's going to pull that thread hard to come up with a charge. I won't be able to protect you once that rug starts to unravel."

I blinked up at him, head tipped. He couldn't protect me from Mike Tran's investigation, but what if we could stop it from getting that far? "Unless we can figure out who *really* had a motive to kill Gilford Dupree."

Nick looked at me as if I had lost my mind. "No! Whatever you're thinking, Finlay, shut it down right now!"

"Why not? It wouldn't be the worst idea I've ever had."

"It's definitely the worst idea you've ever had! Did you not hear what I just said about keeping your distance?"

We both fell silent as my parents emerged from the house. My mother took the children's hands and walked them toward the playground at the end of the block. My father followed behind her, carrying a picnic cooler and a diaper bag.

One of the older children playing soccer on the street corner paused his game to watch them. He called out to his friends, "Check it out. Those are the kids whose dad slept with the dead guy's wife."

My mother covered Delia's ears as my father nudged the children along. My face heated with rage. The rumors about Steven had gone too far. I couldn't care less if my neighbors wanted to gossip about my ex-husband, but I drew the line when it hurt my children. I was determined to get to the bottom of this once and for all. If Gilford Dupree's wife was lying, she'd better be ready to set the record straight.

"Where are you going?" Nick called after me as I opened the door of my van.

"To Penny Dupree's," I snapped, "to ask her if she slept with my husband."

"Finlay, stop!" He put a hand on the window when I slammed the door between us. "You can't just show up at her house asking her those kinds of—*Christ*," he said as I started the engine.

I put the van in gear, leaving Nick standing in my driveway as I peeled out.

I drove with one hand, googling Penny's address with the other. Before I made it out of the neighborhood, Nick's Impala rolled up behind me. My cell phone rang in my lap. His name flashed on the screen. I ignored it, pulling a hard right out of South Riding and hitting the gas, not bothering to check my blind spots as I merged into oncoming traffic.

Nick's face was livid in my rearview mirror when he caught up to me again. He grabbed the mic from the radio under his dashboard and put it to his mouth, his voice booming from the speakers. "Pull over, Finlay," he said in his cop voice. "Please," he added when I didn't comply.

I accelerated through a yellow light. He rolled through it as it turned red, sticking close to my bumper. "Pull over so we can talk about this like rational adults."

I was too angry to be rational. I shifted over a lane, putting distance between us.

He shifted over, too, blue lights beginning to flash in his front grille.

My phone vibrated again. This time, Vero's name appeared on the screen. I connected the call.

"Finn? Where the hell did you and Nick go racing off to? One minute you were practically making out behind the van in the driveway, and the next both your cars were gone."

"We were not making out! We were just talking."

"Mrs. Haggerty says it looks more like the two of you were arguing. So does your sister. Cam thinks so, too. Wait—" she said, muting the phone against her body, "your mom wants to know what you and Nick were arguing about. She's very concerned. She wants to know if this means she should plan Georgia and Sam's wedding first."

"There is no wedding!" I snapped. "Were you all watching us?"

"Not all of us," Vero clarified. "The rest of us were too busy starting a pool about whether or not Steven is lying. I hate to break it to you, but the odds don't look good."

"I don't care what it looks like! I'm going to Penny Dupree's house to find out the truth!"

"You can't go to that woman's house!" Vero cried. "If a sharp object accidentally impales her and she dies a slow horrible death while you're standing in her living room, who do you think is going to get blamed for her murder? The scorned then-wife of the douchebag she was sleeping with. That's who! You're not going there alone, Finlay!"

"I'm not going alone. Nick's right behind me." His siren whooped twice in warning. "Shit," I murmured, catching his eyes in my rearview mirror. "I have to go. I'll be home before the kids' bedtime. There's leftover meatloaf in the fridge. And don't worry," I said before she could ask, "I don't have any sharp objects in my purse."

"That's probably smart. Also, remember to tuck your thumb under your fist before you—"

I disconnected the call and tossed my phone in the drink holder. My van shook as it struggled to meet the demands of my angry foot. It's not like I didn't already know Steven was a cheater before today's shiny new revelation. Hell, apparently everyone did. But I was sick of people talking about me and the kids as if Steven's mistakes defined us. I didn't want Delia to grow up as the *cheater's kid* or the *murderer's kid.* Or the *daughter of the woman who'd had no idea what her husband had been doing under her own damn roof.* Every bet against Steven felt like a bet against me, like I was too foolish or too naive to have seen through all of his lies from the beginning.

Nick's Impala surged after me until he was right on my bumper. He eased his car a few feet to the left, making sure I could clearly see his police lights in my driver's side mirror.

He lifted the mic to his lips. "Finlay, please. This is a bad idea." I shook my head, certain he could see me, too. He was going to have to arrest me for evading a traffic stop or wait until I was done confronting Penny. Either she was lying or Steven was, and there was only one way to find out who.

I turned left onto Mrs. Dupree's street, temporarily losing Nick to the rush of oncoming traffic. I slowed down, angling forward in my seat to search the mailboxes for her house number. It didn't take me long to find it.

I pulled over and shut off the engine while I glared at her front door. It was the same one I had remembered from the images on the news. I tried to picture Steven's truck parked in her driveway. His hand on her door as he knocked. I had hoped it would be harder to imagine than it was.

Nick's car screeched to the curb behind me. He killed the blue lights and got out, jogging to intercept me as I opened my door. "Stop," he said, cornering me as I got out of the van. "I know you're hurt and you're angry, but you don't have to do this."

"Neither do you." The look on my face told him he was welcome to go.

"Can you at least tell me what you plan to do?"

"Why? So you can arrest me for intent?"

"If it's for your own good, yes."

"You'll just have to trust that I know what I'm doing."

Nick swore under his breath as I turned toward Penny Dupree's house. He put a hand on either side of me, boxing me against the side of my hood before I could start walking. "Just promise me you won't do anything that will give her grounds to press charges. Whatever she says, violence is not the answer."

"Except when it is."

"Finn!"

"Fine, I promise."

"Then I'm coming with you." When I didn't object, he let his arms fall. "We're going to identify ourselves. *Politely,*" he emphasized, keeping pace with me as I stormed up the walkway to her door. "We're going to tell her why we're here and ask her if she'd be willing to step outside and talk to us. We're not going in," he said firmly as I smacked her doorbell. "And if she asks us to leave, we're going to respect that decision and—"

Mrs. Dupree's door swung open.

If I had seen her face on the news I hadn't bothered to remember it, but seeing it now stole the words right off my tongue.

Penny's blond hair hung in casual waves. She wore close-fitting jeans that showed off her long, toned legs and a deep V-neck sweater that revealed a hint of cleavage. Steven definitely had a type, and Penny was it. She wasn't a young woman, by any stretch—maybe ten years older than me, if I had to guess—but her similarities to Steven's ex-fiancée were undeniable. I could tell by the sudden shift in Nick's posture that he noticed them, too.

"Hello, Mrs. Dupree. I'm Detective Nicholas Anthony with the Fairfax County Police Department, and this is—"

"Finlay Donovan," I said, once I'd managed to recover. "My ex-husband is Steven Donovan, the landscaper who delivered your mulch the summer before your husband went missing. I'd like a word with you," I said, taking a step closer to the threshold.

Nick cut his eyes to me, a warning in them.

Penny held the door open and stepped aside. It took a moment for my brain to catch up. I had fully expected her to tell us to leave. Had visions of throwing a foot in the door to keep her from slamming it in my face. But she just stood there, politely waiting for me to enter her home. "I figured you might find your way here eventually. You're welcome to come in."

Nick's hand tightened against the small of my back. "Maybe it would be better if we speak outsi—"

I walked through the door, forcing him to follow me into her home.

"Sorry for the mess," Penny said, leading us into an immaculate living room. Every surface was spotless. Every magazine and coffee-table book felt intentionally placed, every potted plant and flower vase perfectly staged, every book on her elaborate shelves organized by color and height. I skimmed the spines as I walked past them on my way to her designer sofa. The books were all popular bestsellers, a curated collection of commercial Oprah-and-Reese–approved titles that had probably been chosen as much for their shelf appeal as their content. Her interior could have been showcased on a Home & Garden TV program.

"Please, sit down." She gestured to the sofa, taking the love seat for herself.

Nick sat beside me, close enough for our elbows to brush.

Penny sat at an angle to face us, her legs crossed at the knees, her fingers laced and resting loosely atop them. "I'm assuming you're here because you want to know if your husband was unfaithful. You want to know if he slept with me while he was married to you."

The casual way she said it took me off guard, and frankly stole some of the wind from my sails. I had expected her to be defensive. To be offended. To refuse to discuss it. But Penny didn't seem to mind.

I nodded once. Then again, more certainly this time. "Steven was taken to the station a few hours ago for questioning," I said. "The police seem to think he knows you."

"He does."

"Because he delivered mulch to your home five years ago," I suggested.

"Because I invited him inside when he was done, so I could write him a check. It was hot. I offered him a cold beer, we talked for a while, and one thing led to another." There was no shame in the woman's confession. Only an elegant shrug. She wasn't outraged or emotional the way Steven had been when he'd sworn up and down he'd never touched her. Her reaction was all painfully matter-of-fact. It was also suspiciously vague.

"What if I don't believe you?"

Her smile was both sympathetic and sad, and not nearly guilty enough. "You don't have to believe me. The police do, and Steven knows the truth. I suppose that's all that matters."

"Prove it," I said.

"Excuse me?" She batted a set of perfectly false lashes at me, as if she must have misheard.

I leaned forward, perched on the edge of my seat, fully intending to press my advantage. "If you and my ex-husband were as intimate as you're suggesting, tell me something you could only know if you'd been with him."

A nervous smile broke over Penny's face. It cracked in tiny lines at the corners of her mouth, revealing the truth of her age. It wasn't the fact that she was significantly older than Steven that made me think she was lying—I'd be a hypocrite to assume that after my fling with a twenty-two-year-old law student last fall. Julian Baker and I had only briefly dated, but those few short weeks had been fiery enough. It wasn't Penny's age. It was something else. Something I couldn't quite put my finger on.

She looked back and forth between Nick and me. "I don't think you really want me to do that."

"Oh, but I do."

"Finn," Nick whispered. I held up a hand, holding Penny Dupree's stare. Steven was as average as they come, in every possible way. If you were to strip him naked and stick him in a lineup, you'd be hard-pressed to find anything uniquely memorable about him.

"Well," she said with a hesitant look between us, "there was that one thing . . ."

"Go on," I prodded. She was bluffing. I had her on the ropes.

"There was that noise he would make . . . right before he . . . you know . . ."

The air left my lungs as Penny looked away.

I did know. On the rare occasions when Steven and I did have sex, I used to have to close our bedroom windows to keep the neighbors from hearing him. The only way Penny could know that about him was if she had heard those sounds, too.

I stood up and pointed a finger at her. "Just because Steven screwed you once doesn't mean he murdered your husband." At the very least, she could acknowledge *that* accusation against him was bullshit.

Her face flushed with shame. "If it had only been once, I might agree with you."

Nick put a steadying hand on my back. "We should probably go," he said quietly. He stood, but I couldn't make myself walk out with him. While none of this was sitting right with me, there was one thing about her confession that felt entirely wrong.

"If you suspected back then that Steven had something to do with your husband's disappearance, why wait until now to tell the police?"

Penny shook her head, confusion knitting her brow. "I never told them about my tryst with Steven."

I frowned. "If you never told them, how did Detective Tran find out?"

"I asked him the same thing. He told me he heard it on a podcast, some true crime show run by a couple of local college kids. They said they got an anonymous tip from someone who claimed I'd been cheating on my husband. Detective Tran came to my house a few days ago and asked to see my financial records. That's where he found the check I had written to Steven for the mulch. He noticed the address on Steven's invoice—that it was on the same street where Gilford's body was found. He confronted me about it once he made the connection. I never told him about my fling with Steven until he asked."

The podcasters had to be Riley and Max. But who had been their anonymous source?

"Thank you for your time, Mrs. Dupree." Nick nudged me again.

I didn't look at her as I stood. Penny Dupree had been courteous enough, but she'd slept with my husband while I'd been eight months pregnant, and I didn't owe her any pleasantries. I stormed past her and out the front door.

"I'm sorry," she called after me. "I know what we did was wrong. But maybe you're better off without him."

I didn't give her the satisfaction of admitting she was right.

Nick jogged after me as I tromped over her lawn to get to my van. "Finn, wait. I'll follow you home."

"Don't." I stepped out of his reach, unable to stand the sympathy in his wince. This was nothing I hadn't been through before. "I don't need a police escort. I'll be just fine on my own."

I got in my minivan and slammed the door.

Nick's Impala had followed me most of the way home, though he'd been careful to maintain his distance. I hadn't tried to shake him, but I hadn't slowed down for him either. His headlights disappeared from view once I made the turn into South Riding, flashing twice in farewell before he continued on.

My street was dark, my driveway vacant except for Steven's abandoned pickup. The barrage of cars that had flanked both sides of the driveway when I'd left the house earlier—my sister's sedan, my mother's Buick, Joey's Explorer—were all gone when I finally pulled in.

Vero had texted me an hour ago to let me know the house was (mostly) empty, my parents had taken the children to their place, and there was a hot meal and a stiff drink waiting for me when I was ready to come home.

Mrs. Haggerty's ancient Lincoln loomed like a ghost in her driveway, which meant Cam was probably still in my living room.

Sure enough, I unlocked my front door and was greeted by a barrage of gunfire and squealing tires. The house smelled faintly of garlic and pepperoni. Cam and Mrs. Haggerty sat shoulder to shoulder in the dark, their oddly matched shapes silhouetted by the bright light of the TV screen. An empty pizza box sat on the coffee table in front of them. Neither of them looked up from their game as I came inside and shut the door.

Grateful not to have to talk to anyone, I slipped off my shoes and headed upstairs.

Vero's door was shut. I listened before knocking, hoping she was awake, but her low voice suggested she was on the phone, probably with Javi. I retreated to my bedroom instead, not bothering to interrupt her.

The room smelled slightly of Mrs. Haggerty's arthritis cream. I switched on a single lamp by the bed and then closed the door, muting the sound of the TV downstairs while I hunted in my dresser for clean clothes for the morning. I gathered a pair of clean underwear and some pj's, too, not caring if any of my selections matched. My hand paused on the red negligee. The silk and lace spilled like water through my fingers as I dropped it back in the drawer.

When I had everything I needed for the night, I switched off the lamp and turned to go.

Light flashed through the blinds, twice in quick succession, the burst of it casting shadows over the wall.

Hugging my clothes to my chest, I walked to the window and peeked around the blinds, wondering if Nick had changed his mind and followed me the rest of the way home.

A car idled at the foot of my driveway with its headlights off, and though I couldn't make out the model or color of the small hatchback in the dark, I was certain it wasn't Nick's Impala. Someone was sitting in the driver's seat, pointing a flashlight at my window. The driver lingered in front of my mailbox before slowly driving off.

Just like Friday night, when Mrs. Haggerty had gone on her patrol of the neighborhood.

I set my clothes on the dresser and hurried down the stairs, careful not to attract Cam or Mrs. Haggerty's attention as I slipped on my shoes on my way out of the house. I opened the mailbox and found a folded note inside it.

I'm ready to join the club. See you on Tuesday.

I sighed at the ridiculousness of it all. Here I was, trying to keep my ex-husband out of prison for a crime that had happened in Mrs. Haggerty's backyard. Meanwhile, she was playing video games in my house, oblivious to everything, sneaking out in the middle of the night to deliver secret messages to her friends and scheduling social calls she couldn't even drive herself to. It was like living with a teenager.

I carried the note back up to my room and set it on my nightstand, beside Mrs. Haggerty's cell phone, where she'd be sure to see it. The image of the cell phone and the book club message sitting side by side struck an odd chord in my brain. I paused there for a moment after switching off the lamp.

Why were these women delivering handwritten notes? Mrs. Haggerty had a cell phone, and she knew how to use it. Why hadn't she and her friend simply called each other?

"Where the hell have you been?" Vero whispered behind me. "I was getting worried."

I clutched my chest and whirled around to find her standing in the doorway.

"And what are you doing in here in the dark?" she asked, eyeing me suspiciously.

"Nothing." I collected my clothes and met her in the hallway.

"How did it go?" she asked. "Are the neighbors going to post reels of your catfight on Instagram tomorrow?"

"There was no catfight. Penny was perfectly pleasant about the whole damn thing."

Vero dragged me into my office and shut the door. The rollaway bed was neatly made up for me and she sat down on the edge of it, pulling me down with her. "What did you find out?"

I flopped back against the pillow. "Steven and Penny were definitely involved. She knew something about Steven. Something she only could have known if they'd slept together."

Vero's nose crinkled with disgust. "Like that crazy noise he makes right before he—?"

I sat up and gasped. "How do you know about that?"

"Are you kidding? The playground moms were all talking about it for months last year after you two split up. Mrs. Zimmerman heard him and Theresa going at it one afternoon while she was walking her dog past Theresa's town house. She told Reanne, and Reanne told Stacey, and Stacey's got a big mouth so she told everyone. Paula said there were some nights she could hear him from her—"

"Wait . . ." I said, getting up to pace the room. Theresa's town house was only a few blocks down the street. I turned back to Vero. "If everyone in the neighborhood knows Steven is noisy in bed, who's to say Penny wasn't lying about the whole thing? What if she was just repeating something she'd heard to make her story more convincing?"

Vero pulled a face. "Why would she lie about sleeping with Steven?"

"Maybe she's trying to deflect suspicion from someone else." Vero listened while I told her about the podcasters who'd broken the news of the affair. "Don't you think it's a little convenient that as soon as the police found Penny's husband, some anonymous person tipped off a podcast, claiming she cheated on her husband five years ago? And suddenly Steven's a suspect because she happened to hand over a receipt for some mulch?" If someone needed a patsy to take the fall for this murder, Steven was the perfect choice—he lived directly across the street from the place where they'd found the body. He had a reputation for being a cheater, he had worked on Mrs. Haggerty's garden just before Gilford went missing, and only a handful of months ago, he had been all over the news because five bodies had been exhumed from his farm. "What if Penny killed her husband and she's framing Steven to cover it up?"

"But if *she* killed Gilford, how did his body end up in Mrs. Haggerty's backyard? The police said they couldn't find any connection between the Duprees and the Haggertys."

"The police missed a connection before," I pointed out. "Who's to say they didn't miss another?"

Vero looked doubtful. "If *they* missed a lead, how are we supposed to find it?"

"I think we need to figure out who placed that anonymous call."

CHAPTER 7

Vero and I hovered over her laptop in the kitchen an hour later. The YouTube logo framed Riley and Max's faces on the screen. We had watched every episode we could find related to the Dupree murder, including the most recent one in which Riley and Max revealed the details of Mrs. Dupree's secret affair with the "newest suspect in the case."

"We can't just post a comment under their video asking them who their anonymous source is," I pointed out.

Vero drummed her nails. "I say we show up at that little shit's dorm, tie him to a chair, and beat the answer out of him." She turned to look at me. When I didn't outright reject the idea, she bolted out of her seat. "I'll get the duct tape. You figure out where he lives."

"Sit," I said, pushing her back down into her chair. I glanced at the living room, where Cam and Mrs. Haggerty were engrossed in their game, careful to keep my voice down. "I'm not suggesting we resort to violence, but maybe the threat of violence isn't the worst idea."

"I don't understand."

"Riley and Max aren't going to reveal their source without the right motivation. What would motivate two podcasters who are desperate to become famous?"

"The promise of two black eyes and several broken teeth?"

"A lead for a story that no one else has reported on." I pointed out a phone number at the bottom of the screen. "Do you still have the burner phone you bought when we were at the police academy?" Vero nodded. "I think it's time we phone in an anonymous tip."

"What are you going to do? Make up a crime?"

I shook my head. "It needs to be a real one. If Riley and Max have connections within the police department, they might vet the lead. If they suspect it was a crank call, they won't bother showing up."

"What about those warehouse murders last year? No one was convicted."

"Only because the guy who did it got off on a technicality. We need a cold case. Something that promises a big payoff if these two can solve it."

Vero's eyes locked on mine. A familiar spark lit inside them.

"No," I said, slapping my laptop closed. "I know what you're thinking," I whispered, "and we are not calling Riley and Max with a lead on Ike Grindley's case."

"Why not? They were obsessed with it! They'll jump at the chance to investigate the missing nephew of a dead loan shark from New Jersey. And the investigation here has already gone cold. The police in New Jersey are taking the lead on it now. What do we have to lose?"

"You really need me to answer that? We watched the man get crushed by a car, Vero!"

"He was trying to murder us!" she hissed over the squeal of tires coming from the television.

"That doesn't negate the fact that we asked the Russian mob to get rid of his body!"

"Exactly! We can tell Riley and Max anything we want because no one's ever going to find him. Think about it," she whispered. "We know things about Ike's case that were never revealed to the public. Riley and Max will definitely fall for it. It'll be like taking candy from a baby."

I chewed on that as I gnawed on my thumbnail. On one hand, I could see this playing out exactly as Vero had described it. On the other, given our intimate knowledge of Ike Grindley's death, it felt like too much of a risk to take.

"This could actually work in our favor, Finlay. If *we* come up with the lead, *we* control the narrative. And if we wear disguises, Riley and Max will never know who they're dealing with. We'll make them surrender their phones as a security measure, copy the data, feed them a false lead, and send them on a wild goose chase to New Jersey. At the very least, it gets them out of our hair."

I threw up my hands. "Fine."

Vero leapt out of her chair and raced to her bedroom. She hurried back down with her burner phone in her hand. She typed the podcast's tip number into a text message and handed me the phone. My fingers hovered over the keys as I considered what to say.

"Where should we meet them?" I asked. It couldn't be anyplace we could be tied to. Or anywhere someone might accidentally stumble upon us. A remote farm in a distant county seemed like the safest option.

I started typing.

There's more to the Grindley case than the feds are letting on. Meet me where they found his car if you want to know more. Tonight. 10pm.

Vero looked down her nose at me. "Ten o'clock?"

"What's wrong with ten o'clock?"

"It screams, *I'm a tired middle-aged mom who needs to be in bed at a reasonable hour.* Real criminals schedule secret meetings in the middle of the night."

"And you know this how?"

"Give me that," she said, snatching the phone and deleting the last part of my text. *Tonight. 1am.*

"Technically, that's tomorrow," I pointed out.

Vero rolled her eyes at me, then added: *Turn your phones off and come alone. If I even smell a cop, we're done.*

Vero and I left Cam and Mrs. Haggerty in front of the TV with firm instructions to stay inside the house and keep the doors locked. I gave Cam twenty dollars in cash and asked him to keep an eye on the house until we got back.

We drove Vero's Charger to the meeting. It was more reliable than my minivan, faster if we needed to make a quick getaway, and Riley and Max weren't likely to recognize it since they hadn't seen it before.

The farm where police had found Ike Grindley's burned car was nearly an hour from South Riding—far enough from both Loudoun and Fairfax's jurisdictions to seem removed from the Dupree case and remote enough that we wouldn't have to worry about being spotted. Vero avoided the highways, sticking to the lesser-traveled county roads, until we eventually turned down a long gravel drive between two neglected farm fields.

Vero took the rutted road slowly in the dark. She turned off the headlights, navigating the bends by moonlight. It reflected off a ramshackle barn in the distance, and she parked in the shadows behind it.

She killed the engine and looked around before grabbing her backpack and getting out of the car. We closed the Charger's doors as softly as possible, but the sound was drowned out by the rustle of wind through acres of high, brown grass. The sky above us was coal black and spattered with stars. It would have been beautiful if I hadn't been so terrified of being caught there.

Vero turned on her phone light and scanned the overgrown field, pausing over a patch of scorched earth at the center of it. "This is definitely the place. That must be where the police found Ike's car."

"Should we be talking to Riley and Max in the open like this?" The rural location had seemed perfect a few hours ago, but now that we were standing in the middle of it, it felt too exposed.

Vero's light cut a path through the weeds and we followed it to the front of the barn. It was a rustic, wooden shed-like structure. No locks, no lights. The massive door screeched on its hinges as she hauled it open and peeked inside. We both shrieked and ducked, covering our heads as a flurry of bats flew out.

The inside smelled like damp metal and moldering hay. Vero aimed her phone into the cavernous spaces, grabbing my hand when something scurried to avoid the light. A length of rotting rope hung ominously from the rafters and a disconcerting assortment of rusted tools had been left leaning against the splintered walls. Vero nodded a little too rigorously and swallowed when her light landed on a desiccated pile of fur and bones that I was pretty sure had once been a rabbit. "Yep, this is exactly how I pictured it."

"Pictured what?"

"Our untimely demise. Maybe you were right. This was probably a bad idea."

We backed slowly out of the barn, freezing at the sound of tires on gravel.

"Shit, they're early," Vero whispered. "What do we do?"

"Turn off the light!"

We scurried around the barn just as headlights fanned over the landscape. Vero dumped out the contents of her backpack, and we crouched in the weeds, scrambling to put on our wigs, ski masks, and gloves. Vero fluffed the ends of the blond nylon waves that protruded from the bottom of her mask, then she turned to me and fidgeted with my thick, dark curls. The wigs had been purchased from a novelty store in an Atlantic City casino. We looked like Cher and Farrah Fawcett preparing to rob a convenience store. I slapped her hand away. An electric engine hummed somewhere close before finally falling silent.

The headlights cut off. A car door opened, then another.

Vero and I peeked around the side of the barn. Riley's tiny green Prius was parked at the edge of the field, its mud-spattered hubcaps glinting in the moonlight. Riley held his cell phone in the air. We ducked back behind the barn as a bright white light shot past the side of it.

"Hello?" he called out. "Is anyone here?"

"The barn is open," Max said. "Maybe they're inside."

Their footsteps rustled through the grass. The barn door creaked.

"Hello?" Max's voice echoed from the rafters as she shined her phone light through the opening. The beam sliced through the structure, then the walls, penetrating the aged wooden slats and casting daggers of light around us. "Come out where we can see you. We want to hear your story."

Vero and I peeped through the cracks as Riley followed Max into the barn.

"We must have beat them here," Max said.

"It was a good call, coming early. We can record the intro while we wait for them. I can edit it when we get back to the dorm. Turn off your light and stand over there." Riley kept close to the door, aiming his phone light at the center of the barn, directing Max deeper inside it.

"This place gives me the creeps," she said, turning in a slow circle before switching off her light. She positioned herself in the center of his spotlight. Dust motes stirred around her. Riley's beam caught the cobwebs that dangled from the rafters above her. Max shielded her eyes against the glare. "Hurry up, let's get this over with."

He tapped his screen and held it in front of him. "Three, two, one, aaaaand . . . we're recording."

"This is Riley Bernbaum and Max Sievers, and you're listening to *In Your Backyard*, a true-crime podcast where everyday civilians like you and me investigate unsolved crimes and bring justice to victims in our local community."

"You've got to be kidding me," Vero whispered. "I told them no phones!"

"We're reporting on location in Culpeper County," Max said, "where we're pursuing a promising new lead in a developing case. Less than a month ago, Riley and I attended a citizen's police academy where we worked side by side with law enforcement. Now, we're back, armed with new skills *and* new technology. And, thanks to our sponsor . . ." Max paused, as if she was looking up a name, ". . . Donut Bliss in Bristow, Virginia, we enjoyed some steaming hot coffee on our way to solve this ice-cold case. We can't wait to dive into the box of glazed crullers that's waiting for us in the car—"

"They get free donuts for this?" Vero whispered.

"—but first we have a missing persons case to crack."

"Forget the donuts," I whispered. "What do we do about their phones?"

"At least they're not live streaming."

"That doesn't mean they won't."

"I have an idea." Vero nudged me back toward her Charger as Riley and Max continued recording. Silently, she opened her trunk, retrieving two canvas grocery totes and a roll of duct tape.

"You have duct tape in the trunk of your car?"

"I thought we could try using it to keep Zach from taking his pants off. What?" she asked at my mortified look. "Do you have a better suggestion?" She slung the tape around her wrist and handed me a grocery bag, signaling for me to follow her lead before she tiptoed back to the barn.

Riley and Max were still recording inside.

". . . The vehicle was discovered, burned beyond recognition, mere feet from where we're standing," Max said. "While the driver of the car has yet to be found, local police were able to trace the VIN and registration to a man from Pleasantville, New Jersey. Ignacious Grindley's wife reported him missing only hours before—"

"Now!" Vero launched herself at Riley, surprising him from behind. She pulled her grocery tote over his head, knocked him to the ground, and yanked his wrists behind him. His phone slipped from his hands and tumbled to the dirt, the beam shining into the rafters.

Max blinked as the light shifted away from her. She gasped as I rushed her, her sneakers slipping in the hay as she scrambled away from me. "What are you doing!" she shouted as I pulled my grocery tote over her face. It took all my weight to hold her down until Vero could get to us and tape Max's hands together.

"What do you want?" Max shouted through the tote.

Vero and I grabbed her under her armpits and hauled her through the hay, dropping her on her butt beside Riley. I retrieved his phone from the ground as he cried and sputtered. The screen was cracked, but it was still recording, and I quickly erased the footage.

I turned on his phone light, shining the beam at the green canvas grocery totes covering their heads. Riley screeched, thrashing wildly as a field mouse scampered over his ankle. "Oh, god! Did you feel that? Something was crawling on my leg!"

"Why are you doing this?" Max cried.

Vero pitched her voice deep, giving it a harsh rasp to disguise it. "We told you, no phones."

Max's grocery tote tipped curiously to the side. "Wait, are you doing Batman?"

"I am Batman," Vero rasped. She leaned close to my ear and whispered, "I've always wanted to say that." Vero searched Max's pockets for her cell phone. Max kicked out blindly as Vero took it and tapped the screen. She held it up to me, pointing at the security prompt.

"Give me the code to your phone," Vero demanded.

"Your Batman voice is pointless," Max said. "It isn't even scary."

"Are you kidding?" Riley cried. "It's terrifying! Give them your freaking passcode before they kill us, Max!"

"No!" The grocery tote rose with the stubborn lift of her chin.

Vero ripped the bag off Max's head and held the phone in front of her face, waiting for the facial recognition technology to unlock the home screen. Max crossed her eyes and stuck out her tongue, refusing to cooperate.

"We can do this the easy way or the hard way," Vero hissed through the hole in her ski mask.

Max screwed up her face and twisted away. "I'm not giving you the code to my phone."

Riley screamed, "It's 0–9–1–1! Please don't murder us!"

Vero secured the tote back over Max's head. She typed in the code, flashing me a thumbs-up as the home screen opened. She worked fast, skimming through apps and messages on both of their devices.

"I swear on Max's life, we didn't tell anyone we were coming!" Riley said.

"Shut up, Riley!"

"There's a noose in the ceiling, Max! And I'm still a virgin!"

"I think I know why," Vero said, momentarily forgetting her Batman voice. She squinted at his phone with a look of disgust. I jabbed her in the ribs. She cleared her throat and rasped, "You sent *all* of these dick pics to these women?"

Riley sniffled. "Too many?"

"One would have been too many. But twenty?"

"I thought it would increase my odds."

"So would a few inches."

"Would you please just tell us what you know about Ike Grindley?" Max snapped. "You said you had an anonymous tip!"

Vero pulled me outside the barn as Riley and Max began to argue. "I checked both their phones," Vero whispered. "There's nothing here. We'll have to try something else."

"We can't ask them for the name of their source. They might figure out who we are. We'll have to make them think it was their idea to give it to us."

"How are we going to do that?"

"Follow my lead," I said, heading back into the barn.

Riley and Max were still bickering through their totes when we came inside.

I cleared my throat and lowered my voice to the deepest register

I could manage. "Okay, you two. Listen up." I kicked their feet to get their attention. "I've conferred with my associate. We had planned to give you the tip about the Grindley case, but you broke our trust when you brought your phones, so you'll have to earn it back or we'll take our information somewhere else."

"How?" Max asked bluntly.

"Quid pro quo," I said. "You trust us with your secrets, and we'll trust you with ours."

"My penis wasn't enough?" Riley cried.

"You really want me to answer that?" Vero rasped.

"Those pictures are hardly secrets after you texted them to all those women," I pointed out. "Tell us something you *haven't* revealed to anyone."

"Like what?" Max asked.

"How about one of your sources? Give us the name of the anonymous caller who told you about the Dupree affair."

"And a donut," Vero added. I shot her a death glare. "What? You can have one, too."

"We're not giving up our source," Max said firmly. "If we reveal their identity and people find out, no one will take us seriously. Riley and I will get canceled."

"Would you rather get dead?" Vero asked.

"No!" Riley shouted. "We definitely don't want that!"

"They're not going to kill us," Max scoffed. "Batman's bluffing."

"That's it," Vero said, rolling up her sleeves and shoring up her gloves. She marched to the corner of the barn and picked up the rotting rabbit corpse by its ears.

"Ew. Seriously?" I whispered.

"It worked for Glenn Close." She grabbed a rusty hay hook in her other hand and stood in front of Riley, the fraying rope hanging within reach above her head. She jerked her chin at me and rasped. "Take off his bag, Robin."

"Robin?" I protested.

"You're not exactly Wonder Woman. Hurry up. I'm hungry."

I yanked the grocery tote off of Riley's head. His eyes were squeezed tightly shut and sweat poured down his temples.

"Open your eyes," Vero snapped.

He gave an emphatic shake of his head. "I don't want to see your face!" he cried. "You'll have one more reason to kill me, and I don't want to die!"

"Open your damn eyes, or I'll have Robin gouge them out and feed them to the mouse!"

Riley's eyes flashed open. They widened into black holes of terror as Vero held the rabbit's corpse inches from his face, its mouth stretched into a Munch-like scream. Riley shrieked loud enough to wake the dead. "The keys are in my pocket! Take all the donuts you want!"

"Tell me your source!" Vero bellowed.

"Don't do it!" Max shouted through her tote. "They're only trying to scare you!"

Vero dropped the rabbit and reached for the rope. Riley's eyes rolled up in his head and he passed out cold. He fell over sideways and slumped against Max's shoulder.

"Riley?" she said in a small quaking voice. "Riley! What did you do to him?" she cried.

"Tell us your source."

"We don't know! She never told us her name!"

She. The anonymous caller was a woman. "But you know who she is," I pushed. If Max didn't know who the source was, she wouldn't have fought so hard to keep it a secret.

"I don't know for sure," she sputtered. "It's only a suspicion."

"Spill it," Vero said in her Batman voice.

I could hear Max's swallow through the canvas. "I'm pretty sure the caller was Penelope Dupree."

Vero and I locked eyes through our ski masks.

Vero dropped the rusted farm hook. Riley stirred when she ripped the duct tape from his wrists. She dug around in his pocket for his car keys, pressed a button to unlock his car, then tossed his key ring into the hay.

"Let's get out of here," she said, laryngitis wearing at the edges of her Batman voice. "We'll grab the donuts on the way."

"What about our anonymous tip! You promised us a story!" Max cried.

Vero shrugged at me, as if to say *What the hell*? We'd be long gone by the time Riley woke up, freed Max, and they managed to find his car keys anyway. Might as well toss them a bone. If we threw it far enough, maybe they'd chase it out of the state.

I cleared my throat and affected my Robin voice. "You'll have to ask the Pleasantville police. The cops found a piece of evidence at Ike's house. The investigation has moved to New Jersey."

CHAPTER 8

I slept in too long the next morning. The sun was too high and too bright outside my window for the house to be so quiet. I bolted upright in bed before remembering the children were with my mother. Flopping back down, I buried my face in the pillow, still exhausted after our long drive home from Culpeper last night.

When Vero and I had returned to the house at two thirty in the morning, Cam was already gone. According to my phone, he'd Venmo'd himself money for an Uber just after midnight, and Mrs. Haggerty had been snoring softly in my room when Vero and I had finally crept upstairs to our beds.

Vero's door was still closed. I slipped quietly past her room and headed downstairs. Mrs. Haggerty didn't look up from the newspaper she was reading when I came into the kitchen. I hadn't even realized newspapers were still printed anymore, and I could only assume—since she could no longer drive—that she had walked across the street and taken it off her own front porch.

A glimmer of hope lit inside me as I remembered it was Sunday.

"Good morning," I said, trying to sound chipper. Mrs. Haggerty returned my greeting with a quiet grunt. "Any word from Brendan? He did say he would pick you up by Sunday. And . . . well, it's Sunday," I reminded her. "Did he mention what time he might be coming?"

"I wouldn't know. I haven't heard from him," she said tersely.

"Not at all?" That didn't bode well. It was one thing not to return my calls, but entirely another not to call his grandmother.

"Brendan's got enough to worry about. He doesn't need to be concerning himself with me."

"Don't you want to know when your house will be fixed? I haven't seen a single contractor come out to take a look."

"My grandson said that he would handle it, and he will on his own time." She snapped to the next page of her newspaper, making it clear this conversation was over. Which would have been fine if Brendan's time wasn't also cutting into mine.

My phone vibrated and my mother's name flashed on the screen. My stomach bottomed out and I hurried to answer it. "Hey, Mom. Are the kids okay?"

"Everything is fine. The children are doing great," she reassured me. "But your father is contemplating duct tape to keep Zach's pants on."

I laughed, wondering if that had been his idea or Vero's. "Thanks for taking them last night. How's Delia handling everything?" I said in a low voice, carrying my phone into the next room.

"She's doing better today. I hope it's okay that I told her a little fib. She asked what would happen to her father, and I didn't know what to say. I told her he was being suspended and he would only be gone a few days. Your sister says they can't hold him much longer if they're not pressing charges. What does Nick think?"

"I don't know. I haven't talked to him today."

"Why not?"

"I've had a lot going on."

"Georgia says you two are fighting."

"Georgia needs to keep her mouth shut."

My mother sighed. "You can't let whatever is happening with Steven interfere with your relationship, Finlay. You and Nicholas have a good thing going."

"I know."

"Then why are you pushing him away?"

"I'm not pushing him away," I said bitterly. I was keeping him at arm's length. That wasn't the same thing.

"Promise me you'll call him. If you want me to keep the kids an extra night, I can bring them home tomorrow morning on my way to water aerobics. Delia's not going to school anyway."

"No, it's okay," I insisted, rubbing my eyes. "Vero and I have everything under control. I'll come over tonight and get the kids before bedtime. I just have something I need to do first."

Like figuring out what Penny Dupree was up to.

I squinted through the windshield of my minivan just after sunset. "This is never going to work." Vero and I had parked nearly a block away from Penny Dupree's house, and even with the binoculars, I couldn't see a damn thing through her windows. They were all dark, except for a dimly lit room on the main floor. "She probably isn't even home. Her car isn't in the driveway."

"It's probably in the garage." Vero tugged on her wig. Which was actually *my* wig. Forced to decide between the ash-blond 1970s winged monstrosity she'd worn under her ski mask last night or the tangled blond wig scarf in my office desk drawer, the wig scarf had seemed like the more sensible choice. She smoothed it in place, then pulled down her visor to check her lipstick in the mirror. "How do I look?"

"No wonder I got kicked out of Panera."

"Hardy-har," she said, snapping her mirror closed. "It's either this or Farrah Fawcett." She slipped on a pair of oversized sunglasses.

"It's dark outside. How are you going to see anything in those things?"

"Would you rather Penny see my face?"

"Where's your voice recorder?" I asked.

"In my pocket."

"Let's get this over with. What's the plan?" I asked.

"I'm going to sneak around the back of her house and unlock the back door to the garage."

"It should probably bother me more that you know how to do that."

"Then we're going to steal a move from Penny's own playbook. I'm going to call her house and tell her I was having an affair with her late husband. I'll tell her I was the one who made the anonymous call to the podcasters. I'll say I have information about what really happened to Gilford and I want to go public. Then I'll tell her to meet me at the playground down the street so we can talk."

"What if she doesn't fall for it?"

"She'll come anyway. Her curiosity will get the best of her. And when she does, she's sure to trip up and say something to incriminate herself. As soon as she leaves her house, you sneak inside and start snooping." Vero adjusted her wireless earbuds, making sure they were concealed under the wig scarf she had tied around her head. She tapped the screen of her cell phone. My phone vibrated in my pocket, and I connected the call. Vero's voice came through my earbuds in stereo as she fidgeted with her settings. "Am I loud enough?"

"Painfully."

"Great, let's do this." She grabbed a set of lockpicks from her purse that probably belonged to Javi. "Get in there fast, look for anything that proves she was lying about Steven, and get out. Let me worry about getting a confession."

Vero got out of the van and crept off into the shadows. Her breaths were quick in my ears as she disappeared around the side of Penny's house. "I'm here," she whispered. "Penny's watching TV in the living room."

"Don't let her see you," I whispered. Why was I whispering? I was the one sitting in the van.

I heard a soft scrape and some quiet swearing through my earbuds. Then a soft click. "The back door is unlocked," Vero said. "I'm heading to the park. I'll make the call to Penny as soon as I get there. Tell me when she's on her way."

I tucked my phone into the pocket of my hoodie and slipped out of the van. A cold breeze sliced through my black yoga pants as I followed Vero's path between the houses. I could just make out the flash of a blond wig as Vero crossed briskly under a streetlight on her way toward the park. Lamplight filtered through the sheer curtains covering the back windows of Penny's house. I knelt under them, listening. The light of a huge television flickered on the far wall as the deep voice of an anchorman reported the local news.

A cell phone rang somewhere inside. The television went silent, the images still moving on the screen as a figure passed in front of it.

"Hello?" Penny's voice was muffled, barely audible through the windows. "I'm sorry. Do I know you?" Vero had placed a block on her number so it wouldn't show up on Penny's caller ID. I could just make out her uneasy response. "Who is this?" The curtain lifted above me, the light from inside spilling across the lawn. I pressed myself flat against the siding, breath held until the window covering fell closed again.

"Give me one good reason I shouldn't call the cops," Penny demanded.

Vero and I had planned for this possibility. An innocent person would be smart to report the call to the police. But Penny was definitely hiding something.

There was a prolonged pause before Penny spoke again. "Where? . . . I'll meet you there in five minutes."

I rose up on my knees and risked another peek through the curtains. The TV screen went dark. I nearly jumped out of my skin as Penny smacked the remote down on the coffee table and stormed to the foyer. She yanked on her boots and wrestled on a long coat, tying the sash tightly around her. The whole house shuddered as she slammed the front door.

I peered around the corner of the house as Penny's boots ate huge bites of her driveway then headed toward the park.

I dialed Vero. "She's on her way. I'm going in."

I opened the back door and crept into Penny's cavernous garage. My knee smashed into the bumper of her car as I groped around me, afraid to turn on a light. I felt along the wall, searching for the service door. When I finally found it, the doorknob wouldn't budge. "The interior door is locked."

"Look for a screwdriver. You can disassemble the knob and just take the whole damn thing off."

"I can't do that! What if she comes back and catches me?" Slivers of light leaked around the edges of a small rectangular opening at the bottom of the door. I knelt down and traced the pet door with my hand. It swished open when I pushed against it, and I had a sudden rush of panic as I listened for a dog.

The house was silent.

The faint smell of ammonia wafted somewhere close. I got down on all fours, cat litter pressing into my knees as I put my arm inside the pet door and reached above me for the lock. With a painful twist, I flipped the latch, nearly falling into the house when the door swung open. "I'm in."

A light was on over the sink in the kitchen. Another in the living room just beyond.

"I think I see Penny," Vero said in a low voice. "And she does not look happy. Better hurry. I'm not sure how long I can keep her distracted."

I flapped my hands like a frantic chicken as I tried to figure out where to start. What the hell was I supposed to be looking for?

Penny's voice was faint through my earbuds. "Who are you and what do you want?"

"I already told you," Vero answered in a cagey tone.

I opened cabinets and cupboards, moving through the kitchen at a furious pace. I checked the log of incoming and outgoing calls from her house phone. No calls to or from Riley or Max's phone numbers.

"I don't know who you *think* you are, but you definitely aren't the person who made that anonymous call about my affair."

"What makes you so sure?" Vero asked as I tossed aside notepads and grocery lists.

"Because no one knew about my relationship with Steven except for Steven and me, and I don't know you."

"*You* don't," Vero said, "but I knew your husband, and he was onto you."

"If you knew him, prove it."

"Fine."

"Are you crazy?" I hissed. "We don't know anything about Gilford Dupree that wasn't already in the news!"

Vero spoke slowly, over-enunciating every word. "I will prove it to you by telling you something that was *not* in the news."

Oh, god. She was talking to me. I ran through the first floor, my eyes skipping fast over every surface of the house, frantic for any scrap of information about Penny's husband.

"They have a piano," I blurted.

"Gilford loved the piano," Vero repeated.

Penny barked out a laugh. "He *hated* the piano! He didn't speak to me for a month after I bought the damn thing. He made me wait until he left the house to practice it."

"That's what he told you!" Vero said. "But when *we* were together, he *loved* the piano. He loved it so much, he listened to Rachmaninoff *in the bedroom*!"

The bedroom! I tore up the stairs, checking behind every door, searching for Penny's room.

"Well?" Penny prodded, clearly growing impatient when Vero was slow to produce another kernel of proof.

I scrambled into the last room at the end of the hall and flipped on the light. A figure leapt off the top of the highboy dresser. It hurled toward my face with a vicious hiss.

I screamed.

Vero screamed.

Penny Dupree's cat screamed. I grabbed it by the scruff and held it away from me before it could scratch my face off.

"What's wrong?" Penny sounded shaken.

"Nothing's wrong! I'm just trying to think! This isn't easy, you know!"

"They have a cat," I cried as the tabby's hind legs spun like tiny circular saws. "It's orange." I held it up to check its parts, unsure if it was a boy or a girl. Its collar wasn't much help. "Its name is Mozart."

"Not helping," Vero whispered.

"What?" Penny asked.

"Nothing," Vero snapped. "I must be suffering from post-traumatic amnesia. Gilbert's loss devastated me. Remembering him is very painful."

"Gilford."

"What about him?"

"My husband's *name* was *Gilford*!"

"Whatever! You know that's what I meant!"

I ran to the nearest nightstand and dragged it open, hoping if Gilford or Penny had any secrets, they'd be hidden where everyone else kept theirs. A chewed-up ballpoint pen rolled to the front of an empty drawer along with a tiny green capsule. "Mint Tic Tacs! He liked Mint Tic Tacs!" I said, grasping at straws. Vero repeated it as I ran to the closet. Both sides of it were filled with Penny's clothes. The shelves on top were stacked with popular romance novels. I rifled around behind them, knocking a pile of them to the floor. I scooped up two Colleen Hoovers, a copy of *Outlander*, and an Emily Henry rom-com and stuffed them back on the shelf beside a tower of shoeboxes. I yelped when the taped-up spine of a tattered Agatha Christie book fell and hit my toe. I pulled down the nearest shoebox and ripped off the lid. A heavy class ring rolled around inside it. I squinted at the inscriptions. "He played tennis at UVA," I blurted as I searched another box.

Vero repeated me word for word and Penny scoffed. "Anyone could have found that on the internet."

I ran to the bathroom and flipped on the light, shrieking

when I came face-to-face with a foam head on the vanity. I clutched my chest, bracing against the sink as I waited for my pulse to slow.

"It's just a wig stand," I told myself. The stray hairs in the basin were short and chestnut colored, a far cry from the blond waves Penny had been wearing the day before.

I took a calming breath and began rummaging through Penny's makeup drawer. A glossy real estate magazine had been stuffed inside. The magazine was folded open to a photo of a woman. I picked it up, the last of my anxiety giving way to unease as I recognized the face that was staring back at me.

It was Steven's ex-fiancée.

Theresa Hall posed casually in the living room of one of her pricey real estate listings. Her hair fell in long blond waves over the shoulders of her cashmere sweater, and her French-manicured hands were draped casually over her knees. She wore a pair of formfitting designer jeans that still managed to look dressy, and like everything else about Theresa, her makeup was flawless.

My gaze slid back to the counter. An open box of false French nail tips rested beside a bottle of eyelash glue. I picked up a tube of shimmery pink lip gloss. It was the same shade Theresa was wearing in the magazine.

The shock I felt at seeing Penny in person earlier that day suddenly made sense.

"She was wearing a wig," I whispered.

I ran back to her closet. The turtlenecks and generic-brand slacks hanging inside it were nothing like the designer jeans and loose-fitting sweater she'd been wearing when she'd greeted Nick and me at the door earlier that day. Except for Penny's age, everything down to the shade of her lipstick had reminded me of Theresa, as if Penny's entire appearance had been curated to make her affair with Steven more believable.

"A what?" Vero cleared her throat to get my attention.

"She's wearing a blond wig!" I shouted.

Vero chuckled darkly. "I may not remember much about Gilford," she said to Penny, "but I do know something about you. You're not really a blonde!"

Penny gasped. "Neither are you!"

"What are you doing? That's my hair! *Ow*!" Vero cried.

"I knew you were lying!" Penny shouted. "You're not fooling anyone. I know exactly who you are. You're one of those true-crime people. I already told your little friends, I'm not interested in being interviewed for your stupid podcast! Leave me alone. If I see you again, I'll report you to the cops."

I didn't wait for Vero to tell me Penny was on her way home. I dropped the magazine in the drawer, sprinted down the stairs, and bolted out the back door.

An hour later, Vero and I sat in the back of my van in the Dairy Queen parking lot, drowning our feelings of failure in two extra-large Oreo Blizzards and a double order of chili fries. We had listened to the recording of Vero's conversation with Penny three times and come to the painful conclusion that we had gleaned absolutely nothing useful from it.

"I don't get it," Vero said, propping her feet on the armrest in front of her between bites of her ice cream. "Why would Penny try to make herself look like Theresa?"

"Because Steven clearly has a type. His last two girlfriends both fit a very specific mold. Bree and Theresa were both very attractive, well-groomed blondes. They both wore their hair long, they liked designer clothes, and they both wore lots of makeup."

"How'd he wind up with you?"

"Not helping."

"I'm just saying, your argument doesn't hold up. You don't fit that description at all and he *married* you."

"Maybe so, but he left me because he was planning to marry someone else. If Max's hunch was right and Penny was the anonymous caller who told the police she was having an affair with Steven, then painting herself to look like a woman he'd be tempted to cheat with would make her bullshit story more believable."

Vero's feet dropped to the floor. She turned to me, dumbfounded. "You still don't think he actually slept with her."

"No, I don't," I said firmly.

Chocolate stuck in the corners of her open mouth as she threw a balled-up napkin at me. "After all the times that man has hurt you, why do you insist on coming to his rescue? You don't have to believe in someone after they've lied to you, Finn. Why do you keep pretending he's redeemable?"

"Because if I can't find a reason to believe him, what hope do I have that Nick will do the same for me?" I threw my french fry back in the bag, my appetite lost. "I've lied to him, Vero. Over and over. How does that make me any better than Steven?"

Vero slumped back in her seat, thoughtful as she scraped the last of her ice cream from her cup. "Let's assume you're right and Penny's framing Steven for Gilford's murder—why? Who is she protecting?"

"Maybe she's protecting herself."

"You think Penny murdered her own husband?"

"Why else would she go to so much trouble to point the finger at someone else?"

Vero dumped her empty cup in the bag. "Maybe you should talk to Nick about this."

"And say what? I kidnapped two college students and broke into a woman's house? I can't go to Nick with this. Not until we have actual proof that Penny lied about Steven." All the evidence we had managed to gather so far was hearsay or circumstantial. Between Max's uncertain hunch that the anonymous caller had been Penny, a wig stand, some press-on nails, and a photo in a magazine, all we could conclude was that Penny was up to something. And we couldn't even prove that much.

"What now?" Vero asked.

I checked my phone. No missed calls. No texts. Nick and I hadn't talked since I'd left him standing in front of Penny's house yesterday. I hated that his silence since had felt worse than fighting. At least when we argued, I knew where we stood.

I climbed into the front seat and started the engine. "Let's go to my parents' house and pick up the kids. We'll take them home and get them ready for bed. Once they're down for the night, there's something I need to do."

CHAPTER 9

Vero and I bathed the children and put them to bed. Then I changed into a pair of jeans that didn't smell like cat litter before driving to Nick's apartment. He had given me his address right after we'd returned from Atlantic City, but between the hours he'd been keeping at work and the nights he'd spent at my house, this was my first time actually seeing the place.

I parked my van beside his car. A lamp glowed in a window of his ground-level unit. It was nearly ten o'clock on a Sunday night. Too early for him to be sleeping, but too late to call and ask permission to come over.

I got out of the van and walked to his apartment before I could talk myself out of it. The door opened as I raised my hand to knock.

Nick stood in the doorway, wearing a loose-fitting tank top over a pair of faded sweatpants. I wondered if he'd been preparing for bed.

"Hey," he said, studying my face.

"Hey," I said, feeling foolish for coming. I wasn't entirely sure why I was there. Only that I hadn't wanted to leave things the way we had the day before. "Can I come in?"

He stood aside, making room for me to pass, our shoulders brushing as I entered the narrow hallway into his apartment. The galley kitchen to my right was dark, the dishwasher humming quietly. The pass-through above the sink overlooked a cozy lamplit living room, the one I'd seen glowing from the parking lot outside.

The apartment was smaller than I had expected it to be. A glance down the hall revealed a door to a single bedroom. In my daydreams of his home, Nick had taken up more space, or maybe it was only that he had been taking up so much room in my mind in the short time since I'd met him that I had expected his home to be larger. He'd texted me his address late one night, after he'd been out drinking at Hooligans with my sister and his entourage of cop friends, with an open invitation to come over anytime. When I saw the missed text the next morning, I recognized it for the drunken, hopeful booty call it had been, but I had given in to curiosity anyway and googled his address. I'd been surprised by the pictures of the aged, run-down apartment complex, unable to reconcile why a successful detective in his mid-thirties hadn't chosen to buy a home in a nicer neighborhood. It hit me in that moment how little we actually knew about each other. How many questions I had about him. How much more I wanted to know. And how much he might still want to know about me.

A file folder sat open on the leather sofa, the reports inside spilling out alongside a yellow legal pad and an uncapped pen. He beat me to the living room, shutting his open laptop and scooping up the papers and handwritten notes. "Sorry, I wasn't expecting you," he said as he set them on the coffee table, as if it was his fault and not mine that I had come unannounced. "Can I get you something to drink?"

A half-empty bottle of an imported lager sat on a coaster on the table. "A beer would be great." I slipped off my coat and hung it over the back of a chair.

Nick disappeared to the kitchen. He hadn't made an effort to hide the file from me, so I tipped my head to read the notes on his pad, surprised to see the names Dupree and Haggerty scrawled among them. The fridge opened and closed, then a whisper of air escaped the bottle as he twisted off the cap. He came back into the room, his expression still wary as he handed me the drink and gestured for me to sit down.

I cleared my throat and stared into my beer. "I wanted to apologize for yesterday," I said as he sat down beside me. "Thanks for not giving me a ticket."

"A ticket," he repeated.

"I was reckless. I should have slowed down. And I'm sorry I sped through that yellow light, but in my defense, you probably shouldn't have followed me through it."

He stared at me, dumbfounded. "That's what you're apologizing for? You think I was upset about your driving?"

"You had every right to be," I admitted. "I could have hurt someone. Any other cop probably would have arrested me."

He set his beer on the coffee table a little too hard. "You're right, they would. And I most definitely should have. But I wasn't thinking about anyone else. I was thinking about *you*!" He pinched the bridge of his nose and lowered his voice. "I was worried because you were upset. Because you were angry and hurt and you weren't thinking clearly."

"And you didn't want me to do something stupid," I sassed.

"I didn't want you to be alone! I wanted to be there for you, Finn, but you didn't give me the chance!"

"What do you want me to say?" I cried. "I'm sorry I ran out on you back at Penny's! I'm sorry if that made you feel left out! I just needed . . ." I rubbed my eyes. "I don't know what I needed, Nick! You're right. I was angry and upset and I wasn't thinking clearly, and I didn't want you to see me like that."

"Like what?" He leaned into my field of vision. "What don't you want me to see, Finn? The fact that you're hurting or that you're hiding something from me?" His jaw tensed when I didn't answer.

"Look, I get it," he said earnestly. "After seeing what Steven did to you, I get why you don't want to open yourself up to that again. But I was lying to myself before when I said I could be okay with the way things are between us." A familiar knife blade twisted inside me as I braced for what he'd say next. "I was kidding myself when I said there were things about you I was okay not knowing. That maybe I didn't want to know them. Because that look on your face killed me yesterday. Not when Penny told you she'd been having an affair with your husband, but the moment she answered the door—the expectation in your eyes, like you knew the betrayal was coming. Like you *knew* in your heart he was going to let you down. It's the same way you look at me sometimes, when I want to be there for you or when I want to help you. You want to confide in me, but you won't. You want to believe I would never do anything to hurt you, but you can't. Because Steven broke that trust, over and over, and I can't stand seeing you look at me that same way. Like you're scared to talk to me." His voice shook with barely restrained emotion.

"And it's the trust part that's killing me, Finn. You can't ask me to only fall in love with the pieces of you you're willing to show me.

I want you. Not part of you. *All* of you. I don't want you to run away when you're afraid. I want you to come to me. When I ask you a question, I want you to feel like you can be honest with me. When you look at me, I want to know beyond the shadow of any doubt that you believe—*truly believe*—I would never do anything to betray that trust."

"I do trust you!" I *wanted* to.

"Then tell me something. Anything. Tell me one thing that scares you," he pleaded.

I watched him, a deer caught in headlights. I opened my mouth but didn't know what to say. Why couldn't I give him this one small thing without risking everything? "You first," I said. "You know as much about me as I know about you."

"What do you want to know?" He didn't flinch, didn't blink, didn't look away. Whatever question left my mouth next, I'd better be damn sure I was ready to hear the answer.

I gestured to the file on the table. "Where did you get that?"

He hesitated a second before answering. "From the LCPD file room."

"How?"

"Joey made me a copy, and he'd get in a lot of trouble if anyone found out, but he did it because I asked him to."

"Why?" I knew I was pushing my luck, but Nick never said I only got one question.

"I wanted to make sure your name's not anywhere in it."

"Is it?"

He pushed the file toward me, not expressly granting permission but not withholding anything from me. I picked it up and opened it. He sipped his beer as he watched me thumb through the Dupree case notes. Penny had been cleared from the preliminary list of suspects after her husband's disappearance five years ago. According to the original investigator's notes, a neighbor had seen her leave for their beach house in Florida the night before Gilford had gone missing. She'd been alone in her SUV when she'd driven out of her garage, and her husband's coupe had been inside it when the garage door had closed behind her. The next morning, the same neighbor had seen Gilford leave for work, only that afternoon he hadn't come back.

Penny had placed a call to the Loudoun County police from the Duprees' beach house the following evening, claiming Gilford hadn't been returning any of her calls. She'd requested a wellness check at their Ashburn house. Finding no one at home and no signs of forced entry, no action had been taken by the police, until Gilford's car and phone were found abandoned later that weekend at a local park.

I turned the page, angry at myself for breaking into Penny's house for nothing. Her alibi had been verified by her neighbors in both Virginia and Florida, and she'd been cleared as a suspect very early on.

The next reports were more current, including the discovery of the body and the medical examiner's findings concerning the cause of death—blunt force trauma to the back of the head. Mike Tran's notes were also copied in the file. Margaret and Owen Haggerty had been listed as possible suspects early on, but over the course of the investigation, both were discounted. *No known association with the deceased* had been noted beside each of their names. Brendan's name had also been crossed out.

The remainder of the file was mostly about Steven, beginning with the report Mike Tran had filed when Riley and Max had broadcast the anonymous tip, followed by the invoice for the mulch delivery with Steven's address on it and a copy of Penny's voided check.

There were interdepartmental reports about the bodies found on Steven's farm last fall, taken from the joint task force investigation of the Russian mob. Redacted sections had been marked *confidential* and blocked out in thick black bars.

I turned to the last page of the file and felt a hot rush of blood to my face. Mrs. Haggerty had provided a statement detailing the exact dates and times when she'd observed Steven's extramarital activities while we'd been married. I was mentioned once on that page, identified only as Steven's spouse. A handwritten question mark had been scribbled beside my name, presumably by Mike Tran.

Nick reached out and delicately took the file from me. He closed it quietly and set it back on the table, as if he'd known what page I'd been reading by the look on my face.

"Are you finished grilling me?" he asked indulgently.

"Not even close." My throat burned, and I sipped my beer as I considered what to ask him next.

He cracked a smile, but I could tell his patience was wearing thin.

I looked around the room, at the tiny water stain on the ceiling, at the worn spots in the thin gray carpet and the cracked pane in the window, grasping at every surface for a question. Anything to put off the moment when the tables would be turned and he would expect me to answer one of his.

"Why do you live here?" I asked. "You're a detective with thirteen years on the force. Why not buy a house in a decent neighborhood?" It felt like low-hanging fruit, or maybe like I was baiting him, but it was the question that had been nagging at me since he'd opened the door. Even my sister, with all her commitment issues, rented a nicer place in a better neighborhood than this.

Nick took a deep swig of his beer, polishing off the last of it before answering. "I moved into this apartment eighteen months ago," he said quietly. "I never bothered to buy a place of my own before that because I had been living with a woman for the past five years, and I assumed Tonya and I would eventually get married. She came home from work one day and told me she was sleeping with a cop named Wade Coffey. Wade and I had worked in the same precinct together for years, and I wasn't sure which of them I was angrier with.

"I moved out that night. I crashed on your sister's couch for a week and signed a lease for the first vacant apartment I could find. This was it," he said, setting down his empty bottle.

My stomach clenched with a jealousy I had no right to. All I had known about Nick's last girlfriend was what little his former partner had told me, and what Wade Coffey himself had inferred when he'd been my handgun instructor at the citizen's police academy. But to hear Nick say this woman's name gave the vague notion of her a solid form. It took up an uncomfortable space in my mind. I looked down into my beer, wishing I hadn't asked.

"Your turn," he said.

He wanted me to talk about myself. To confide in him things that scared me. But in that moment, I was consumed by only one.

My throat constricted around the words, but I couldn't hold them back. "I hate knowing her name," I blurted. "I hate knowing you shared a home with her, I hate knowing what she was to you, I hate wondering who she is and where she is now, if you work out at the same gym, and if you pass each other in the grocery store. I'm scared there might be some part of you that's still in love with her."

There was a razor-sharp gleam in Nicks' eyes. "Why does that scare you?"

"Because I'm afraid one day you're going to realize that I'm not the person you want to be with!" The confession rushed out of me, taking all my breath with it. I forced myself to hold his gaze. It was only one small truth, and maybe not the one he'd been looking for, but in that moment, it felt like the only one that mattered.

He reached for me, taking my face in his hand, his thumb stroking away a tear as he pressed his forehead to mine.

"Your turn," I whispered. "What scares you?"

I felt his brow crease as he leaned in to kiss me. His lips were warm, his tongue cool and hoppy from the beer.

He reached for my bottle and set it on the table beside his. The leather creaked as he pulled me onto his lap, our kisses becoming deep and greedy. I did want all of him, even the honest and scary parts, but this was the part of him I needed right now.

He wrapped my legs around his waist as he stood, every part of us tangled together as he carried me down the hall to his room and let me down slowly, a soft, controlled fall onto his bed in the dark. His mouth took probing passes at mine, his arms keeping just enough distance between us for me to work off his shirt and pull it over his head. I dug my nails into his shoulders, wanting more of him, my hips rising, seeking him out.

"Tell me something that scares you," he murmured when we were finished.

His bedroom was a dark cocoon. I wasn't even sure what time it was. Only that I was hungry and spent.

I curled into his side, my smile wide against his damp skin. In that moment, there was only one thought that truly terrified me. "It might be too late to order a pizza."

His laughter was warm in my hair. He kissed the top of my head. "I'm a little afraid of that, too."

CHAPTER 10

The bell on the toaster chimed the next morning, and the smell of waffles wafted from the kitchen, which meant either Delia was awake and fixing herself breakfast or Vero was doing it for her.

I sat up and reached for my rumpled yoga pants, turning them right side out before dragging them on. I had them halfway up my thighs and froze as I registered the deep voice coming from the kitchen. "Two waffles, coming up."

"With syrup?" Delia asked in a voice that was unusually sweet for her, given the early hour.

"Know where your mom keeps it?" Nick asked.

"In the pantry."

"Roger that. What time does she usually take you to school?"

"Eight o'clock," Delia answered around a mouthful of food.

"How about we let her sleep and I'll drive you?" I peeked into the kitchen, relieved to find him fully dressed, his shoulder holster framing his tie and his neatly tucked dress shirt.

"I'm not going to school today," my daughter said matter-of-factly.

"Why not?" he asked.

"I got sup'ended for beating up a boy," she explained. Nick frowned to hide his amusement as he drizzled syrup on her waffles. "But Vero and Daddy said it's okay because Cooper wouldn't stop pulling my hair. I told the teacher, but she didn't believe me." Delia cast curious glances at the badge on Nick's belt. "Do you think I should have gotten sup'ended?"

He thought about that as he poured himself some coffee. "I think if you told the teacher someone was hurting you, then your teacher should have listened. What did your mom say?"

"She took me out for ice cream."

Nick's mouth curved into a smile. He hid it behind his coffee mug when he spotted me leaning on the doorframe behind her.

"Good morning," I said, taking his mug as he held it out to me. I closed my eyes, savoring the fact that he knew just how I liked my coffee. It was almost as good as his preferred method for waking me up. He knew exactly how I liked that, too. "What are you doing here?" I asked cryptically enough that Delia wouldn't grasp the subtext. Nick had driven me home five hours ago and had ended up staying the night.

"Figured I'd let you sleep and take Delia to school. How long until she can go back?" he asked me over his shoulder as he popped a waffle into the toaster for himself.

"Two weeks."

"Must have been one heck of a beatdown."

"Two bruised ribs and six stitches."

Nick looked impressed but did a good job of hiding that fact from Delia, who was too busy licking syrup from her empty plate to notice. I reached to take it from her before she could get any more syrup in her hair.

"Mommy," she asked as I wiped her face and hands, "will the police let Daddy come over today?"

I paused, her question taking me off guard. I wasn't sure how long they could keep Steven without bringing up charges, but I didn't imagine Mike Tran would be eager to let him go. I wiped her sticky forehead and kissed the wrinkle between her eyebrows. "I don't think so, sweetie. I think Daddy might be suspended for a little while longer. But we'll take him out for ice cream when he gets home." She brightened a little. "Go wash up," I said, dabbing at her bangs. "And remember to use soap. You've got syrup all over you."

"Are you and Nick going to take a bath, too?" she asked cheerfully.

Nick cocked an eyebrow as I shooed her up the stairs.

"Don't ask," I said as he handed me an Eggo and put his arms around me.

"I'm sorry," he said in a low voice. "I forgot to set my alarm and I overslept. Delia has no idea I spent the night. I was dressed and making coffee by the time she got up. I told her I just got here."

"Thanks," I said, grateful that he had spared me the need to have any more conversations with Delia about my choice of bathtub partners.

While I wasn't hiding the fact that Nick and I were dating from my children—and they had seen their father living with someone else within weeks of our divorce—I wasn't ready to share that piece of our relationship with them yet. Some part of me still felt guilty for enjoying it as much as I did. Maybe it was the lingering doubt that I deserved this much happiness. Or maybe it was the fear that it couldn't possibly last. They had already lost so much. And if Steven went to jail for murder, they were about to lose a whole lot more.

"Morning, Detective," Vero said, rubbing her eyes as she shuffled into the kitchen.

"Hey, Vero." Nick checked his watch and reached for his coat. "I hate to run, but I've got some things to do before I head to the station." He poured his coffee into one of my travel mugs and came to stand in front of me. "Today," he reminded me, pointing toward my bedroom where Mrs. Haggerty was still sleeping. He leaned down to steal a kiss on his way out the door. "I love you. I'll call you in a couple of—" He froze, his face inches from mine, wide-eyed and speechless, as we both registered what he'd just said. He scrubbed a hand over his mouth, his fingers rasping over the stubble. "I should go," he said softly. "I'll call you later." He dropped a tentative, quick kiss on my lips. I stood motionless in the kitchen as the front door closed behind him.

"*That* was an interesting development," Vero said as she poured a mountain of sugar in her coffee.

"That wasn't a development. He obviously wasn't thinking and it just slipped out." I dropped an Eggo in the toaster for Vero and wiped the crumbs from my hands, as if none of this mattered. Which was a big fat lie. It totally mattered, and I was pretty sure I'd spend the next few hours playing back Nick's parting words, dissecting every syllable. "It was probably force of habit."

"Force of *habit*?" She cocked a hip against the counter, her low-riding pajama bottoms dragging on the floor. "You think he gets up every morning before dawn to make coffee and breakfast and say *I love you* to someone else?"

"It doesn't matter what I think. He clearly didn't mean it."

"Just because he wasn't ready to say it doesn't mean it wasn't true. Look at Javi. He was in love with me for three whole years and never once said it. Face it, Finn. Detective Hottie is head over heels in love with you and it just slipped out because he happened to let his guard down."

"Thank you, Dr. Ruth."

Vero's phone vibrated on the counter. Javi's name flashed on the screen. She jabbed it, sending his call straight to voice mail.

I raised an eyebrow. "If you're such an expert on relationships, why did you just hang up on your betrothed?"

"He's not my *betrothed*. And I hung up on him because he's being an idiot."

I frowned. "What did he do?"

"He refuses to tell me how many women he dated before we got back together."

"Are you sure you want to know?"

"Of course I want to know! What if he slept with a hundred people while I was away at college?"

I doubted that. Javi had been madly in love with her since they were kids. "Maybe he didn't sleep with anyone."

"Have you *seen* him? He's ninety-nine percent pheromones, Finlay. He should come with a warning label. There had to be *someone*. Oh, god . . ." She clutched the counter like she might be sick. "That's even worse. What if there was only one. What if they were serious? What if she met his *mom*?"

"What if you're worrying for nothing?" I plucked the waffle from the toaster and shoved it in her hand. "Maybe he just doesn't want you worrying about something neither of you can change and he wishes he could take back?"

A door opened upstairs. Mrs. Haggerty came down, wearing a

brightly colored coordinated knit set and her big orthopedic shoes. She seemed a little less dour. Her gloom from the day before apparently had lifted, and I hoped that meant she had finally heard from her grandson.

She pinched the wire frames of her glasses, squinting through the narrow lenses at me as she took in my sleep-disheveled hair and wrinkled shirt. "Are you ill?"

"No."

"Good. Then I'd like two eggs, poached, with a slice of wheat toast. And some orange juice," she added, puttering toward the table.

"And that's my cue to go," Vero said under her breath, taking her coffee and waffle upstairs with her as the children came bursting into the kitchen. Delia's hair was wet and her feet were bare. Zach was still wearing his pajamas.

"What's this?" Mrs. Haggerty asked, frowning at Delia as the children zipped past her and opened the pantry. "It's Monday. Why aren't you at school?"

"I'm not allowed," Delia said, putting a foot up on a shelf so she could reach the fruit snacks for Zach. "I got in trouble for hitting a boy because he pulled my hair, and I have to stay home for two whole weeks."

"Two weeks!" Mrs. Haggerty tsked. "You go right upstairs, young lady, and get ready for school."

Delia blinked at the woman.

So did I. "Mrs. Haggerty, Delia was suspended. She'll be staying home with us today."

"My hearing is just fine," Mrs. Haggerty said stubbornly. "The girl was perfectly clear, but this is unacceptable. A young woman's education should never be hindered by the actions of a poorly behaved boy. Shame on that school. I should call the principal and give them a piece of my mind. Your daughter *will* be attending class today. Only she'll be doing it here with me."

I shook my head, wondering if *my* hearing was the problem. "With . . . you?"

"I'm perfectly qualified, if that's your concern. You have writing implements and notebooks, I presume?"

"Yes . . . but—"

"Then we'll get started right after I have my breakfast. Let's get on with it!" Mrs. Haggerty clapped her hands impatiently. Delia raced upstairs to finish getting dressed, with Zach in hot pursuit.

I sighed and set a pan on the stove. If nothing else, it would keep them both busy for a while. Maybe I could get a few loads of laundry done and sneak in a few hours of work. I took out the eggs, grabbed a tube of orange concentrate from the freezer, and dropped a dollop of butter in the pan while Mrs. Haggerty settled in at my kitchen table to wait for her meal. She set her massive cell phone in front of her and turned up the volume as loud as it would go.

. . . a new person of interest in the Gilford Dupree murder investigation. Steven Donovan of South Riding, owner of Rolling Green Sod and Tree Farm and former resident of the house located directly across the street from the property where the body was found, has been detained by Loudoun County police for questioning. According to an anonymous source, Donovan had been secretly involved with Penelope Dupree, the victim's wife . . .

I rushed to the table, frantically turning down the volume on her phone, hoping the children hadn't heard any of it. Max was on the screen, detailing what they had uncovered about Steven and Penny's affair.

The smell of burning butter shook me from the phone. I dropped it on the table, leaping to the stove to slam a lid on the smoking pan. I turned down the heat, wiped out the blackened butter, and started Mrs. Haggerty's breakfast over.

"I always said that man was worthless," she grumbled.

"That's none of your business," I said, cracking her egg hard enough to leave a little shell in it.

"It was everyone's business, the way he paraded his affairs around, always traipsing that real estate woman in and out of your house. He certainly wasn't quiet about it."

I gritted my teeth as I plucked two slices of singed bread from the toaster.

"I hope they lock him up. You and those children would be better off for it."

I snapped off the stove, scraped her egg and toast onto her plate, and dropped it in front of her.

Nick was right. Mrs. Haggerty needed to go. Today.

I carried her phone upstairs with me to Vero's room and banged on the door. Vero opened it, one eyebrow raised as she gestured for me to come in. She sipped her coffee while I dialed the number Brendan had left me. If he wouldn't answer my calls, maybe he would answer his grandmother's.

Brendan's phone rang no less than a dozen times. I let out a frustrated growl. "His voice mail still isn't picking up."

"He's probably avoiding her," Vero said. "The woman's a royal pain in the ass. I wouldn't blame the guy for wanting to get as far away from her as possible."

"He was in a hurry to get home when he dropped her off here. Maybe he just miswrote the number."

"*Hurry* is an understatement. He couldn't get out of here fast enough. The guy laid enough rubber in the street to outfit the tire department at Costco. I'm telling you, Finn, he's ditching his grandma."

"I don't think he would do that. They're very close."

"If they're so close, why didn't he come pick her up first thing this morning? You saw the news. By now he's seen it, too. If he was so worried about his grandma, do you really think he'd leave her here, living under Steven's old roof with you?"

She took Mrs. Haggerty's phone and opened the contact list. There were only a handful of entries in it. Vero held it between us as she scrolled to Brendan's name. "See? That's the same number he gave you. Face it, the guy's ghosting her, Finn." Vero thrust the phone back in my hand and reached for her laptop.

"What are you doing?" I asked as she opened a search engine. She typed Brendan's full name into the search bar as I looked over her shoulder.

"I'm finding out where he lives so we can go to his place and escort his ass back here." Vero reached for a notepad and jotted down an address. "This must be it. You get Delia ready to go. I'll go find Zach's shoes."

"We can't leave Mrs. Haggerty alone." The woman was far too nosy. Giving her unfettered access to snoop inside my house seemed like a dangerous idea. Especially given the secrets Vero and I were keeping. It was bad enough that my ex-husband had been publicly implicated in a murder case. But if Mrs. Haggerty was to discover Vero was living under an assumed identity to avoid an arrest warrant in Maryland, that would only make things worse, and we didn't need that fun fact coming up in a neighborhood watch meeting. We'd be on Mrs. Haggerty's radar for the remainder of her days, and with our luck, I was pretty sure she was going to outlast both of us.

"I'll go talk to Brendan," I said. "You stay here and keep an eye on Mrs. Haggerty. And don't let her anywhere near my office." The last thing either of us needed was for the woman to read my unfinished manuscripts and recognize the plot of my own life inside them. Hell, she could probably write my novels herself, given how much she'd seen through her kitchen window over the years.

"What am I supposed to do with her while you're gone?"

"Nothing. When she gets tired of playing homeschool, put on the TV and let her watch reruns of *Jeopardy!* Just keep her busy, and don't let her snoop."

CHAPTER 11

Thirty minutes later, I pulled my minivan into the parking lot of a three-story building in a condominium complex halfway between the Metro station and the mall. I squinted to read the number on the sign out front. There had been several Brendan Haggertys listed in Northern Virginia, but only one had a public profile that presented a likely match. Brendan had told me he lived in a one-bedroom condo on a third floor, though after a quick loop through the parking lot, I hadn't seen his white Volvo anywhere.

I parked in front of the address Vero had written on her notepad. A vicious wind sliced across my face as I climbed the three-story stairwell to what I hoped was Brendan's unit. I shivered, teeth chattering as I rapped on the door. There was no sound on the other side, and I knocked again, louder this time.

My phone buzzed with an incoming text.

Vero: *Did you find him?*

Finlay: *I'm at his condo, but his car's not here and no one's answering the door.*

Vero: *Try opening it.*

Finlay: *That's against the law!*

Vero: *It's only breaking and entering if it's locked. Otherwise, it's only entering, which is probably a misdemeanor.*

I didn't justify that with a response.

Vero's ringtone blared from my phone. I connected the call, desperate to silence it. "Look in his windows," she said before I could speak. "He's probably pretending he's not home."

I leaned around the side of the building and peeked over the railing. "The blinds in the windows of his balcony are open, but I can't see inside. The angle's all wrong."

"How far away is it?"

"At least four feet."

"That's nothing. Get closer."

"It's three stories up, Vero!"

"So? You climbed out our dormitory window at the police academy!"

"We fell!"

"You survived."

"And what happens if Brendan's home?"

"Then you can drag his lying ass back here to pick up his damn grandma."

Wind whipped my hair over my face as I peered over the ledge. Brendan's balcony was only a few feet away, and the railing looked sturdy. I'd traversed far more terrifying terrain in the ceiling of a chop shop in Atlantic City. At least here, no one was trying to shoot me.

I checked the stairwell again. Then the ground below. There wasn't a soul in the parking lot. No one coming or going from the building, as far as I could see. "I can't believe I'm doing this."

I slipped my phone in my pocket before I could talk myself

out of it, muffling Vero's voice inside the thick layers of my coat. I climbed onto the ledge. The ground wavered below me, much farther down than it had seemed a moment ago. I gripped the side of the building for balance, shut my eyes, and swung a leg out sideways, clinging to the brackets of a drainpipe as I searched for the metal railing with my foot. The heel of my sneaker caught the slick surface of the top rail. My stomach dropped as the rubber sole slipped, the force of my sudden lurch pulling the drainpipe away from the wall.

I yelped, groping for a fingerhold as brackets and screws tumbled to the sidewalk below with soft *clink*s. My nails raked the brick façade, mortar and grit collecting under my nails until they caught the edge of a shutter.

"Don't look down, don't look down, don't look down," I whimpered, my heart flapping furiously against my ribs as I eased a foot back onto the railing. With one final sideways step, I threw myself over the top of it and collapsed onto Brendan's balcony.

"Finlay! Say something. Anything!" Vero's shouts were frantic and tinny in my pocket as I lay motionless on the cold, wet decking.

My hands shook as I retrieved my phone from my pocket. "I'm not dead," I said between ragged breaths. At least, I didn't think I was.

"Where are you?"

"On Brendan's balcony."

"See anything?"

"Other than my life flashing before my eyes?" I pushed myself to my feet and peered through the slats in Brendan's blinds. A single lamp was on in his living room. The kitchen was dark, the counters clean of clutter. I could just make out one side of his crisply made bed through his open bedroom door. "No sign of Brendan. I don't think he's home." I tested the doorknob. "But we have a problem."

"What kind of problem?"

"I'm stuck on Brendan's balcony."

"Can't you just go back the way you came?"

"The drainpipe broke. My only hope for getting out of here is a fire truck ladder or a key to his condo."

"Good idea. Stay where you are. I'm calling the maintenance office."

"You're doing *what?!*"

"They'll send someone out to help you. All you have to do is pretend you live there. Tell them you're Brendan's girlfriend and you went outside to get some air and accidentally locked yourself out of his condo."

"No!"

"You have a better plan?"

I peeped over the railing. The balcony below Brendan's was at least fifteen feet down. A low rumble of thunder echoed in the distance.

"There is *one* other way," Vero suggested, "but only if you're willing to be flexible on that whole breaking-and-entering thing."

A fat raindrop plunked down on my head. "Absolutely not!"

"Would you rather I call *your* boyfriend to come save you?"

"Fine. You can call Javi, but tell him to hurry. It's starting to rain and it's freezing out here. The last thing I need is for the cops to find my frozen corpse on Brendan Haggerty's balcony."

"Look at the bright side," she said as the sky opened and it started to pour. "At least you won't stink."

Exactly twenty-eight minutes later, a white panel van eased into the condominium's parking lot, its windshield wipers slapping away the heavy rain. It made a slow pass through the complex and parked beside my minivan. The driver's side door opened and Javi got out. He wore a pair of dark sunglasses, a grease-stained pair of blue coveralls, and his baseball cap low over his eyes. I rocked back and forth to stay warm, watching from Brendan's balcony as Javi retrieved a toolbox from the back of his van. His eyes climbed the side of the building, searching for me as he approached. I hugged my knees against the driving rain, my teeth chattering. I considered getting up and waving to him, but my clothes were plastered to my body and I couldn't feel my toes. Javi's steps faltered when he spotted the drainpipe dangling from the side of the building. He quickened his pace to the stairs.

The next few minutes felt like an eternity. The balcony door swung open. Javi pulled me upright and dragged me into Brendan's condo. My face tingled at the rush of warm air as he closed the balcony door behind us and quickly shut the blinds. He took a throw blanket off the back of the sofa and wrapped it around me.

"Sit down," he said, depositing me in an armchair and turning up the thermostat on the wall. The digital display illuminated as Javi adjusted the temperature, cranking it up to seventy degrees from the cool fifty-five it had been set to. "It's fucking cold in here," he said with a shudder as he knelt in front of me.

I managed a hoarse laugh. Compared to the temperature outside, Brendan's living room felt like a spa. My whole body had started shaking and my skin prickled as the blood crept back into my extremities.

"How long have you been out there?" he asked, pushing back my wet sleeves.

"F-f-feels like f-f-forever." I could hardly feel my face, and my words came out in a stutter.

He took my hands in his, turning them over to examine the pads of my fingers. His were probably still warm from the car, but if they were, I couldn't tell. "You'll be fine," he said, peeling off my drenched sneakers to examine my toes. "Do I want to know what you were doing out there?"

"Probably not."

A muscle worked in Javi's jaw. He had a history of scrapes with the law, and I hated the idea of involving him in any more of mine. "Don't move," he said, securing the blanket around me. "I'll find some towels."

Touching anything inside Brendan's condo didn't feel wise, but I was too cold to care as Javi left me in the living room while he searched Brendan's closets. Doors opened and shut down the hall, followed by the sound of a dryer tumbling to life. The heat had clicked on and warm air rustled the fringed edges of the blanket. Sinking to the floor, I pressed my hands to the nearest vent, relishing the rush of warmth to my fingertips. Under the light from the lamp on the table beside me, I watched the color slowly return to my skin.

I paused, my gaze catching on the lamp cord. It was connected to a timer, the kind that turned lights on and off at preprogrammed intervals. The same kind Vero and I had used the night we'd snuck out to bury Harris, when we'd wanted to trick Mrs. Haggerty into thinking we were home.

I winced at the needles of pain that shot through my toes as I stood and shambled to the thermostat. It had been set low—economically low—as if Brendan hadn't planned to be home anytime soon. I peeked in the kitchen. The counters and sink were spotless, the coffeepot clean. I hobbled inside and opened the fridge, finding only condiments, pickles, jams, and jellies. No leftovers. No fresh produce or sandwich meats. Nothing that might spoil.

The trash can under the sink was empty. All of them were. Even the one in Brendan's bathroom.

No toothbrush or toothpaste in the holder.

Vero was right. Brendan had skipped town and abandoned his grandmother.

Pain lanced through my feet as I made my way back to the sofa.

Javi emerged from the laundry room, his phone pressed to his ear and a pile of hot towels in his arms. "I've got her. She's fine . . . Well if you're feeling that grateful, I can think of a few things we could—Vero . . . ?" He frowned at the screen on his phone and shoved it in his pocket. "She wants you to call her," he said, arranging the hot towels around my feet. "I've got to go. I promised Ramón I'd be at the shop thirty minutes ago. Do you have your phone?"

I nodded. "Thanks, Javi."

He gathered his toolbox but hesitated when he reached the door. "Hey, can I ask you something?"

"Sure."

"If someone you really cared about asked you a question, and you swore to them you'd never lie to them or do anything to hurt them, but you knew the answer might really mess things up, would you tell them?"

"Oh, wow. I really don't think I'm the best person to ask." I was still struggling with that question myself.

"You're the only person I *can* ask. And you know Vero as well as I do."

"What about Ramón?"

Javi pulled a face. "I can't ask Ramón. He'd remove my nuts with a bolt cutter if he even *thought* I'd say anything that would hurt Vero, but she's pissed at me because I won't tell her anything about the people I dated after she left for college." He shook his head.

"I don't know what to do, Finlay. I want to be honest with her—I promised her I would—but having that conversation with her feels like walking through a field of land mines. If I tell her everything, she'll probably hate me. But if I don't, she'll think I'm trying to hide something from her. Either way, I'm screwed. I don't know what she wants from me."

"Maybe all she wants is a little reassurance. Maybe she just needs to know you're *willing* to be honest with her, even if it feels like a risk. She's taking a risk, too," I reminded him. "Maybe she just needs to know that it's worth it. That no matter what happened in the past with someone else, nothing is more important to you than your future with *her*."

He looked down at his hand, flexing his fingers as he stared at his purple bat ring. "People keep giving me shit about it, but I haven't taken off this ring since the day I put it on. I meant every word I said to her that night. I just want her to trust me."

"Then you have to trust her, too," I pointed out. "Tell her why you're holding back. Then let *her* decide how much she's ready to hear."

He nodded, his shoulders rising and falling with a sigh, as if he'd come to some decision. "Thanks," he said, giving the condo one last look. "Remember to wipe the place down before you go." He drew his baseball cap low over his eyes, slipped out the door, and locked the dead bolt behind him.

I pulled my phone from my pocket and speed-dialed Vero.

"You were right," I said when she answered. "Brendan's gone. It looks like he plans to be away for a while."

"We are *not* getting saddled with that woman. Go through his things and figure out where he went. He's probably hiding out at some fancy hotel with room service, celebrating the fact that someone else is watching his grandma."

"There's not much to search," I said, carrying my phone through Brendan's condo. He was tidy for a bachelor. It was almost suspicious how little there was, come to think of it. Who doesn't have some bills sitting on a counter? A stack of crumpled receipts or a notepad left beside a phone? I picked up the receiver in the kitchen and thumbed through the menu to access the call log, but like most landlines, it contained a dozen telemarketing calls, scam numbers, and one from a time-share resort in Florida.

I hung up the receiver, hugging the blanket around me. The condo was spotless, not a single crease in the hotel-quality duvet or a crumb on the counter. Not a speck of spit on the bathroom mirror or toothpaste in the sink.

The only stray item in his bedroom was a newspaper left on the dresser. It had been folded open to the local politics section. I picked it up, doing a double-take at the photo on the page.

Brendan smiled brightly in the image, his crisp black suit jacket and burgundy tie standing out against the pale blue backdrop of his headshot.

Executive Director of Local Non-Profit Announces a Run for City Council.

"Huh," I mused. "Riley and Max were right. Brendan's running for local office. Looks like he submitted his petition to the city in January. The official announcement hit the paper last week."

"Maybe Brendan's campaign manager would know where he is."

"There's a number in the article. Hold on. I'll call you right back." I disconnected from Vero and dialed the number for the campaign office I'd seen in the article. I got routed through several phone trees before a human finally answered.

"I'm trying to reach Brendan Haggerty," I said. "I'm a close friend of his grandmother and it's urgent that I speak with him but he's not answering his phone—"

"Mr. Haggerty is on leave for a personal matter."

"Do you know where I might find him?"

"I'm sorry, but I don't have that information."

"Did he say when he'll be back?"

"I don't expect him until next week. Would you like to leave a message?"

I had already left him several, including one from his grandmother's phone. Brendan obviously didn't want to be found. "No, thank you."

I disconnected and called Vero back. "No luck. All they would tell me is that he's away on personal business." The timing felt awfully suspect. Who takes a week of personal leave on the heels of a major career announcement?

I remembered Riley's warning to me behind Mrs. Haggerty's house . . . that Brendan Haggerty was running for office and the public deserved to know what had happened in his grandmother's community. But why? Had they only been concerned with his transparency as a candidate? Or had they suspected there was more to Brendan Haggerty's story?

I skimmed the rest of the article, which contained a brief rundown of his qualifications, including a mention of his participation in the citizen's police academy a month ago. If he was posturing for an election, his participation in a program like that would look good on his platform. And the fact that he'd attended it with his elderly grandmother would have held promise as a heart-tugging human-interest story before she'd been arrested. I searched the article for any mention of Mrs. Haggerty, but her name was noticeably absent.

"Check in the closet," Vero suggested. "That's where all the sleazy politicians hide their skeletons."

I opened Brendan's closet and riffled through his hangers. His shirts had been pressed and sorted by color. His loafers were polished and organized on racks. "Nothing odd in here. It's neat as a pin."

"There's no such thing as a clean politician, Finlay. Keep looking."

Hangers screeched as I pushed aside his suit jackets, revealing a small cardboard filing box in the corner of his closet. I lifted the lid. There was a collection of newspapers and clippings inside it. "I think I found something." The headlines of most of the news articles were recent, dated within the last few weeks.

"What is it?" Vero asked as I picked one up and skimmed it.

Body of Missing Local Man Is Found Buried in South Riding. Under the headline was a photo of Gilford Dupree. There were several clippings in the box about the silver-haired businessman, some containing photos I'd already seen on the TV news, others containing grainy shots that appeared to be screen grabs from social media pages. Below them, I found a handful of articles that predated the discovery of Dupree's remains. Most had been published the year he went missing. Human-interest pieces about the quiet mortgage broker who'd mysteriously disappeared from a local park, each article culminating in pleas for witnesses to call his wife with any information.

"There must be a dozen articles here. They're all about Gilford Dupree."

Vero's laugh was bitter. "Of course Brendan was following the news. The lying jerk was probably praying his grandma would be indicted so he'd have an excuse to get rid of her."

"He wasn't just following it, Vero." I struggled to convey in words why this hidden stash of articles was so disturbing to me. "It's like he was collecting details about the case. Like he was scouring the news for information about the crime." Like he was studying it. Names and dates had been circled. Every small detail of the case that police had disclosed had been highlighted. Notes had been furiously scribbled in the margins—odd forms of shorthand that were hardly legible.

Was he trying to exonerate his grandmother by solving the investigation himself?

Or was he trying to stay one step ahead of it?

The observation Vero had shared with me earlier that morning began to take on new significance as I stood in Brendan's closet.

He couldn't get out of here fast enough.

"What if Brendan isn't hiding from his grandmother?" I asked. "What if he's running from the cops?"

"What do you mean?"

"Brendan said he was the only relative of Mrs. Haggerty who lived close by. He used to visit her all the time. What if *he* needed a convenient place to hide a body? Somewhere familiar. An easy place to dig on a privately owned lot where no one was likely to go looking?" Hadn't Vero and I done the same thing when we had accidentally become saddled with Harris Mickler's corpse? We'd buried him on my ex-husband's sod farm. The unplanted ground had been soft, recently tilled. It was the easiest, safest solution we could come up with, and it had worked for us, too, at least until someone dug him up. "What if Brendan killed Gilford and hid the body in his grandparents' yard?"

"I thought you said the police ruled him out."

"That's what the file in Nick's apartment suggested, but it didn't say anything about an alibi."

"Well that's just great," Vero said through an exasperated sigh. "If Brendan's the killer, there's no way he's coming back to pick up his grandmother. I vote we call the damn detective's number on that business card, tell him Brendan Haggerty skipped town, his grandmother is a pain in our ass, and let the cops figure out what to do with both of them."

"We can't call the police about this! What are we going to say? That I broke into the man's condo, snooped around, and found something suspicious when I searched his closet?"

"We'll just have to give them a compelling reason to search it themselves. Put everything back where you found it, wipe the place down, and come home. It's almost lunchtime and I can't think on an empty stomach."

My heart leapt into my throat. "Wait, what did you say?"

"I said, I'm starving and I—"

"Not that! What time is it?"

"Eleven fifteen. Why?"

"No, no, no, *shit*!" I looked down at my drenched clothes, as if by some Cinderella magic, they might turn into something suitable to wear. "I'm going to be late to my meeting with Sylvia!"

"You didn't tell me you were meeting with—"

I disconnected the call, put the articles back in the box, and frantically straightened the hangers.

There was no time to run home to change. No time to stop at the mall to go shopping for clothes. I had forty-five minutes to wipe down every surface in this condo and get to Union Station before my literary agent killed me.

CHAPTER 12

Sylvia was easy to spot in spite of the crowds in Union Station. Elevated by what I could only assume was a pair of four-inch stilettos, the leopard-print fedora atop her bouffant coif stood out like a tacky Vegas billboard. I stood on my toes and waved, catching her attention over the masses of commuters. She started toward me, her red leather handbag slung over one arm and held out in front of her like a phalanx. The other dragged a carry-on suitcase behind her. She smiled wide enough to reveal the lipstick on her teeth when we got within clear sight of each other. She peeled off an enormous pair of sunglasses that, coupled with her faux-fur stole, made her look like the cartoon version of some nocturnal jungle creature I'd seen in a Disney movie with my kids. Sylvia slowed, her smile collapsing as she scrutinized me from head to toe.

"Oh, god. It's worse than I thought," she said. For one interminable, hopeful moment, I thought she might cancel the meeting and get on a train back to New York. She rose up on the toes of her shoes and held her glasses in front her eyes, squinting through the lenses to the far corners of the terminal. "There!" she said, pushing her way past me with her wheelie bag in tow. It bounced unapologetically past briefcases and over other people's feet as she forced her way through the crowd.

"The exit's the other way, Syl. Where are you going?" I had little choice but to follow her as her heels clacked ferociously through the depot and into the nearest ladies' room.

"It's a good thing I brought a suitcase. See? I knew there was a reason I couldn't find a train back to New York tonight. It's kismet. Put this on," she said, digging into her carry-on and shoving a wad of nylon and spandex at me.

I felt the blood drain from my face. "What do you mean, you couldn't find a train back?"

"All they had was coach. You know I don't do coach. I booked my return trip for tomorrow. I'm spending the night at your house. I hope you got everything on the shopping list I sent you. I only drink Evian. And I don't sleep on anything that doesn't have at least five hundred thread count."

"Sylvia—!"

"Have you seen the prices of hotels in DC? If you wanted me to stay at the Ritz-Carlton, you should have written a better book." She pushed me backward into an empty stall, slammed the door shut, and slung a pointy, heavily padded bra over the partition. She dropped a pair of stilettos on the floor and kicked them under the door.

"Those are never going to fit me."

"Small breasts are nothing to be ashamed of, Finlay."

"I was talking about the shoes!"

"So we'll tighten the straps. On the bra, too. Please tell me you at least shaved your legs. Never mind," she said when I didn't answer.

"It's a nice place we're going to. I'm sure they'll have tablecloths. Just don't let him play footsie with you unless he's wearing socks."

"Sylvia!"

"I'm kidding. Sheesh! I'm your agent, not your pimp. I would never let him put a hand on you . . . unless he can get us Joe Manganiello to play the cop. If he can pull that off, he can have me, too."

"That's not funny."

"Just put on the damn dress and let's go! We're going to be late."

I stared at the dress, then down at my damp clothes. Then at the wall behind me, praying there was a window I could crawl out of so I could go home.

This will be fine, I told myself.

It was just a meeting over a meal with a powerful man who wanted to negotiate a deal with me. At least this guy had a pulse, which was a step in the right direction.

With a resigned swear, I stripped off my sweats and sports bra and kicked them out from under the stall. I fed my arms through Sylvia's bra and cinched the straps as far as they would go. "There are still gaps in the cups."

"The universe only gives us as much as we can handle. Try these." My balled-up socks flew back over the partition, and I scrambled to catch them before they could fall in the toilet.

"You want me to stuff my bra with socks?"

"Men stuff their underwear all the time. *Especially* celebrities."

"I'm not a celebrity."

"Not yet. But after this meeting, you will be. I feel it, Finlay. This lunch is going to be your big break."

Assuming a sock ball didn't come bursting out of my bra when I shook the producer's hand. "Great. No pressure," I said, pulling the dress over my head. My hair crackled with static as I adjusted the stretchy material to cover as much of Sylvia's undergarments as possible. "What's that smell?" I asked, wrinkling my nose at the disturbingly familiar scent that wafted from a sock ball as I stuffed it into place.

"It's lavender. I told you I came prepared. It's great for masking odors."

A dark laugh bubbled out of me. This did not bode well. I gritted my teeth as I stepped into her shoes.

She beamed at them when I opened the door. Her smile crumbled as her gaze climbed up to my hair. "Come here," she said, rummaging through her handbag. She pulled a bottle of Aqua Net from its depths like it was Mary Poppins's carpetbag. I forced myself not to contemplate murder as she ran her hands under the faucet, then through my hair, and scrunched. The jail time wouldn't be worth it. At least that's what I told myself as she sprayed a cloud of hair spray around me that could have raised the global temperature by at least five degrees.

"Can we please just not?" I swatted her hand away as she swiped ruthlessly at my mouth with a tube of burgundy lipstick.

"You're right. I shouldn't push my luck," she said, returning her arsenal of cosmetics to her bag and checking her handiwork. "Let's get out of here. Hollywood awaits."

Ten minutes, a twisted ankle, and three blisters later, we were standing on a street corner in front of a restaurant called The Palm. I'd heard of it before, mostly through local name-droppers. It was a popular lunch spot among politicos and the who's who of DC, the kind of place an aspiring politician like Brendan would probably want to visit, if only to tick it off his bucket list.

I stepped aside, making room for a group of businesswomen in

Ann Taylor suits as they left the restaurant. I could do this, I told myself. The producer would take one look at the ridiculous getup I was wearing and change his mind about wanting to meet with me at all. There was no way he'd want to turn my book into a movie. At worst, he'd take pity on me and make an unreasonably low offer. That wouldn't be so bad, right? Those kinds of deals never made it into the headlines. And nobody bothered to watch low-budget films, anyway.

Sylvia took me by the arm and dragged me inside the restaurant.

"There he is," she said, standing on her toes and waving her fingers at a man seated alone in a far corner of the dining room. The man stood to greet us as the hostess led us to his table. Randall Wolfe looked exactly how I expected a Hollywood producer would. His teeth had been bleached an unearthly shade of white, his wrinkles and crow's-feet had been spackled over with fillers, and the plugs in his hairline were the only remaining evidence of his age. I was quick to shake his hand when he offered it, if only to fast-forward the nightmare to the part where I got to sit down.

"See? Tablecloths," Sylvia whispered as she claimed the seat beside me.

Randall held his silk tie to his chest as he sat. "I can't tell you what a pleasure it is to finally meet you, Fiona."

Sylvia nudged my leg under the table.

"Oh, right!" I said. "Please, call me Finlay."

"Fiona Donahue is her pen name," Sylvia explained. "Randall Wolfe, meet Finlay Donovan, your future star."

Randall leaned in. "A secret identity! How apropos."

I choked on a laugh. "If you only knew."

Randall folded his ring-laden hands atop his menu. "You have such a gift, Finlay. The danger, the intrigue, the sexual tension. It all feels so real. So authentic! I love how you put me so deeply inside the head of a killer. It's all so inspired." He leaned closer. "Tell me everything. You must have an inside source."

"Nope. No source," I said, snapping open my menu and hiding behind it. "It's all just . . . right up here." I fired a finger gun at my head.

"Don't be silly," Sylvia said. "Of course, she has a source. Tell him about Nick."

Randall raised an eyebrow. Sylvia pushed my menu down and jabbed an elbow in my side.

"Sylvia, I really don't think—"

"Nick is a detective," Sylvia said with gravitas. "And he's every bit as hot as the cop in her book."

Randall rubbed his hands together. "Now we're getting somewhere. That's just the kind of angle that could help me pitch this as a series."

I could practically see the dollar signs twinkling in Sylvia's eyes. She gestured above her to an imaginary marquis. "Steamy legal drama featuring a star-crossed romance?"

"Better," Randall said with a flourish. "Gritty, sexy procedural based on real-life events. The networks will eat it up. Tell me, Finlay, how do you feel about the small screen?"

My mouth went dry and I nearly dropped my menu. "I guess that depends . . ." *on how small the TV screens are in prison.* I reached for my ice water, spilling some down the front of my dress. The smell of wet lavender hit me square in the face as I sucked down a huge gulp.

"I think what Finlay means," Sylvia said coolly, passing me a napkin, "is that it really depends on the deal your studio is prepared to make. We have several other parties interested in her book."

If we were counting crime lords, detectives, the IRS, and my ex-husband's divorce lawyer.

An ice cube clanked against my teeth. I held up my empty glass and looked around the room for a server. With any luck, they'd sense my desperation and bring me something with booze in it.

"I'm sure you do," the producer said as he perused his menu. "But not everyone can attach the kind of talent that I can to a project like this."

Sylvia narrowed her eyes. "What kind of talent?"

"We'd plan to go out exclusively to A-list actors for reads."

"Keep talking."

"And of course, there's the issue of expense if we want to stay true to the source material. Between the set pieces, the pyrotechnics, the extensive stunt work, and the high-end sports cars, it would require quite an investment to get it off the ground." He stared at me as he stroked his chin. "Not just any production company can commit to that kind of budget, but I'm prepared to make a big up-front commitment for this."

"How big?" Sylvia asked eagerly.

"I can get Finlay fifty thousand for the rights if you take it off the table today."

"A hundred," Sylvia countered.

I fought back a laugh. *That* might *be enough to cover my bail bond.*

"Seventy-five," Randall said. "But I'd insist on bringing in her source as a consultant."

Great. Maybe they can hire Nick to consult at my criminal trial, too.

"Throw in executive producer fees with her own card in the opening credits, the surf and turf with the tiramisu, and we'll call the whole thing good."

"Sure you didn't miss anything?" I deadpanned to Sylvia.

"You're absolutely right. I almost forgot." She turned to the producer. "We want a cameo in the pilot, too."

"Done," he said, shaking her hand across the table. "I'll even throw in a bottle of bubbly to celebrate." I covered my face as Randall signaled to a waiter.

Sylvia clutched my knee under the table and whispered, "See? The socks really did the trick. You're going to be huge, Finlay. The talk of the town. In a few months, you'll be headline news. *Hometown Mystery Author Locks in a Killer Deal for Her New Hit Series.*"

I just hoped my killer deal included a decent plea bargain.

"Would you excuse me?" I slid out from behind the table as the waiter popped the cork, leaving Sylvia and Randall to toast their victory without me. I hurried between the rows of tables, desperate to get to the ladies' room and splash water on my face. How was this happening? How had I just accepted an offer to adapt a television series based on my own crime?

My feet wobbled in Sylvia's gaping heels. I stumbled, nearly tripping over them, when a set of familiar hazel eyes found mine across the dining room.

Julian Baker did a double take. His bored, tuned-out expression grew suddenly intense and alert. The attractive older man seated across the table from him didn't seem to notice. I pretended not to notice, too, as Julian rose from his seat.

I covered the side of my face as he navigated between the tables toward me. Julian and I had only dated for a few weeks last fall. Our relationship had been hot and liberating and refreshingly honest, but I had known early on it wasn't going to work. He was nine years my junior and still in law school, and I was a single mom in the aftermath of a divorce. We were at very different places in our lives, and yet somehow the universe kept throwing us together.

He called my name before I made it to the ladies' room. I turned, crossing my arms self-consciously over the sock balls in my bra.

"Julian! What a surprise," I said, pretending I had not just sprinted through The Palm to avoid him. The smell of lavender bloomed from my sweaty cleavage and I discreetly stuffed the errant sock ball back inside its cup. "What are you doing here?" I asked, trying and failing to ignore his befuddled glance at my chest before he forced his eyes back to mine. He had seen under my brassieres enough to know exactly what I was (and was not) packing inside them.

"Business lunch," he said, hitching a thumb toward the table he'd just escaped from.

"Going well?"

"Yeah, great. You?"

"Very." We were both terrible liars.

He glanced over his shoulder at the colleague he'd been meeting with. The man bore a striking resemblance to Julian, with the same athletic build and sun-kissed skin, but the man's honey-blond curls were streaked with silver.

"Come on," Julian said, hooking an index finger around my pinkie. He led me to the emergency exit at the back of the restaurant. We emerged in an alley behind the building. A weight seemed to fall from his shoulders as he leaned back against the brick.

His tie fell askew, the late February wind tossing a curl over his eyes. They closed with relief as he took the first full breath either of us had probably drawn since we'd entered the place.

"That bad, huh?" I asked, slumping against the wall beside him.

His laugh was as dry as his sidelong look. "My father," he explained. "Courtland Baker. Senior partner at Baker & Stratton." The title sounded sour on his tongue. "He thinks I'm wasting my talent. Why should I sling drinks at a bar after slaving away at the county courthouse all day as a public defender when I could be following in his footsteps, doing lunch with investment bankers and highbrow clients at The Palm? He thinks it's beneath me." Julian sighed and shook his head. "Forget it. I haven't seen you in weeks and here I am, wasting a perfectly good five minutes in an alley with you to bitch about my dad." He rolled sideways on one shoulder, smiling as he tugged the edge of the sock ball peeking out of my blouse. "I'd say you look great, but honestly, you look like your meeting is going about as well as mine. Everything okay?"

I cringed. "I think I just accepted an offer for a TV show."

Julian's eyebrows disappeared under his curls. "Seriously? That's amazing. So why don't you look happy about it?"

I considered kicking off my shoes, sitting down on the pavement, and venting to him about everything. He was the only person aside from Vero who knew the truth about what had happened between Harris Mickler and me. Or how closely aligned that story was to the book I'd written. I knew he would listen—and probably give me great advice—but it didn't feel right to use him as a sounding board for things I hadn't confided to Nick. "It's . . . complicated."

Julian nodded as if that somehow made sense. "How are things with Detective Anthony?"

"Good. I think. I don't know," I confessed, resting my head against the wall. "That's also complicated."

He nodded as if he understood that, too.

"How about you? Are you seeing anyone?" His roommate, Parker, was a brilliant young prosecutor. She was gorgeous and crazy about him, and I had assumed it would only be a matter of time before they got back together.

His shrug was noncommittal. "No one I'd accept a ride in a minivan with."

I laughed, careful not to hold his gaze too long. I didn't have any regrets about ending things with Julian, but I would probably always hold a soft spot for him. By the look on his face, he'd hold one for me, too.

"I was going to call you last night," he said. "I got worried when I saw the story on the news, but I didn't want to overstep. I read up on the Dupree investigation, just to make sure . . ." He paused.

"That I wasn't the new person of interest in the case?" I asked. A guilty flush rushed to his cheeks, and I shook my head. "This murder, at least, has nothing to do with me."

"What about your ex-husband?"

I stuck a finger in Sylvia's shoe and rubbed the blister on my heel. "I don't think so. I suspect someone else, but I don't have any evidence to prove it."

"Then I guess I can't be mad about you dating a police officer," Julian teased. "That doesn't mean I have to like it, but at least I know you'll be safe if there's a killer running loose in your neighborhood. Maybe Nick can help get your ex off the hook, assuming that's what you want." It came out like a question, and honestly, I wasn't sure I knew the answer. To some degree, Steven had made his own bed, and a broken, bitter piece of me wanted to watch him sleep in it. The same piece of me that wanted to believe that Penny and Mrs. Haggerty were right—that I would be better off if he wasn't in the picture. I wanted my kids all the time, not just some of it. I wanted the security that came with not having to pay my ex-husband rent, and a life that didn't necessitate coparenting strategies and custody agreements.

But my gut—the piece of me that had been niggling at me since I'd left Penny's house—was screaming at me that Steven didn't do this. And I didn't want my kids' relationship with their father to be reduced to visiting days once a month within the walls of a state prison.

"I don't think there's much Nick can do for him. Steven insisted on using one of his buddies to represent him—a divorce lawyer. The guy's good, but I'm worried."

"Want me to make a few calls?" Julian offered. "I can at least make sure he's in capable hands."

"I can't ask you to do that."

He tipped my chin up to look me in the eyes. "You can, and I would. Let me know if you change your mind."

I released a held breath. "Thank you."

He pushed himself off the wall and extended a hand, helping me upright. "I should get back inside before my dad leaves me with the check." He opened his arms for a parting hug. "I'm happy for you, Finlay. Nick's a great guy." Julian's smile was wistful when he finally pulled away. "If things get too complicated, you know where to find me."

I watched him walk back into the restaurant, feeling both lighter and heavier than I had in a long time. Talking to Julian was like confessing to a hot priest. I felt cleansed and absolved after every conversation with him (and wouldn't have minded occasionally worshipping under his cassock), but I couldn't make myself feel about him the way I felt about Nick.

There was only one man I truly wanted to be with, and confessing my sins to him wasn't an option.

Steeling myself, I walked back into the restaurant. Nick wanted me to tell him something that scared me. This damn TV series was only the start.

CHAPTER 13

"So let me get this straight," Vero said, fingers pressed to her temples. "You had a meeting with a TV producer and your agent, and you wore *that*," she said, pointing to the drooping gaps in the top of Sylvia's spandex dress that had contained my socks less than an hour ago, "and you did not tell me?"

I sat down at my kitchen table and massaged the blisters on my feet. If it had been any closer to five o'clock—and if Mrs. Haggerty and my daughter had not been in the next room—I would have poured myself a very large glass of wine after the day I'd suffered. "It didn't seem as important as nearly dying of hypothermia."

"I saved you from hypothermia! I could have saved you from this!" She threw a balled-up sock at me while I gestured for her to keep her voice down. "Please tell me the producer was visually and olfactorily impaired." She pulled a face as she sniffed her hand. "Is that *lavender*?" she whispered. "Seriously? Did you learn nothing in Atlantic City about covering up foul—"

"Randall Wolfe offered me a TV deal."

Vero went unnaturally still. The only sound was Delia's quiet counting in the dining room, where Mrs. Haggerty was giving her a lesson in math. Vero blinked at me. "Can you repeat that last part? I think I misheard you."

"He and Sylvia negotiated it over lunch."

Vero eased slowly into the seat beside me, as if she'd lost the feeling in her legs. "How much?"

"Nothing is signed yet."

"Spit it out."

"Seventy-five."

"Thousand? That's it?"

"And an executive producer credit." Vero gasped before I got to the tiramisu and surf and turf. "But there's a catch."

"I knew it. You never should have gone without me. What did Sylvia screw up this time?"

"They want Nick to consult on the script."

For a moment, Vero gaped at me. Then a low laugh rumbled in her chest.

"It's not funny, Vero!" I dropped my voice to a frantic whisper when Mrs. Haggerty shushed us. "It's one thing to read my book and notice a few subtle coincidences. It's another to market the show as being inspired by a true crime and invite the lead detective from the case to the set to make the whole thing feel even more authentic! Especially considering the fact that my ex-husband is being detained on suspicion of a *new* murder that will bring everything that happened in that book—and his farm—back under scrutiny."

Vero's laughter died. "What are you going to do?"

"I don't know yet. I put Sylvia up at a hotel for the night. I'll deal with her tomorrow." After the bottle of champagne she'd split with

Randall, she'd been too tipsy to argue when I'd pulled over in front of a Hampton Inn and put a room on my credit card.

Zach streaked through the kitchen, naked as the day he was born. He zoomed into the dining room and tugged on Mrs. Haggerty's pant leg. "Me do school, too!"

"Absolutely not," she replied. "You must be properly dressed to attend school. Come back when you can behave like a young man."

Zach stomped his foot. He tore out of the room like his tiny ass was on fire, ran to the playroom, and slammed the door.

Vero sighed. "We should probably find him before he pees on the floor." We did a quick game of rock, paper, scissors to see who would get elbowed in the boobs while holding him and who would get kicked in the face while wrestling his pants on.

Then we walked in solemn procession to the playroom and opened the door. Vero scooped him up before he could stuff himself inside his sister's dollhouse, while I attempted to wrangle him into his clothes. The doorbell rang.

"Do you mind answering that, Mrs. Haggerty?" I called out. "Our hands are full."

I couldn't make out her muttered retort over Zach's tantrum as I dressed him, but that was probably a good thing. She had made it clear every day since she'd been here that she didn't approve of my parenting methods, and if I had to listen to one more lecture from her, I was going to pack up my kids and move to Missouri.

I emerged from the playroom holding a writhing, fully dressed Zach in my arms. He quieted, arching up to get a better look when he noticed the two strangers standing on our front porch.

The woman held up a slip of paper in one hand and rested the other on her son's shoulder. He looked about Delia's age and I faintly recalled seeing them both in her classroom at career day a few months ago. The woman was speaking in sharp tones while Delia cowered behind Mrs. Haggerty's legs.

"What's this?" Mrs. Haggerty asked the woman.

"*That* is a bill for our medical expenses. My son suffered several serious injuries after your granddaughter assaulted him at school last week."

I passed Zach off to Vero and stepped forward to intervene. "It's fine, Mrs. Haggerty. I'll handle it."

Cooper's mother blanched and took a small step back from the door. "*You're* Margaret Haggerty? From the news? The one who was arrested and sent to jail?"

Mrs. Haggerty scowled at the woman. "What business is that of yours?"

"I'm sorry . . . It's just . . . I didn't expect—"

"What *did* you expect?" Mrs. Haggerty snapped. "An old lady with prison tats?" Vero nearly dropped Zach as Mrs. Haggerty pulled aside the neckline of her blouse, revealing the three-leaf clover tattooed below her collarbone. She let Cooper's mother get a good, long look at it before tugging her shirt back in place. "Now that you know who you're dealing with, it seems we have a different understanding of what transpired on the playground last week. According to Delia, your son was pulling her hair."

"He was just being a little boy," Cooper's mother stammered.

"He was being a little bully! And don't give me that *boys will be boys* nonsense. That's a load of horse dookie!" Mrs. Haggerty looked down her nose at Cooper. "Were you pulling Delia's hair?" Cooper looked cautiously to his mother. They both flinched when Mrs. Haggerty raised her voice. "Your mother wasn't on that playground, boy! I want to hear it from *you*. Did you or did you not pull Delia's hair?"

Cooper nodded. His mother stood mute with shock beside him.

"How many times did she ask you to stop?" Mrs. Haggerty asked him.

Cooper held up three fingers, using his other hand to hold his fourth one down.

"Look here, young man." Mrs. Haggerty pointed to the stitches in his forehead. "Bad things happen to poorly behaved boys who don't know how to stop when they're told. Next time, it might be worse. Delia's a quick study, and I learned a thing or two during my stint in the cooler." Mrs. Haggerty nudged Delia forward. "I believe you have something to say to my granddaughter."

The woman prodded her son. "Apologize to Delia," she said in a wobbly voice.

Cooper mumbled an apology.

Mrs. Haggerty cupped a hand beside her ear. "Speak up, boy! I can't hear you."

"I'm sorry, Delia," he said, clear as a bell.

"Good," Cooper's mother said, pasting on a diplomatic smile as she patted her son's shoulder. "Now Delia will accept your apology, and the grown-ups will settle the matter of the bill."

"Delia doesn't have to do any such thing! And neither does her mother. The consequences of your son's actions are no one's responsibility but his and your own." Mrs. Haggerty tore the medical bill in half, then tore it once more for good measure. "Your business is done here. Tomorrow, you're going to march yourself right back to that school and tell them none of this was Delia's fault. If you don't, I might have to show up at *your* home unannounced with a little business of my own." Mrs. Haggerty slammed the door.

Delia beamed up at her with a wide toothless smile. I suppressed my shocked laughter behind my hand.

Vero let out a low whistle. "Nice tat, Mrs. Haggerty. What'd you have to do to get it?"

Mrs. Haggerty harrumphed. "I didn't get it in jail, if that's what you're asking. I got that tattoo three years ago, but I didn't see any reason to tell Cooper's mother that. Let her think whatever the heck she wants." She turned to Delia and Zach. "We're done with school for today. Time for chores." When the children whined about having to clean up their playroom, Mrs. Haggerty thrust a dustpan at Zach and gave Delia a hand broom. "In my school, you follow *my* rules. Everyone has a job to do. Everyone contributes."

Vero and I watched in quiet fascination as Mrs. Haggerty marched the children to the playroom.

Vero burst into hysterical laughter as soon as they were out of earshot. "I might have passed judgment too quickly. That woman is one badass mama bear! She absolutely shredded Cooper's mother."

My own laughter died, and I tipped my head.

If Mrs. Haggerty was a mama bear, then Brendan was the closest thing she had to a cub. Which made me wonder how far she might go to protect him.

I reached for my phone.

"What are you doing?" Vero asked as I scrolled through my contacts.

"I'm calling Cam."

Vero frowned. "Why?"

"We need to find Brendan," I said in a low voice. "Mrs. Haggerty has been very cagey about where he went and why he's not returning my calls. I feel like she's hiding something. She could be covering for him. And if she's covering for him, there's probably a reason." If he was involved in any way in Gilford Dupree's murder, then the sooner we found him, the better.

Cam picked up on the second ring. "What's up, Mrs. D?"

"I need a favor."

"Name it."

"It's really important that I find someone. Today."

"How important?"

"I did save your life, you know."

"Which is why I'm willing to offer you a generous discount. A hundred bucks. That's half my usual rate."

I was surprised he hadn't already Venmo'd it to himself. "Fifty."

"And dinner?"

"Chicken casserole."

"Send me everything you've got on your missing person. I'll be there in an hour."

I texted Brendan's name and address to Cam, along with a brief description of the few things I knew about him—approximate age, line of work, his vehicle make and model, and a link to the article about his run for office, which also contained his photo.

I gave my phone to Vero. "See what you can find about Penny Dupree. Look for any connection between her and Brendan. While you search, I'll start working on dinner." I dug around in the pantry, the fridge, then the freezer, cobbling together a hodgepodge of ingredients for a casserole.

Vero opened a search engine and began scouring the internet for information about Gilford and Penny Dupree. For a few minutes, the kitchen was quiet except for the scrape of the whisk against the mixing bowl, the clatter of Vero's computer keys, and Mrs. Haggerty barking out orders in the playroom.

"Look at this," Vero said, zooming in on one of the articles. "According to the news, Gilford and Penny had purchased a vacation home in Boynton Beach and were planning to retire there before he went missing. Didn't you say you'd found a Florida area code in Brendan's call log?"

"Just some vacation company. Probably a marketing call. Why? What else does it say?"

"Penny sold their house in Florida later that winter. She decided to hold on to the house in Ashburn because the police were still searching for Gilford here."

"Did they have any leads?"

"Not according to the news. All the articles say the missing persons case went cold pretty quickly. No witnesses. No signs of foul play. Nothing missing from Gilford's car or his home. No enemies or conflicts his family was aware of. And according to police, no known ties to any of the Haggertys."

The part about *no conflicts* didn't sit right with me. Every murder was rooted in conflict. Conflict was the engine that drove every story. It's what propelled a thriller forward. Murders didn't happen by accident to anyone other than me. There was always a motive: greed, self-preservation, jealousy, money, revenge . . . there had to be a conflict in Gilford's past that no one had uncovered yet.

"There must be a tie to Brendan in all this. We just need to find it."

Vero resumed her search and I returned to my casserole. At some point, Mrs. Haggerty puttered out of the playroom and turned on the television. I had just popped dinner in the oven when the doorbell rang. I hurried to answer it, pulling Cam and Arnold Schwarzenegger with me into the kitchen.

"Did you find anything?" I whispered as Arnold Schwarzenegger ventured to the oven and sniffed.

"This Brendan guy is about as vanilla as they come," Cam said.

"No priors. No aliases. Not so much as a ding on his credit report. He's squeaky clean."

Which was precisely the problem with Brendan's condo. "Any idea where he is?"

"Just his car. He's got an app on his phone. His Volvo's parked way out in the economy lot at Dulles."

"Great," Vero muttered.

Brendan's choice to park in the economy lot of an international airport didn't bode well. "He could be halfway around the world by now."

"Doubt it," Cam said. "His ticket was for West Palm."

Vero and I both turned to stare at Cam. "West Palm? As in Florida?" I asked.

Cam nodded, helping himself to a Coke from my fridge. "The guy cleaned out his savings account at the bank a few days ago, then charged the flight to his AmEx—one checked bag, no upgrades. What's your beef with this guy, anyway?"

Vero slapped her laptop closed. "He's a no good, lying, mur—"

"He abandoned his elderly grandmother," I cut in quietly. The last thing I needed was to involve Cam in a murder investigation. I'd already asked him to do more than I should have.

Cam looked horrified. "What kind of an asshole would abandon his grandmother? That's elder neglect!" I gestured frantically for him to keep his voice down. His blue eyes widened as he registered my quick sideways glance into the living room. "Holy shit, his grandmother is Mrs. H?" he whispered. "I should call Uncle Joey right now and report that fucker to the cops."

I paused as I considered that. Maybe reporting Brendan to the police wasn't such a bad idea after all. It was beginning to look like he and Penny could be in on this whole thing together. I couldn't just waltz into Mike Tran's office and accuse the two of them without any proof, but maybe I could plant a seed.

"I'll handle it," I said to Cam. "You go keep Mrs. Haggerty company until dinner's ready. But don't say anything to her about this. It might upset her."

He made a zipping motion over his lips and carried Arnold Schwarzenegger with him to the living room while I called his uncle.

Joey sounded frazzled when he answered the phone. "Hey, I was just getting ready to call you. I'm trying to get in touch with Nick, but he's not picking up. Is he with you?"

"No, why?"

"He asked me to let him know about any developments in the Dupree case. I just got a call from a buddy of mine in Loudoun. Steven's being charged. They're booking him tonight."

CHAPTER 14

I left Vero at home to keep a close eye on Cam and Mrs. Haggerty while I hightailed it to the Loudoun County Police Department. I entered the building with the confidence of a woman who'd walked in and out of countless police stations before, but it didn't change the fact that I didn't know a single cop in this one.

"I'm here to see Detective Mike Tran," I informed the officer behind the desk.

She gave my sweatshirt and jeans a quick once-over through the glass. "Is he expecting you?"

"No, but it's very important that I speak with him—"

"I'd be happy to give you his extension and you can leave a him a message."

"I don't want to leave a message."

"I'm sorry, but Detective Tran isn't here."

"I *know* he's here because he just filed charges against my ex-husband! Just . . . please," I said, lowering my voice when two other officers behind the partition paused their conversation to look at me. "My name is Finlay Donovan. My ex-husband's name is Steven Donovan. I need to know if he's still here and if I can speak with—"

The door beside the partition opened. I turned, hoping to see Mike Tran, but it was Steven's divorce lawyer who came barreling through it. I almost didn't recognize him. The last time I'd seen Guy Folsom had been at our wedding. He'd been Steven's best man and had gotten drunk enough on cheap champagne to tell me exactly how long he predicted our marriage would last. He'd been right, and it wasn't until Guy had sent a courier to deliver our separation and custody papers that it occurred to me that he'd known Steven much better than I ever had. He looked more or less the same as I remembered him, with a few extra wrinkles, a little less hair, and several more inches around his middle.

He stormed out of the back offices into the waiting area, his knuckles white around the handle of his briefcase. His fancy suit jacket hung open, revealing sweat rings under his arms. A button had been torn from the collar of his dress suit and his tie was askew.

"Guy?" I called out as he blew past me.

He paused, frowning as if it had taken him a minute to register who I was and what the hell I was doing there. I held up a finger to the officer at the desk to let her know I'd be back to finish our conversation, then I pulled Guy aside, into a corner of the small reception room. His hair was mussed and his lower lip was puffy.

"What's happening?" I asked. "Is Steven okay?"

"Is he okay?" Guy's sardonic laugh revealed a smear of blood on his front teeth. He wiped the corner of his mouth with the back of his hand and swore under his breath when it came away pink. "No, Finlay. Steven just assaulted a cop. He's far from okay. He was only a few short hours from walking out of this place. Now he'll be lucky if they don't throw him in prison."

"He assaulted a cop?"

"Not just any cop—Mike Tran," Guy said, pulling a handkerchief from his breast pocket and dabbing at his lip. "We were in the interrogation room, answering the same damn questions they'd been grilling him with for the last two days. I had just finished telling Tran to file charges against my client or get off the pot. I told him we'd been more than cooperative and this was the last question I was giving him before I filed a complaint for false imprisonment. The next thing that came out of Tran's mouth was about you."

"Me?"

"Steven flew off the handle. He launched himself over the table at Tran. I took an elbow in the face trying to pull him off. Next thing I know, two uniforms are hauling him out in handcuffs and Tran's pushing for assault charges."

"But not murder?" I asked as Guy blotted his lip.

"Not yet. But let's just say Tran didn't look too upset about his fat lip. Might not have been the charge he was hoping for, but at least now he's got one that'll stick. And you know what? Maybe a little time in the cooler will be good for Steven. The guy's a fucking hothead."

I couldn't argue with that. "Where is he?"

Guy jutted his chin toward the door he'd just come through. "They're booking him now. When you talk to him, tell him I've done all I can do."

"Wait!" I called after him as he headed for the exit. "You're just dropping him?"

"I was trying to do Steven a favor. But if he wants to be an idiot and throw his life away, he'll have to do it on his own."

I didn't have a chance to ask Guy for a referral, or what would happen to Steven now, before he was out the door.

Stunned, I returned to the counter. "I'd like to see Steven Donovan," I said with a forced calm.

"No family is allowed. Attorneys only," the officer said bluntly.

I claimed a hard plastic chair in the waiting area and stared at my phone. Against my better judgment, I sent a quick text to Julian.

Finlay: *Steven is being charged. I'm at the LCPD. They won't let me see him without a lawyer.*

My knee bobbed an impatient rhythm as I waited for his reply.

A text message pinged.

Julian: *Sit tight. I'm on my way.*

I was getting ready to text Vero and fill her in when the inner door buzzed open again. Detective Tran held it wide as he scanned the room. One side of his face was shiny, his eye slightly discolored. "Mrs. Donovan, would you come with me, please?"

I hurried to my feet and followed him into a labyrinthine maze of hallways flanked by small offices. He directed me into an empty interrogation room.

"Have a seat," he said, gesturing to the table in the middle of it.

"Thank you, but I'd like to see Steven."

Detective Tran closed the door. "It'll be a few hours before the magistrate can get to him. You might as well take a seat." He pulled out a chair for me, claiming the one across the table for himself.

"I've called an attorney," I said. "He'll be here any minute."

"Mmm," Detective Tran acknowledged with a nod. "Yes, I heard Steven's lawyer quit. That's unfortunate timing."

"For who?" The detective glanced up from his notebook. I hadn't meant to say it out loud, but Tran looked amused. "I'm sure this was all a misunderstanding," I said, careful to keep my tone civil.

"There's no misunderstanding. Steven is here because he's a suspect in a murder investigation. We can demonstrate that he had means, opportunity, and a motive to kill Gilford Dupree. We can also prove he has a violent streak." He didn't bother pointing out the indisputable evidence on his face.

"Steven can't be the only suspect!" I argued. "I mean, has anyone bothered to investigate Brendan Haggerty in all this?"

"Brendan Haggerty?" Detective Tran laughed, making me feel as if I'd been left out of some inside joke.

"Brendan left his grandmother at my place on Thursday night," I explained. "He was supposed to pick her up before the end of the weekend, but no one has heard from him since. He's not answering his phone, and his car is parked in the economy lot at Dulles. Given that he was supposed to pick up his grandmother yesterday and he didn't tell anyone he was leaving town, don't you think that's a little suspicious? I mean, *I* certainly have questions."

"I have a few questions, too. But mine are for you." Tran's expression sobered as he uncapped his pen and turned the page of his notebook. My name was written inside it. "It's lucky for me you came in tonight. I was planning to stop by your house tomorrow, but it seems you've saved me the trip."

My palms began to sweat. "What kind of questions?"

"Mrs. Donovan—"

"Ms.," I corrected him.

"Right," he said, his mouth twitching around a smirk. "*Ms.* Donovan. The address where you currently live . . . Did you live in that same home with your ex-husband during the period when you were married?"

"Why do you ask?"

"It's a simple question."

"Yes, we lived together while we were married. Why is that important?" I insisted, growing impatient.

"And at the time you were living together, were you aware that your husband had signed a contract to complete a landscaping project for Mr. and Mrs. Owen Haggerty?"

"It was a long time ago," I said, flustered. "I don't remember. I was pregnant and trying to finish writing a book before my due date. And, frankly, I don't see what any of this has to do with—"

"That book you were writing . . ." Detective Tran flipped a page in his notebook. "*Sinister Regrets*?" He glanced up at me without bothering to wait for confirmation before continuing. "That was an interesting story. I'm not much into reading *those* kinds of books—I'm more of a Tom Clancy man myself—but when Mrs. Haggerty told me you were a romance novelist, I couldn't help but be a little bit curious about them. You can tell a lot about a person by their taste in books." He leaned back in his chair, studying me as he stroked his chin. "Turns out, there's quite a bit of action in those novels—and not just in the sheets. Before I knew it, I'd spent my whole weekend reading. I managed to get through quite a few of your books, and I noticed some intriguing parallels."

My spine tingled as if someone had blown an icy breath down the back of my neck.

I shot to my feet. "It's getting late. Thank you for your time, but if you're not going to let me talk to Steven, then I'm going to—"

"Sit down, Ms. Donovan. We're not finished." When I didn't sit, he hooked a foot around the leg of my chair and gave it a sharp tug, dropping me into it as it swung into the back of my knees. "See, there's a particularly interesting scene in one of your books—the one you must have been working on around the same time Gilford Dupree disappeared—about a woman whose lover accidentally kills a man in defense of her honor, and she—loving him as deeply as she does—comes up with a plan to hide the body. I'm just curious what might have inspired that idea."

"It's a common trope."

"Seems awfully coincidental under the circumstances, doesn't it?"

"I wouldn't know. At the time, I had no idea what was happening at Mrs. Haggerty's house."

"Did you know what was happening in yours?" My stomach soured. Detective Tran raised an eyebrow when I didn't answer. "Did you know your husband was having an affair, Ms. Donovan?"

Voices argued in the hall, growing louder until they culminated in shouts. I started as the door to the interrogation room flew open and Nick barged inside, flushed and breathless. "Don't answer that," he said to me as Detective Tran rose from his seat.

"Pretty sure you're in the wrong office, Officer Anthony . . . Oh, wait," Tran said, getting a look at the badge on Nick's belt. "Make that the wrong *county*."

Joey leaned on the open doorframe, rolling a toothpick in his mouth. "Give it a rest, Mike."

Nick pulled out my chair for me and handed me my purse. "Come on, Finlay. It's time to go."

Detective Tran stepped in my path as Nick steered me toward the door. "This is my case. She'll go when I say so."

"Are you charging her with something?"

"Haven't decided yet."

Nick pressed forward until he and Tran were toe to toe. "Unless you have a reason to hold her, she's leaving."

Tran lifted his chin. "Aren't you the same detective who found all those bodies on Steven Donovan's farm?" He gestured between Nick and me, his tone dry as tinder. "Is that how the two of you met? Or were you sleeping with each other before?"

“Ask me that one more time,” Nick said through his teeth. There was a dare in his eyes as he stared Tran down.

“Funny. Steven said the same thing when I asked him that question. I guess we all know how that turned out. The guy’s got a mean jealous streak.” Tran tapped his shiner. “Speaking of which, the magistrate should be here any minute about those assault charges. You’ll be hearing from me, Ms. Donovan.” He winked at me with his good eye on his way out the door.

Nick’s hands clenched at his sides. I took him gently by the arm to keep him from doing something he’d regret.

“You two better get out of here,” Joey said once Tran was finally gone.

“Thanks for the heads-up, Joe. I owe you one.” Nick squeezed Joey’s shoulder and followed me into the hall.

Right into Julian Baker.

Julian steadied me with a hand on my arm as we collided. “Finlay, what are you doing back here? I came as soon as I got your text. You should have waited for . . .” His eyes lifted to Nick behind me and Julian quickly shut his mouth. He acknowledged Nick with a quick, professional nod and assumed a more reserved tone. “I brought Parker with me,” he said quietly. “She’s meeting with Steven now. I don’t know that she’ll agree to represent him, but she can help him through his hearing with the magistrate tonight and we can figure out what to do from there.”

Julian’s roommate, Parker, wasn’t very fond of me. This wasn’t the first time Julian had called her to get me out of a jam, but hopefully she wouldn’t hold that against Steven.

“Don’t worry,” Julian assured me. “He’s in good hands.”

“Thank you,” I said.

"Can you tell me anything about what happened?" he asked Nick.

Nick waited for two uniforms to pass by before answering in a low voice. "Mike Tran is looking at Steven's affair with Penny Dupree as a motive for the murder. Tran was trying to prove Steven can be violent when he's jealous. He played dirty during the interrogation and brought up Finlay's relationship with me. Steven took the bait and reacted. Frankly, I'm not sure you being here is the best idea right now." It was coolheaded, rational advice, but there was a steely undertone to it.

Julian nodded, color rising in his cheeks. "Got it. I'll fill Parker in and wait outside." He turned to me. "I'll text you after the meeting and let you know how it went, but I doubt the magistrate will let him leave here tonight. She'll probably want to keep him in custody until his bond hearing. You going to be okay?"

"I'll be fine." I forced myself to smile, resisting the temptation to ask him for a referral to an attorney for myself. After my discussion with Mike Tran, I was convinced I was going to need one.

I opened my arms to hug Julian but thought better of it when I felt Nick's palm on my back. I extended a hand to Julian instead, settling for a shake. "Thank you for everything."

"I'm glad you called me." His eyes flicked to Nick's before he let me go.

Nick didn't say a word as we exited the station. I started toward my minivan, too exhausted to deal with the argument I felt brewing. He took me by the hand and marched me to his Impala instead. He opened the passenger door and deposited me inside. I braced myself as he rounded the hood, got in the driver's seat, and slammed the door.

I waited for the inevitable lecture to start, the one where he asked me how I could be so foolish showing up here, after he'd told me to stay as far away as possible from Tran. The longer Nick didn't say anything, the more my stomach tied itself in knots.

"Why did you call Julian?" he asked without looking at me.

"I needed a lawyer."

"He *isn't* a lawyer."

"I didn't know who else to call."

"You could have called me."

"Joey said you weren't answering your phone."

His eyes snapped to me. "I would have for you! When are you going to start trusting me?" The silence stretched between us. He rubbed a hand over his mouth and lowered his voice. "How certain are you that Steven didn't murder Gilford Dupree?"

"Completely." I waited for him to ask me why. To ask me for proof.

He stared out the windshield for an intolerable length of time. His voice was thick with gravel when he finally spoke. "Tell me you have Mrs. Haggerty's house key."

"It's in her purse, back at my—"

He held up a hand. "Tell me she gave it to you." It wasn't a question. He wasn't looking for an answer. He was looking for permission. An excuse to make a decision he wouldn't be able to if my answer was no.

I nodded. "She gave it to me."

"Good," he said as he started the engine. "You and I are going to solve the Dupree murder before this case gets out of hand. We're starting at the crime scene, and we're doing it tonight."

CHAPTER 15

Nick and I pretended to have tickets to a late show at the movies, while Vero stayed at home to keep an eye on Mrs. Haggerty and the kids. Nick drove us out of the community, checking his rearview mirror through the first few turns, making sure Mike Tran hadn't assigned an unmarked car to stake out my house. Once he was satisfied we hadn't been followed, he took another entrance into South Riding and parked on the street behind Mrs. Haggerty's house.

We cut through the neighbors' backyards on foot, past a line of tall hedges that hid us from view. Nick knelt at the base of Mrs. Haggerty's fence.

"Should you really be doing this?" I asked as he laced his fingers together.

"Would you rather go in the front door?"

The last thing either of us needed was for Mrs. Haggerty to look out my bedroom window and see us breaking into her house.

Nick gave me a boost and I scrambled over the fence, freezing as

I waited for a set of motion-sensing security lights to expose us before I remembered Mrs. Haggerty's power was still out. Nick landed on his feet on the damp grass beside me. He took my hand, leading me around the gaping hole at the edge of Mrs. Haggerty's rose garden. I watched the neighbors' windows while he used Mrs. Haggerty's key to unlock her back door.

The house was pitch-black inside.

"Why are we starting here?" I asked as I waited for my eyes to adjust. "The police already searched the whole place. And they already determined that Mr. and Mrs. Haggerty didn't know the victim. Maybe we should be starting somewhere else." *Like Brendan Haggerty's condo.*

"I'm not buying it," Nick said, leading me deeper into the house. "If neither of them knew the victim, why'd the killer bury the body here?"

"Probably because her garden was an easy place to dump it."

I could just make out the shake of his head. "There's nothing easy about hauling a two-hundred-pound corpse into the backyard of a house in a residential neighborhood without being seen, Finn. Especially when the property lines are less than thirty feet apart. Someone went to a lot of work to bury Dupree here, and I'm betting they did it for a reason. Either the Haggertys knew him or they knew the person who killed him."

"What about Brendan?" I suggested, latching on to the opportunity to point Nick in the right direction. "He's strong enough to move a body. And he would have had access to this house."

"Tran already ruled him out as a suspect."

"He ruled out Mr. and Mrs. Haggerty, too, but we're here, aren't we?"

Nick didn't look convinced. "Whoever it was, there might be

something here the investigators missed." Nick pulled his penlight from his breast pocket, careful not to let the beam veer too close to the windows as he passed it to me. "You start inside. I'll check the garage."

He took a small flashlight from his belt and disappeared through the kitchen. There was a soft click as the service door closed behind him.

I looked around Mrs. Haggerty's first floor, unsure exactly what I was supposed to be looking for. I moved through the living room, fanning my light over her end tables and bookshelves as I slid picture frames and knickknacks aside to search behind them.

I pulled the cigar box on the mantel closer to the edge. It felt heavier than it looked, or at least heavier than a box of cigars was likely to weigh. I tried to peek inside it, but the lid was sealed shut. I aimed my penlight at the engraving on the gold plate. A pair of dates was etched below a set of initials. A framed photo of Mrs. Haggerty's husband had been placed behind the box.

I shook out my hand and wiped my palm on my jeans as I realized what (or, more accurately, who) was *in* the box.

I remembered very little of Owen Haggerty. Only that he had been about as pleasant as his wife and that he had passed of a heart attack around the same time Delia had been born. He had been fit for his age when the photo had been taken. And tall, with eyes like Paul Newman's, that gathered deep smile lines from the sun. I studied the cigar box with sick fascination. It seemed impossible that such a large man could be reduced to fit into such a tiny vessel. I wondered if there was more of him, scattered somewhere else.

I backed away, nearly tripping over a cardboard box on the floor. I knelt and lifted the lid. It was filled to the brim with family memorabilia and photo albums, all carelessly tossed inside. A sticker on the side of the box declared it was evidence—Property of LCPD.

The investigators must have found nothing of value in the old photo albums and returned them after their search.

I dug through a handful of loose pictures, uncovering a stack of spiral notebooks at the bottom of the box. Their covers had been labeled with dates in Mrs. Haggerty's shaky handwriting. I thumbed one open, recognizing it immediately as one of her neighborhood watch diaries.

My heart skipped a beat. I glanced around the corner to the kitchen, making sure Nick was still in the garage as I removed them from the box and read the dates on the covers.

They were all more than six months old.

I checked them again, searching for her entries since October, but the one diary I needed wasn't there.

The rest of the notebooks went back five years, the earliest dated just after Mrs. Haggerty's husband had passed away. I wondered if there was a correlation there. If she had become so obsessed about the safety of her neighborhood because she was an elderly widow living alone, or if there had been some other reason she had chosen to become so vigilant then. After all, that had also been around the same time Gilford Dupree had been buried in her yard.

I thumbed through the notebooks. They contained what I had expected, a litany of minor offenses she'd gone out of her way to record: teenagers who drove too fast, cars that played their music too loud, Girl Scouts who came to the door to sell cookies without parental supervision, door-to-door solicitors who'd been rude, and the occasional odd noises that had apparently come from my bedroom window . . .

My stomach turned as I spotted Steven's name, and I realized with a stinging pang that his infidelities with our real estate agent had dated back much further than I'd known. Mrs. Haggerty had become obsessed with documenting his "suspicious behaviors," including any time he'd come home in the middle of the workday while the children and I had been out.

Only on closer inspection, not all of the surreptitious meetings at our home had been with Theresa.

He had met someone else there, too. Not once, but on several occasions. I counted at least four visits by a man in an unmarked van, none of which had occurred while I had been at home. Each time, Steven had unloaded several bags of mulch from his truck and loaded them into the back of the man's van. But why have his buyer pick up mulch at our home? Why not deliver it to the man's house? Or have him pick it up at the farm?

I jumped out of my skin as a hand came down on my shoulder. "Find anything?" Nick asked.

I closed the notebook and dropped it in the box. Nick had plenty of lingering suspicions about Steven's truthfulness in all this, and I didn't see any reason to add more fuel to that fire.

"Just a bunch of old photo albums and some journals the police already searched."

"Journals?"

"Nothing useful. Just Mrs. Haggerty's neighborhood watch diaries. Community drama mostly. You know, which neighbors are cheating on their clueless wives, how often, and with whom. That and her weekly grocery lists." I rolled my eyes, if only to hide the fact that they'd begun watering.

Nick pulled me in for a hug. He rested his chin on my head. "I'm sorry you had to see that."

"It's fine," I insisted, eager to change the subject. The diary I was looking for wasn't in the box, and I doubted any of the other neighbors even knew these journals were here. I was certain they would have all been stolen and destroyed (or sold to the highest bidder), depending on which neighbor had found them. Which meant the missing one I was looking for was either in Mrs. Haggerty's possession or in Mike Tran's. I hoped to god it wasn't the latter. "Did you find anything?" I asked Nick.

He shook his head. "The garage was empty. So was the basement. Looks like Mike Tran took just about everything. If you're finished down here, we could try upstairs. But I'll understand if you want to go."

"No." I tossed the lid back on the box. "If you're stupid enough to commit a B&E to help me, we might as well be thorough about it."

"It's not a B&E if she gave you her key," he reminded me. He took my hand and led the way upstairs, winding us around the chairlift that took up one side of Mrs. Haggerty's stairwell. I'd always wondered why she had one. She'd seemed pretty spritely for her age when she'd been kicking my ass on the police academy training course, though that was mostly due to the fact that Brendan was her partner and he was in excellent shape. And she'd certainly had no problem climbing the stairs in *my* house when she'd staked her claim to my bedroom. I could only assume the chairlift had been her husband's.

Nick aimed his flashlight into the first room at the top of the stairs. A set of twin beds bookended one wall. Framed photos hung behind them. The photos were mostly of Brendan. While Brendan hadn't grown up in this house, this room had clearly been where he stayed when he visited.

Nick and I moved through it in tandem, searching drawers and closets, but it was as tidy and spare as Brendan's condo.

"Nothing," Nick said, emerging from the closet. "You?" He came up behind me, putting his hands gently on my waist as he looked over my shoulder.

I shut the desk drawer a little too hard. "Nothing that screams, 'I murdered Gilford Dupree.' I swear, Brendan is involved in this somehow."

"Why do you say that?"

"He was supposed to pick up his grandmother two days ago, but he's not returning my calls, and I'm pretty sure he's skipped town. When I told Mike Tran, he completely ignored me. And I didn't see much about Brendan in that file in your apartment," I pointed out.

"You never saw that file," Nick reminded me. "And be careful before you go throwing accusations around. Brendan's a big supporter of local law enforcement. He's got a solid shot at a seat on the city council and he's in tight with some very big donors—"

I opened my mouth to point out that his political standing had no bearing on his capacity to commit murder, but Nick beat me to it.

"—I know, I know. I'll look into him. Quietly," he added.

"If you find him, tell him to pick up his grandmother."

We moved down the hall, door by door, until we reached Mrs. Haggerty's bedroom. I searched the dresser. Nick checked her closet. The contents were disheveled where police had already searched them: clothes organized by season, rolls of yarn, an assortment of knitting needles and sewing supplies.

I opened Mrs. Haggerty's nightstand. A collection of dog-eared, yellowing paperbacks was tucked inside the drawer, along with a bottle of hand cream, an eyeglass repair kit, and several ballpoint pens. I picked up the stack of books to look beneath them and tossed them on the bed. One slipped off the edge. A folded piece of stationery fell out of its pages.

Curious, I opened it. It was written in the kind of crisp, careful script they used to teach in schools before the advent of computers.

Dearest Maggie,

You'll never know how sorry I am. I know I can't take back what I've done, but I hope you can find it in your heart to forgive me. It was all my fault. You shouldn't harbor any guilt for that night. I take full responsibility.

Yours always,
Owen

There was no date on the letter. The paper hadn't yet yellowed, but the stationery had been pressed flat for so long, it was impossible to tell how old the note really was. Which begged the question: What happened on the night Owen had written about, and what was he taking responsibility for?

I looked over my shoulder for Nick. His light bobbed inside the closet.

"That file you showed me at your apartment," I called out to him.

"What file?" he reminded me.

"The one I never saw and doesn't exist," I called back. "Did it say why Owen Haggerty was ruled out as a suspect?"

"Age and poor health. He would have been almost eighty when Dupree was murdered. The notes said Owen was being treated for hypertension and chronic back problems. Guess Tran figured it was unlikely that Owen could lift two hundred pounds of deadweight and dig a hole big enough to bury a man."

"What do you think?"

Nick grunted as if he was lifting something heavy. "I think desperate people who want something badly enough are capable of all sorts of things. Why?" he asked, dusting off his hands as he emerged from the closet.

"What do you make of this?" I showed him the letter.

He wiped sweat from his brow and frowned as he read it. "I don't know. It may be nothing, but I'll run a background check on Owen and see what I can find." He took a photo of it with his phone, folded the letter, and handed it back to me. I tucked it inside the cover of one of the books. Between Penny's anonymous tip, Brendan's suspiciously timed trip to Florida, Steven's bizarre mulch deliveries, and this strange letter from Owen, I wasn't sure what to make of any of this. There were too many clues, and none of them seemed connected.

"Hey," Nick said behind me, resting his hands on my shoulders. "You okay? You've been a little quiet since you found those journals downstairs."

"I'm fine."

He turned me to face him. "We don't have to do this. Steven's lied to you so many times, Finn. No one would blame you for doubting him."

"He didn't sleep with Penny," I said sharply. "And he didn't murder Gilford Dupree. You don't have to believe me." After all the lies *I'd* told over the last five months, I wouldn't blame Nick if he second-guessed me either. But I was right about this.

I stepped out of his arms and dropped down on my knees beside the bed, ducking to look beneath it.

Nick knelt behind me. "I do believe you," he said close to my ear. "If your gut says he didn't do it, we'll keep looking." He reached around me to grab the mattress. The muscles in his arms strained as he lifted it so I could slide an arm underneath.

"Anything?" he asked.

"There's nothing here."

He let the mattress fall, but his arms stayed around me. He was warm and solid, his body heat chasing away the chill in the room. "This is almost as much fun as that night we went looking for evidence in the dumpster behind Feliks's restaurant," he murmured into my hair. "Only you smell better." He nipped my earlobe when I laughed. "You know, we don't have to go back to your place just yet."

"I'm not getting naked with you in Mrs. Haggerty's bed."

He nuzzled my neck as he unzipped my coat. "How about on the floor?"

"It's freezing in here."

"I can fix that, too." He turned my face to his and kissed me. And in that moment, I was pretty sure he could fix anything. He pulled me against his chest and my knees turned to Jell-O.

Why not? I told myself. Mrs. Haggerty had been doing god knows what in my bedroom for the last four days. If I wanted to feel guilty for something, I had plenty of other sins to choose from.

Nick laid me back on the carpet, his hands finding me under all my layers. I turned my head as he moved down my body, kissing a trail down my neck. One of Mrs. Haggerty's dog-eared paperbacks lay on the floor beside me, the peeling spine label caught in the beam of Nick's flashlight. The title of the book pinged something in my brain.

Goose bumps rippled over my body as I recognized the collection of Miss Marple stories.

It was the same book I'd seen in Penny Dupree's closet.

Detective Tran was right. You could tell a lot about a person by their taste in books.

I just hadn't paid enough attention to Penny Dupree's.

CHAPTER 16

"Tell me you're not serious." Vero looked like she might be sick in the back of my minivan the next morning. It was the only place I could think of where we could talk privately. As soon as Vero had come down to the kitchen searching for coffee, I had shoved her arms in her coat and a travel thermos in her hands and hauled her out to the garage with me. Then I'd stuffed us both inside the back of my minivan, locking us in where no one could hear us.

"I am telling you, I saw the exact same book in Penny Dupree's house."

"I was talking about you having sex in Mrs. Haggerty's."

"Says the woman who still has her own bed! Can we please focus on what's important here? Penny had that same book of old mysteries in her house."

"So?"

"So the woman owns a library of pristine contemporary romance novels. She keeps them in a glass-enclosed case in her living room, so why is there a ratty old collection of Agatha Christie murder mysteries hidden in her closet? And why does Mrs. Haggerty have the same exact book in her nightstand?"

I hadn't mentioned a word of it to Nick last night. I couldn't, not without revealing how I knew about Penny's book. But it might be possible to convince him that Mrs. Haggerty and Mrs. Dupree had both lied when they'd claimed they didn't know each other. "All I need is some thread of evidence connecting the two of them," I told Vero. "I just can't figure out how the book fits into the case."

"Maybe you need to stop thinking about this as a case and start thinking about it like a story. Maybe it'll make more sense to you that way."

"What do you mean?"

She turned sideways on the bench seat to face me. "You've got all these little random plot threads, right? All you have to do is figure out how those plot threads connect. Ask yourself, what do Mrs. Haggerty and Penny Dupree have in common with that book? Figure it out, and that's the solution to your mystery. Anything else is just a red herring. What else did you find?"

"Just a letter from her late husband and a stack of her old neighborhood watch diaries. They were in an evidence box the police left in her house. They must have already searched them all." Vero's eyes went wide. "Not the most recent one," I assured her before she could ask.

"You think Tran has it?"

"God, I hope not."

We both jumped at a loud knock on the window. I craned my head above the captain's chairs to see my sister's face pressed up against the glass. She cupped her hands around her eyes, squinting to see through the tinting. "What the hell are you two doing in there?"

I reached between the seats and unlocked the door. Georgia slid it open and frowned at us.

"The car has to be running for a suicide pact to work, you know."

"We're hiding from Mrs. Haggerty," I explained.

"Don't bother," Georgia said, climbing in with us. She knelt on Delia's booster seat, leaning over the back of the chair to see us. "Mrs. Haggerty was the one who told me you were out here."

"How'd she know we were out here?" Vero asked.

"She said she heard you screaming that it was cold in the garage and why the hell was Finn making you sit in the van in your pajamas."

"Right, that was probably it."

"We might as well not all freeze to death," I said. "Let's go back inside and I'll make everyone some breakfast."

Georgia stopped me before I could wedge myself out of the bench seat.

"You might want to stay put for a minute. I've got some news, and it's probably better if I tell you out here."

I sank back onto the bench, my stomach growing a little queasy at the look on her face.

"Joey called Nick this morning. Nick called me. He thought I should be the one to tell you."

"Tell me what?"

"Steven's bond hearing was this morning. The judge decided to hold him."

Julian had told me to expect that much. "Is that all?"

"Also, some true-crime podcast did a whole episode about Steven last night. They talked up his involvement with Dupree's wife, then rehashed the night we found the dead mafia guys on Steven's farm. They're spinning some serial-killer angle out of it. Apparently, the episode got a lot of attention. Fox, ABC, NBC, CBS . . . they all had reporters sniffing around the station this morning, wanting to know if the sod-farm case was being reopened in light of new evidence. Brendan Haggerty's campaign manager got word of it and called the station. He's putting pressure on Tran to nail Steven for this, probably to get the Haggertys out of the spotlight before the election this fall."

I threw up my hands. "Great. Anything else?"

"Yeah, Mrs. Haggerty says you're out of toaster waffles. And your literary agent just left."

I sat up. "Sylvia was here? What did she want?"

"I don't know. She was talking to Mrs. Haggerty when I got here. She said something about going to the station to look for Nick."

"Oh, boy," Vero said.

"Jesus, Georgia! You couldn't have led with that?!" I bolted out of the back of the van and raced into the house, where Mrs. Haggerty's School for Finlay Donovan's Wayward Children was already in full swing. Delia was hunched over the table, pencil in hand, as she meticulously copied the alphabet onto a sheet of hand-lined paper while Zach stood naked in the corner, screaming bloody murder, his clothes scattered over the floor and snot pouring from his nose.

"I. DO. SCHOOL. TOOOOOOOO!!!!" he shouted at Mrs. Haggerty's back as she rewarded Delia's progress with a sticker.

"Only boys who use the toilet and keep their pants on go to school." Mrs. Haggerty turned to me. "We're out of toaster waffles. I've made you a list to take to the store."

Zach demanded a sticker at the top of his lungs. He was past the point of no return, and there was no sense in trying to calm him. I raised my voice to speak over him.

"I can't go to the store right now," I said, pulling on my sneakers and coat. "Maybe Vero can take you."

"But we're in the middle of arithmetic and toilet training."

"And we all see how well *that's* going," Vero said over Zach's screams.

"I'm sorry, Mrs. Haggerty, but I have an emergency I need to handle right now. I'll take you shopping when I get home." I kissed each of the kids on their heads in case Nick murdered me and I never got to see them again. "Vero's in charge," I told them.

Delia nodded. Zach threw himself on the floor and screamed louder.

Mrs. Haggerty stood in my way as I gathered my purse and keys. "My book club meeting is this evening," she said. "I'll need a ride. Cameron was supposed to drive me, but he's taken my vehicle to the repair shop."

I fought the urge to offer to drive her off a cliff. But maybe this was serendipitous. I could take Mrs. Haggerty to her book club meeting and Vero could stay behind with the kids and search the house for that missing neighborhood watch diary. If she could find it, that would solve at least one of my problems.

I pasted on a smile as I circumnavigated Mrs. Haggerty. "I'm sure I'll be back in plenty of time to take you. What book are you all discussing?" Maybe I could cram the CliffsNotes version before the meeting.

"We're not," she said bluntly.

Vero raised an eyebrow. "You're not discussing a book at book club?"

"On Saturdays, we discuss. On Tuesdays, we vote."

"Vote on what?" Vero asked.

"On the next book, of course! If you let one person choose, you'll be lucky if anyone else bothers to read it. You end up sitting in an empty room with the host, with nothing to do but complain about your husbands and gossip about the neighbors. Regardless, we're not accepting new members, so there's no point in either of you coming. You can wait in the car."

I decided not to point out the note her friend had left in my mailbox the other night about joining her club. Apparently, Mrs. Haggerty didn't want an author who writes *those kinds of books* cramping her style.

"Fine. I'll drive you to your meeting, and I'll wait in the car. We'll stop for groceries on the way home."

And as soon as I got her out of the house, the hunt for her diary was on.

CHAPTER 17

I'd known I was too late the moment I entered the Fairfax County police station. The duty officer at the desk was turned in his chair, facing the room of officers behind him, his shoulders rocking with laughter. I rapped on the window to get his attention.

"Oh, hey, Finlay," he said as he tried and failed to quiet the last of his chuckles. I smiled and returned the greeting, trying not to make it obvious that I couldn't remember his name when I stole a peek at his uniform. Between my frequent visits to this station with Georgia over the years—and, more recently, with Nick—and the week I had spent at the citizen's police academy, my welcome here was a fair bit warmer than the one I had experienced at Loudoun's precinct the day before.

"Is Nick here?" I asked, though, judging by the jovial tone of the bullpen behind him, I feared I already knew the answer to that.

"Yep. Some lady is back there with him. She said she came all the way from New York City to meet—and I quote—'the hot cop named Nick.'" The duty officer's eyes watered as another laugh burst out of him. "I figured she was one of those crazy stalkers that started showing up here after all that PR last fall. Between the interviews and Nick's press pictures all over the news, we've had women showing up here at all hours wanting to 'report a crime' or take selfies with him. I assumed she was one of 'em, but then she said she knew you. I asked Nick if it was okay to send her back. I'm guessing he didn't know what he was in for when he said yes. This is the most entertainment this department has seen for weeks. Jesus," the officer said, shaking his head, "I hope Nick doesn't put my name in for a demotion." He wiped his eyes, still giggling to himself as he buzzed me in.

My stomach dropped as I opened the door and followed an explosion of laughter to the bullpen. A cluster of young patrol officers stood just inside the entrance, blocking my view. I tapped one of them on the shoulder and nudged my way between them, blanching at the scene on the other side.

Sylvia stood by the watercooler, wearing neon-green stiletto heels and a matching spandex dress that was probably restricting circulation to most of her essential organs. Judging by the amount of cleavage on display, there definitely wasn't room for any socks in her bra. Her arm was slung around a young cadet. She towered over him, her shoes leaving him at eye level with her chest. She held out her cell phone, asking one of the other uniformed officers to take their picture. She fluffed her hair, gave each of her breasts a vigorous hoist, and ran a finger over the front of her teeth, checking them for lipstick before the camera flashed. Sylvia took her phone back and frowned at the screen.

"I need someone taller," she called out. "You!" She pointed to Officer Roddy, who was hunched over the coffeepot, discreetly filling his mug.

The quiet, middle-aged beat cop turned around slowly, his face growing red when she beckoned him with an obscenely long, hot-pink fingernail. He lumbered over—all six feet and four inches of him. Sylvia pushed aside the cadet and threw an arm around Roddy's middle. "Here," she said, handing him her phone. She gestured in a sweeping motion over her chest. "But take it high. They look better from above." She sucked in her cheeks and threw her shoulders back. Roddy extended an arm above them and snapped a selfie that probably could have doubled as an aerial shot of the Grand Canyon.

I pushed my way through the crowd of officers, determined to save Roddy before Sylvia could proposition him. He was happily married with twin teenage daughters, and I didn't imagine he had any desire to offer Sylvia a ride-along in *any* capacity.

He looked relieved when I made it to his side.

"Sorry," I muttered, giving him a quick one-armed hug. I whispered in his ear, "Run while you still can."

He was quick to take the hint.

"Sylvia!" I hissed, dragging Sylvia into a corner. "What are you doing here? You can't just waltz into a police station unannounced for no reason!"

"I have a reason!" she said, giving each of my cheeks an air-kiss. "I went to your house first but you weren't there, so I had coffee with your neighbor. She told me where I could find your hot cop. I figured I'd leave the paperwork with him."

"What paperwork?"

"Randall called. He needs you and Nick to sign a preliminary offer letter, breaking down all the terms we agreed to at lunch yesterday. Once he has that, he can go back to the studio's attorneys and have them draft the contract for the series."

"I'm not ready to sign anything, Sylvia. I haven't even had a chance to talk any of this over with Nick."

"Don't bother. I already filled him in. He's got all the paperwork on his desk. You two can read it over and sign it together tonight. I'll pick it up before I head back to New York. But right now, I'm going to see if one of these very attractive policemen would like to have lunch with me. I'm famished." Her false lashes narrowed as she scoped out the handful of officers that remained in the bullpen. "Oh, my," she said, smoothing down her dress. "Would you look at the size of the baton on that one?" She was like a jungle cat in a room of unsuspecting antelope, singling out her next meal. I needed to get her out of here before she pounced. I was pretty sure there were rules about hunting in this place.

"Have you tried the firefighters next door?"

"Firefighters?" she asked as I took her by the shoulders and steered her briskly down the hall.

"They're in the building behind us. You can't miss them. They have very big hoses."

She opened her mouth to protest, then changed her mind. "Color me intrigued," she said as I shuttled her to the exit. "But don't think I don't see what you're doing. I want those papers signed and delivered to my hotel by tomorrow, or I'm coming to your house to pick them up."

"Fine."

Roddy's rookie in training, Tyrese, saw us hustling toward the emergency exit and rushed to get the door for us. I whispered in his ear as he held it open for Sylvia. "Can you make sure she finds her way to the fire department?" He looked a little terrified as Sylvia grabbed him by his biceps and towed him outside with her.

I hurried back to the break room and spotted Georgia's girlfriend, Sam, picking over a box of donuts.

"Where's Nick?" I whispered.

Sam smirked. "Probably hiding at his desk."

"They're never going to let him live this down, are they?"

"Not a chance. Wade Coffey already ordered a life-size poster of Nick's face on Channing Tatum's body. He and Coletti are picking it up from the printshop in an hour. They told everyone to come back this afternoon for a rousing game of 'Pin the Badge on the Hot Cop.'"

I winced. "He's going to kill me."

"Doubt it," she said, taking the last jelly donut. "You can do no wrong in that man's eyes. But," she added, placing added emphasis on the *but*, "considering the morning he's endured in the company of your agent, you might not want to go into his office empty-handed." She passed me a Boston cream. "And maybe get him out of the station before Wade gets back from the printshop."

"I'll take it under advisement. Thanks, Sam." I carried the donut back through the bustling station to Nick's office. He shared the space with a few other detectives. When I poked my head in the door, they got up and filed past me one by one, suppressing mocking smiles on their way out. Nick was the only one who didn't look amused.

I came in quietly and sat in the plastic chair beside his workstation. He glared at my sugary offering before reaching for it, the hard line of his mouth softening a little as he set it on his desk. A stack of files sat by his elbow. His laptop was open in front of him, and a single sheet of letterhead with a fancy Hollywood logo rested in the space between us. My name was printed below one of the signature lines. So was his.

"I'm sorry," I said. "I had no idea she was coming to the station."

"But you knew about this." He slid the contract toward me. I skimmed the bulleted line items of the agreement Sylvia had hashed out with Randall over lunch yesterday.

> *Finlay Donovan writing as Fiona Donahue (hereafter referenced as The Author), and Nicholas Anthony (hereafter referenced as The Consultant) have been made aware and agree that the source material will be adapted for a television series to be marketed and promoted as being inspired by true crimes.*
>
> *Nicholas Anthony hereby agrees to consult on the script with the goal of lending authenticity to the project.*

"You know I can't sign this," he said, his eyes still seething.

"I won't ask you to. I tried to tell Sylvia but she didn't want to hear it. You've met her now. You see how she is."

Nick rubbed a hand down his face. "We talked about this, Finn. It's not just that I can't sign it. You shouldn't sign it either." He got up and shut the door, keeping his voice low. "Mike Tran is already trying to rope you into Steven's case. You saw what he's doing. He's grasping at straws, trying to paint the picture that Steven murdered Gilford Dupree and you helped him cover it up. Joey thinks Mike is going to try to convince a judge that you and Steven were in this together. You know as well as I do that once you sign this form, Sylvia's going to fire off a press release, just like she did before. Mike Tran's going to see the news about your shiny new *true crime* TV deal and dig in his heels. You can't afford that kind of attention."

"I'm not going to sign it," I assured him. I'd just have to find some way to get that through to Sylvia. "I'll make her take your name out of the offer. I'll tell her I'll only agree to the deal if it remains a work of fiction."

Nick took the arm of my chair and slid it gently toward his until our knees were touching. He cupped my face in his hand. "I'm not trying to create obstacles for you. I know how much this deal means to you. I just want you to be smart about it." He stroked my cheek with his thumb. "And you know you can ask me anything you want. I'll consult with you in private," he said, placing a soft kiss at the corner of my mouth, "gratis, any hour, day or night. No producers," he said, pressing a kiss to the other side. "And definitely no agents," he said, kissing me full on the mouth.

I smiled. "Where do I sign?"

He stole a last searing kiss. "I've got to get back to work, but I'll be in touch to discuss the conditions of my offer."

"Sure you don't want to discuss it now? I might have a few conditions of my own."

He grinned as he caught my lower lip between his teeth. Apparently he'd found his appetite, and it wasn't for donuts. "You should go before I feel a need to lock that door," he said in a rumbling voice I could feel down to my toes. "I've got a lot to do if I'm going to get out of here at a reasonable hour tonight."

"Sounds important. What are you working on?"

"I'm checking into Brendan and Owen Haggerty."

I pushed my chair back so I wouldn't be distracted by the hungry way he was still looking at my mouth. "Did you find anything?"

"Brendan called his office on Friday night. He left a message saying he was taking a week of personal leave and would be offline for a few days. That's probably why Mike Tran wasn't surprised when you told him Brendan wasn't returning your calls. He's either taking some time off or he's done a good job of covering his bases. I'm inclined to think the former."

I frowned. "Why?"

"Brendan was at UVA getting his master's degree in public policy when Gilford Dupree went missing."

"So? Charlottesville is only two hours away," I argued.

"I'm not discounting anything. I'm just telling you what I found." Nick didn't have to say he wasn't considering Brendan a likely suspect. It was written all over his face.

"What about Owen?"

"I'm still working on that. Mike doesn't have much on him besides his medical records. Owen's health had been deteriorating for a few years before he died."

"Did you uncover anything about the letter we found?"

Nick's hand rasped against the stubble on his jaw. "Without a date, it's hard to know what it was about. He could have been apologizing for anything. We have nothing to suggest he was referring to anything illegal. For all we know, it could have been a simple argument between him and his wife." I opened my mouth to protest, but he held up a finger. "But I'm looking into it. I promise." He took my hand and kissed my palm, sparking a flare of warmth that shot to dangerous places. "You going to be home later?"

"I promised Mrs. Haggerty I would drive her to her book club meeting."

He raised an eyebrow. "I haven't returned her husband's gun to her yet. I could come over after work and take my chances on the couch."

I laughed. "Find Brendan so I can get Mrs. Haggerty out of my house. When she's gone, I'll leave you a key."

"You drive a hard bargain."

"Those are the conditions of my offer."

"Throw in that red negligée I saw in your drawer and it's a deal."

"Solve the case, and we'll discuss it," I said coyly.

"Finn," he said softly as I stood to go. "I'm not sure there's anything left to solve here. You heard what Penny said—the things she knew about Steven. You saw the receipt for the mulch. I just want you to be prepared for the possibility that we might not find another suspect." He didn't bother saying the rest. That Steven might be guilty. That he might have had an affair with Penny. And if so, the only thing Nick could do for me was try to keep me out of Mike Tran's sights.

I took Sylvia's contract and his donut, and I showed myself out.

CHAPTER 18

Mrs. Haggerty came into the foyer that evening at six thirty prompt. She carried her huge purse over one arm and a foil-covered plate in the other. Vero took a bottle of wine from the pantry. She grabbed hold of Mrs. Haggerty's bag by the straps, nearly pulling the woman over as she tried to steal a glimpse inside.

Mrs. Haggerty gasped as they fought over the handles. "What are you doing?"

"I'm saving your reputation," Vero said, peeking in the bag before dropping the bottle of wine in it. "It's rude to go to a party empty-handed. Besides, everyone knows book clubs are better with booze. You're not driving, so you might as well stay out late and have a little fun."

Mrs. Haggerty looked scandalized as she snatched back her purse. Vero shook her head at me, letting me know the diary we were looking for wasn't inside it. And since I already knew it wasn't in Mrs. Haggerty's house, hopefully that meant her diary was somewhere in mine.

"I would never dream of going empty-handed! I prepared dessert," Mrs. Haggerty said, holding up her foil-covered plate. She slapped Vero's hand when Vero pulled up the corner of the foil, revealing an assortment of cookies and brownies. Vero took one and stuffed it in her mouth before Mrs. Haggerty could insist she put it back.

"We should get going," I said, nudging her to the door. "We know how you hate to be late. And you," I said pointedly to Vero, "have lots to keep you busy while we're gone."

She licked chocolate crumbs from her fingers. "Don't worry about me. I've got everything under control."

Mrs. Haggerty tugged the foil back in place to cover the plate, watching me out of the corner of her eye as we walked to my van, as if she was expecting me to steal a brownie, too.

"Is your babysitter always so strange?" she asked as she fastened her seat belt.

"Trust me, you haven't seen strange." I programmed my navigation app to Viola's address and set the phone in the cupholder on the dashboard.

Mrs. Haggerty scrutinized it through the narrow frames of her glasses. "That's not where we're going."

"Where are we going?"

"Don't be nosy," she said, adjusting the plate of cookies on her lap.

"If you don't tell me where we're going, how will I know how to get there?"

"Just drive. I'll tell you when you need to turn."

"Right." I snapped my seat belt and started driving, nearly killing both of us with every last-minute turn as Mrs. Haggerty fired directions at me like bullets. We made a circuitous route through western Loudoun County and ended up in a residential neighborhood I'd never been in before.

"Drop me off right here," she said, pointing up at a towering three-story town house. I pulled along the curb, looking for signs of her friends. The short, narrow driveway contained only enough room for one car. Several others were parked at various points along the street.

The curtains inside the house were drawn shut, the main floor brightly lit from within.

"You can pick me up in an hour." Balancing her foil-covered plate, Mrs. Haggerty helped herself out of the van and slammed the door. She looked both ways up and down the sidewalk, her wine-heavy purse swinging from her elbow as she navigated the concrete steps to the front door.

A woman answered. I recognized her from the last meeting. She'd been wearing a set of pastel-colored Hello Kitty scrubs. Tonight, she wore jeans and a sweater. She peered through the dark at the windows of my van, offering a tentative wave. I waved back, unsure if she could see me. Mrs. Haggerty handed her the plate of desserts and followed the young woman into the house.

I dialed Vero's number. "Did you find the diary?"

"Not yet. I searched your entire room, your bathroom, and the inside of your toilet tank lid."

"My toilet tank lid?"

"The woman spent a week in the slammer, Finn. Who knows what she learned while she was there." The toilet flushed in the background. "Besides, Zach told me he had to go potty, so I was already in here anyway. I figured it couldn't hurt to look."

"Wait," I said, certain I had misheard her, "Zach *told* you he had to go?"

"I think Mrs. Haggerty's tactics might actually be working. We made it just in time."

"Oh, thank god." I might be arrested and thrown in jail tomorrow, but at least my child would be out of diapers, and today, I would take any victory I could get.

"Don't celebrate just yet. He refused to put his pants back on after he did his business. When I told him he had to get dressed, he ran and hid in Delia's room. He crawled inside her Barbie house and got himself stuck."

I swore and checked the time. Maybe I could make it home and back before the end of Mrs. Haggerty's meeting. "Did you try rubbing him in vegetable oil?"

"No. I used the lube in your nightstand to get him out."

"Vero!"

"Relax. He's fine. I gave him a bath before I put the kids to bed. And before you ask, the neighborhood watch diary wasn't in your nightstand either."

I put a hand to my temple. We only had an hour to find it. Two, at the most, if we stopped for groceries on the way home. "It has to be somewhere."

"Whoa," Vero whispered.

"What is it?" I asked, sitting up in my seat.

"I don't know. I feel a little . . . strange."

"Strange how?" God, I hoped Delia and Zach hadn't brought home any germs from the playground. The last thing we needed was a case of the flu.

"I'm . . . not sure," Vero said. "My head's a little light. And I'm feeling . . . really, *really* hungry."

Uh-oh. "When was your last period?"

"I can't be pregnant, Finlay! I'm on the pill, and Javi and I haven't had sex since . . . *Oh.* Oh, no," she said. Her phone jostled, her breath coming faster as her feet shuffled quickly down the stairs.

"What's wrong?" I asked, listening as she opened and slammed the refrigerator, the kitchen cabinets, then the pantry door.

"I think we have a problem," she sang in a panicky voice. "You know those brownies I bought from Stacey? The ones I hid in the freezer? I think Mrs. Haggerty took them to her meeting."

"No! Are you sure?"

"My lips are going numb and I'm getting the munchies." A chip bag crinkled on the other end of the line, followed by loud crunching.

No! No, no, no!

I looked up at the town house and checked my watch. The meeting had only been going on for fifteen minutes. Maybe it wasn't too late to stop Mrs. Haggerty and her friends before they started sampling the desserts.

I scrambled out of the van.

"What are you doing?" Vero asked as I hoofed it to the house. "You can't go in there and tell them their brownies are drugged! Mrs. Haggerty will probably put it in her damn diary and report us for distribution of controlled substances! Oh, god," Vero blurted between quickening breaths. "Do you think Mike Tran has an unmarked cop watching our house? What if he comes to the door and my pupils are dilated? What if I accidentally confess to something? He might look me up in his police database, see I'm a wanted criminal, and send me back to Maryland. I'll spend the rest of my life in prison making license plates and shivs out of toothbrushes, all because of Stacey and her damn brownies!"

"Now you're being paranoid."

"I'm not paranoid," she said around a mouthful of chips.

Still, she had a point. Those brownies were drugged and they had come from my house. This would not be the first time I had inadvertently drugged an unsuspecting person, and since it was entirely possible Mrs. Haggerty had written in her diary about the night I'd drugged Harris Mickler, it was probably not wise to let any of her friends eat those brownies.

Instead of knocking on the front door of the town house, I took the sidewalk to the end of the row. I checked both ways before darting behind it, then crept along the privacy fences, counting the units until I reached the right house.

"Oh, wow. Stacey wasn't kidding," Vero said. "Those are some killer brownies."

I got down on all fours and crawled to the nearest window, bringing my eye up to the sliver of light that was visible under the curtain. I risked a peep inside. The women sat in a loose circle of armchairs and ottomans, as they had done before, their chairs pulled close, filling in the gaps around the sofa. The open bottle of wine rested on the coffee table.

"I don't see the dessert plate," I whispered. "What if they already ate them all?"

"That meeting is going to be one for the books." Vero giggled at her own joke. It grew into a fit of hysterics.

"That's not funny!"

"Maybe a little funny."

"Vero!"

Her laughter died, the last few chortles bubbling out of her as she struggled to contain them while I shushed her.

I tipped an ear to the window, but I couldn't make out any of the conversation happening inside. I could see all the women, except for a few whose backs were to the window. I recognized most of them from the last book club meeting. One of the women definitely hadn't been there the previous Saturday, but she still seemed vaguely familiar to me. I didn't know her name, but I was fairly certain I'd seen her walking her dog in my neighborhood. This must be the new member Mrs. Haggerty had signaled with her flashlight—the one whose note I had intercepted a few nights ago about joining the club.

The woman's face was red and puffy. She sat in the center of the sofa, holding a wad of tissues. The women on either side of her rubbed her back and patted her shoulders, doting on her as she dabbed her eyes.

The woman who'd been wearing the Hello Kitty scrubs last week gave their newest member a pale blue gift bag with a shiny paw print embossed on the side. I couldn't see what was in it, but the contents of the bag were heavy enough to strain the decorative paper. Viola passed her a mahogany keepsake box, topped with a red bow. Someone else handed the woman an envelope with a logo on the front. Her eyes welled with fresh tears as she peeked at the certificate inside.

The woman looked up at her new friends and smiled, her lips trembling as she thanked them, overwhelmed with gratitude.

I relayed everything to Vero as it was happening.

"That's some welcome party," she said, crunching on a chip. "I don't remember you giving me any presents when you invited me to move in with you."

"I didn't invite you. You invited yourself. And you charged me forty percent of my income," I reminded her.

"I should have held out for forty-five."

A fourth and final gift was placed in the woman's hands. She untied the ribbon and peeled back the tissue paper, revealing a paperback book. She held it to her chest. The women clapped and called out congratulations, and someone declared it time for a toast.

One of the guests got up and poured wine into plastic cups.

Another went to the kitchen, returning a moment later with a charcuterie board in one hand and Mrs. Haggerty's platter of desserts in the other. She set the food on the coffee table and the women attacked the snacks like circling hyenas.

"I see the brownies! I'm going in," I told Vero.

"Finlay, don't—!"

I shoved my phone in my pocket and sprinted to the front of the house. I jabbed at the buzzer and pounded on the door. The laughter abruptly died. Footsteps shuffled inside. After a prolonged silence, the door cracked open.

"Hi! So sorry to interrupt." I smiled brightly and shouldered my way into the house. The women turned to gawk at me as I rushed into the living room. "I know your meeting just started, but I was waiting in the car, and I got hungry. I hope you don't mind if I just help myself to some of your . . . Oh, would you look at that! Brownies."

I hurried to the table, picking the brownies off the plate and stuffing them into my coat pockets. When my pockets couldn't hold any more, I scooped the rest into the front of my sweater. I stole a brownie from one woman's hand as she held it halfway to her mouth. "Thank you, that looks delicious! I'll just take these back to the car so I don't disrupt your meeting. Before I go, may I use your restroom?" I turned eagerly to the host, planning to lock myself inside her bathroom and flush the drugs down her toilet.

She pointed at a closed door with a dumbfounded expression. "Someone is using it. There's another upstairs."

"Great!" I held the front of my sweater closed as I start toward the steps.

"Not so fast!" Mrs. Haggerty called behind me. She turned me around sharply by my elbow. She held the empty cookie plate between us with the same uncompromising look she'd worn when she'd made Zach surrender the thick, black Sharpie he'd stolen off the kitchen counter that morning.

"Mrs. Haggerty," I said, dipping my head close to hers, "I really don't think I should give these back to you. It would be a very bad idea. They're not what you—"

"I know what they are," she snapped. "And I know you didn't bake them."

"You do?"

"Of course I do. Who do you think gave Stacey the recipe? If I'd thought *you'd* made the brownies, I wouldn't have brought any. Now give those back." She thrust the plate at me, looking impatient. "*You* can't have any. You're driving."

With a contrite smile (and more than a little shock), I lowered the hem of my sweater, releasing a cascade of brownies.

"Right, sorry," I said, dusting the crumbs back onto the plate. "I'll just be going, then."

The weepy woman with the tissues shot to her feet, pale and shaken. "I should go, too. Robert doesn't know I'm gone. He'll be angry if I'm not back by the time he gets home." She scooped up the envelope with the logo on it and stuffed it inside her coat. Her hands shook as she tucked her book under her arm. She picked the gift bag up in one hand and juggled the mahogany box in the other, struggling to carry it all as she hurried to the door. She averted her eyes as she raced past me.

"Your book," I said as it slipped from her arm. I bent to pick it up. She scurried to retrieve it, but my fingers held stubbornly to the cover. It was a brand-new copy of *The Tuesday Club Murders* by Agatha Christie—the same collection of Miss Marple stories

I had seen in Penny's and Mrs. Haggerty's houses. I stared at it, open-mouthed.

She jerked it from my hands and ran out the door.

I excused myself from Mrs. Haggerty's book club meeting to wait for her in the car. The longer I waited, the more I regretted not using the bathroom while I had the chance. I hoped the woman who had been locked inside it the whole time I was there wasn't having some horrible reaction to the brownies.

I also hoped there was enough of my sweater fuzz on the ones I'd dumped back on the plate to deter the rest of her book club from eating too many of them.

I tapped the steering wheel, unable to stop thinking about the book the woman had dropped. It was the third time I had stumbled across a copy of that book in less than a week.

That couldn't have been a coincidence, could it?

The only thing that was different about this woman's book was that her copy had been brand-new. The other two books had been old, with creased and faded covers. The breaks in their spines suggested they'd been read countless times. The tape was probably the only thing holding Penny's copy together.

My fingers stopped tapping.

There had been tape on the spine of Penny's book. I had assumed it was holding the cover in place, but what if it had served a different purpose? I thought back to the peeling spine label on the old paperback in Mrs. Haggerty's bedroom. Then to the novel she kept on my nightstand with the sticker residue on its spine. Libraries put tape over their labels to keep them from peeling.

I sat up in my seat.

Penny's book wasn't covered in tape because it was broken. It was taped because it had come from a library.

So had Mrs. Haggerty's.

I dialed Vero's number.

"Why are there no waffles?" she asked in lieu of a greeting.

"Because I haven't gone shopping yet. Listen," I said, hoping she wasn't too intoxicated to manage it, "I need you to go to the Loudoun County Public Library's website. See if they have a book club."

"Why bother?" she asked, the words coming more slowly than her usual rapid fire. "You and I can give each other presents and take edibles at home. But if you're looking for more of a club vibe, Stacey brings samples to the HOA meetings, and some of the dads are actually kind of hot."

I pinched the bridge of my nose, willing myself to be patient. "I'm not looking for a book club for us. Penny's Agatha Christie book came from a library. So did Mrs. Haggerty's."

"So?"

"What if Mrs. Haggerty and Penny were in some kind of book club together?"

"You think that's the connection between them?"

"What else could they have in common?"

There was a prolonged silence as Vero slowly clicked the keys on her laptop. "There's a book club at the nearest library branch. It meets once a month."

"Are the books they've read archived anywhere?"

"Yup. They're all right here."

"Can you see the selections from the year Penny's husband went missing? Is *The Tuesday Club Murders* anywhere on the list?"

More clicking. "Let's see . . . *Gone Girl* was January, Nora

Roberts in February, Kristin Hannah in March, *The Poisonwood Bible* was April, *whoooooa . . . The Tuesday Club Murders* was their selection in May."

Four months before Gilford was murdered.

If Penny and Mrs. Haggerty had been in a book club together, then they had both lied to the police when they'd claimed they hadn't known each other. Penny had obviously been lying to protect herself, but why had Mrs. Haggerty bothered? Who was she protecting? As far as I knew, the only person she cared that deeply for was Brendan.

I glanced up from my phone at the town house, then at the cars parked along the street. Was it possible that one of these other women had been in that same book club? If so, did they know Penny? All I needed was for one of them to come forward and confirm my suspicions.

"What are you doing?" Vero asked as I got out of my van.

"Taking pictures." I slunk around the back of each woman's car, snapped a photo of the license plate, and texted the images to Vero. "Send these license plates to Cam. Tell him I'll give him twenty dollars each if he can get me the names and addresses of the women who own these cars. And tell him I'll throw in a spaghetti dinner if he can get me the information tonight."

CHAPTER 19

Mrs. Haggerty had gone straight to bed when we got home, looking a little tipsy and complaining of a headache. Cam's text message had come just before midnight, a barrage of screenshots from the department of motor vehicles, one for each license plate number Vero had sent him earlier that evening. His final text had simply said, *When do I get my spaghetti*?

I texted him back, *Tomorrow night*.

Vero and I took our phones, her laptop, and a bottle of wine upstairs to her bedroom and quietly shut the door. We sat on her floor, sharing what was left of Vero's bag of potato chips. She sat cross-legged on the carpet, squinting at the front of my sweater. She reached over and picked a chunk of brownie off my boob. "Don't eat that," I said, confiscating it and tossing it in the trash can behind me.

"Maybe I should do the googling," I suggested, reaching for her laptop. It had been nearly six hours since Vero had eaten her brownie, and though she insisted she was already sober, her eyes were still lacking their usual razor-sharp focus.

She slapped my hand away. "I've got it," she insisted. "I could eat twelve brownies and still be better at this than you." She opened her laptop. "Who are we investigating first?"

The plan was to learn as much about the book club members as possible, then look for any connections they might have to the library or Penny Dupree. I read through the list of their names.

"Try Viola Henry," I said. "I think she hosted the first meeting we went to."

Vero typed Viola's name into the search bar. "Says here she's the director of human resources for some tech company in Reston. The bio on their website says she enjoys hiking and reading, and in her spare time she volunteers with several women's advocacy groups. She has two grown children. No mention of a husband."

"I'm pretty sure he's deceased," I said, remembering the urn I had nearly knocked over in her house. "Any links to Penny in her social media?"

Vero typed and scrolled for a minute. "Viola doesn't seem to have any social media. And Penny hasn't updated hers since Gilford went missing."

I read the next name on the list. "Try Gita Chaudhary."

Vero typed in Gita's name. "She owns a flower shop. According to her website, she specializes in formal events and deliveries of large arrangements. All I'm finding is her business page. No personal stuff. You don't think that's weird?"

"You don't have any social media either," I pointed out.

"Because I don't want anybody to find me," she reminded me.

"Let's try the others." I fed Vero one name at a time until we'd nearly exhausted the list. Lola de la Rosa was a nurse practitioner at a nearby hospital, and Kathy Sanderson owned a commercial cleaning company. Neither of them had social media pages, but both women had active profiles on various dating apps. Destiny Roth had an Instagram account. Her grid was mostly photos of her twin daughters, who were cheerleaders at the local middle school.

"Any mention of a partner?" I asked.

"None that I can find."

"Where does Destiny work?"

"Looks like she has two jobs. One in information management at the Office of Vital Records in Richmond and a side hustle doing embroidery and custom engraving for her own Etsy shop."

"I don't get it. The only thing these women have in common is the fact that none of them are married." They were all different ages, different nationalities, with different careers and wildly different interests. And I already knew from seeing Penny's vast collection of romance novels that even her book tastes ran very different from Mrs. Haggerty's. So how had these women all found each other?

"What about Elizabeth Chen?" I asked, reading the next name on the list. "Her car was the one I saw parked in the driveway at the book club meeting tonight. She must have been the host."

Vero started typing. "According to Loudoun County, she's the only person listed on the deed to her house. No social media profiles except for a LinkedIn page. It says she's been working as a vet tech at the county animal shelter for the last eighteen months." That explained the Hello Kitty scrubs and the gift bag with the paw print on it. "Before that, she worked at a shelter in Fairfax . . . *Oh.*" Vero angled her screen toward me. "Isn't this the same shelter where Patricia Mickler used to volunteer?"

I scrolled down to the bottom of the page. Vero was right. The address of the animal shelter where Elizabeth Chen had previously worked was the same one we had visited when we were investigating Patricia Mickler's husband. "If Patricia and Elizabeth both worked there at the same time, they probably knew each other." It wasn't a huge shelter, judging by the number of lockers we'd seen in the staff lounge when we'd snuck into the building last fall. And the employees and volunteers there had all seemed pretty chummy. It's not like the internet was giving us much else to work with.

"Maybe Patricia can tell us something useful about at least one member of Mrs. Haggerty's freaky little circle of friends."

"There's only one way to find out," I said, closing Vero's laptop and corking the wine as she yawned. "Get some sleep. Tomorrow, we're going on a field trip."

It was nearly one in the morning when Vero and I said our goodnights and retired to our beds. I headed to the rollaway in my office, turned off the light, and slipped under the thin blanket. As I lay there in the dark, I could have sworn I heard a door open in the hall. I sat up, ear tipped toward the sound of the telltale squeak in the riser on the third step.

The footsteps were too heavy and slow to belong to the kids. I threw off my blanket and got out of bed, poking my head out into the hall just as Vero opened her door and peeked down the stairs.

Both children's doors were closed. Mrs. Haggerty's door was cracked.

We listened as the front door downstairs quietly opened and shut.

Vero met me in the hall and whispered, "Do you know where she's going?"

"I have a hunch."

"I'll stay here with the kids. You follow Mrs. Haggerty and see what she's up to."

I put my coat on over my pajamas, slipped on my shoes, and

hurried out the front door, following the same path Mrs. Haggerty had walked the last time she had snuck out for her late-night walk. I avoided the streetlamps, careful to stay a block behind her.

Mrs. Haggerty paused in front of the same house she had before. I hid behind a tree trunk as she turned on a small pocket light and flashed it twice at the window. Then she strode to the mailbox and tucked a note inside.

A curtain parted in the window upstairs. Mrs. Haggerty closed the mailbox and started walking back the way she'd come.

I didn't dare to breathe as she strolled past my hiding spot and headed home.

When Mrs. Haggerty was gone, the front door of the house cracked open. A woman I'd seen at the book club meeting stepped out—the one who had dropped her book in her hurry to get home. She shuffled to the mailbox in her slippers and robe, darting cautious glances at the windows of her own house as she retrieved the slip of paper Mrs. Haggerty had left. It occurred to me then that I didn't know the woman's name. But why? Vero and I had looked into every license plate of every vehicle that had been parked on the street near Elizabeth Chen's town house that night, and yet somehow, we had missed the one that belonged to their guest of honor.

Had the woman taken an Uber? Or had she parked so far down the street that I hadn't seen her car?

She read the note, folded it into her pocket, then looked furtively around her as she hurried back into her house. When her door finally closed, I pulled out my phone, dimming the screen and angling it close to my body to keep any of her neighbors from noticing the light.

I typed the woman's street address into a search bar. The home was owned by Robert and Sally Mullen. According to the county department of revenue, they only paid property taxes for one car—a luxury sedan listed solely under Robert's name. I googled him and found a LinkedIn page featuring a robust profile. Robert Mullen, CPA, was employed at a large local accounting firm. When I googled Sally Mullen, I found no more than a brief mention in a church newsletter where she was listed as a volunteer. No Facebook or Instagram accounts. No LinkedIn. Not even a chat group.

Robert doesn't know I'm gone. He'll be angry if I'm not back by the time he gets home.

Sally must have found a ride and sneaked to that meeting to avoid upsetting her husband. That explained all of Mrs. Haggerty's cloak-and-dagger visits to the woman's mailbox, but why come again tonight? What had the note said? The book club had already met twice that week. What more could they possibly have to talk about?

On Saturdays, we discuss. On Tuesdays, we vote.

But what did they do after that?

CHAPTER 20

Vero poured tomato juice and vodka into a coffee mug the next morning and grimaced as she chased two ibuprofen with the hair of the dog. She shuddered, wiping her mouth with the back of her hand, then frowned at her dry toast.

I wondered if the brownie had contributed to her hangover or if it was all the junk food and wine she'd consumed while she'd been stoned. She'd awoken later than usual that morning in a foul mood, if not because of her hangover, then probably because Javi hadn't come over or called the last two nights. He'd claimed he had a big job he needed to finish at the garage, but Vero was convinced he was avoiding her so he wouldn't have to revisit their conversation about the history of his love life.

I carried my breakfast to the table and sat down beside her, leaning close and keeping my voice low so Mrs. Haggerty wouldn't hear us in the next room. She and Delia had been playing homeschool all morning, and they were both engrossed in some kind of art project involving dried soup beans and glue.

"Are you sure you're up for this?" I asked as Vero picked at her toast. She was still looking a little green and I didn't imagine she was looking forward to executing the plan we had concocted the night before.

"We can't just walk into that shelter and ask to speak with Patricia Mickler," she said, careful not to let her voice carry. "Those places have cameras. We can't afford to be seen with that woman. Especially if Mike Tran has doubts about who really killed Patricia's husband. If he gets wind of the fact that you and Patricia know each other, then it won't be Steven in jail on suspicion of murder—it'll be me and you."

"We'll wear baseball caps and sunglasses. No one will recognize us."

"After the last time, you'd better hope not." During our last trip to the shelter, Vero had unleashed chaos, literally, unlocking all the cages and freeing about a dozen cats and dogs to create a distraction big enough to conceal the fact that I was searching the lockers in the employee break room.

"Don't worry. I have a plan." I'd been (mostly) clearheaded when I'd gone to bed last night, and I'd been awake for several hours already, thinking it through. "We'll fit right in."

"And what are we going to do with the kids? We can't leave them alone with Mrs. Haggerty."

"We're not. I called a babysitter." I checked the time on my phone, expecting Cam any minute. I had texted him first thing that morning and told him I'd make a chocolate cake to go with that spaghetti dinner if he came over a few hours early to keep an eye on the children and Mrs. Haggerty.

Vero and I both fell quiet as Zach padded into the kitchen. It was well past noon and he was still wearing his pajamas, but at least he was dressed. He hid behind a wall, peeking into the dining room with a covetous expression as he watched his sister glue brightly colored beans onto a piece of construction paper under Mrs. Haggerty's watchful eye. He toddled closer and tugged on Mrs. Haggerty's pants. She looked down at him over the rims of her glasses and frowned at his rumpled sleepwear.

"I go potty," he said, puffing out his tiny chest. Vero quietly sniffed the air. I set down my coffee, ready to take him upstairs to change his Pull-Up, but Mrs. Haggerty was first to speak.

"Well? What are you waiting for, boy—an engraved invitation? The day's almost over already. Go do your business and come back when you're ready for school."

"This ought to be interesting," Vero whispered out of the side of her mouth.

Zach blinked at the woman, then at his sister, who was contentedly gluing her beans. He tore out of the room, and I considered pouring myself a Bloody Mary as his bare feet thundered up the stairs. Vero and I braced for the inevitable tantrum to start—the slamming doors and thrown toys, clothing being stripped off and tossed down the steps—but it never came.

A toilet flushed.

Vero and I exchanged a worried look. A quiet two-year-old was rarely a good thing. Last time Zach had been alone and quiet in the bathroom, he'd been finger-painting the walls with his own poop. "Think one of us should go check on him?" she asked.

Mrs. Haggerty made a sound of disgust at our exchange. "Zachary is perfectly capable of using the lavatory himself. He'll never learn to be a young man if you don't expect him to behave like one."

"Ten to one?" Vero whispered.

"Why not?" I whispered back. "I bought a box of Magic Erasers at Costco."

"The last time we scrubbed those walls, I wrecked a perfectly good manicure. I vote we hire a painter."

We both turned as Zach scurried down the stairs. Vero and I blinked at him. His jeans were on inside out. So was his Pull-Up, judging by what I could see of it over the exposed tag on his elastic waistband. His Buzz Lightyear shoes lit up gleefully over a mismatched pair of socks as he marched himself into the dining room and tugged on Mrs. Haggerty's pants.

Her mouth pursed as she paused her lesson to look him over. "Did you remember to wash your hands?"

Zach nodded, splaying his damp fingers in front of him.

She scrutinized them through the narrow frames of her glasses. "Very well. Take a seat."

Zach ran to the empty chair beside Delia and scrambled up the side of it, perching on his knees. His wide eyes lit with triumph as Mrs. Haggerty passed him a sheet of construction paper and a bottle of glue.

"How did you do that?" I asked her, coming into the room and staring at my son with an awed sense of wonder.

"People rise to the level of expectation you have of them. If you don't trust them, how are they supposed to prove you can? Your generation coddles kids too much," she grumbled. "You're all so afraid of everything. If you want kids to grow into capable adults, you can't strap them to a padded chair and tell them not to wiggle. You've got to let them fall and make mistakes, and be willing to forgive them."

Vero scoffed. "That's pretty strong advice coming from someone whose own son never comes to visit."

Mrs. Haggerty looked a little stung. "I never said my generation did any better. Our kids survived mostly on their own wits and hose water. And you're right," she said ruefully, "that's probably why my son doesn't come to visit. He and I aren't terribly close after his father ran him out years ago. It was easier on all of us once Owen passed, I suppose. Regardless, Brendan turned out to be a fine young man. I did a much better job with him," she said proudly.

"Speaking of Brendan," I said, sensing an opening, "I still haven't been able to get in touch with him. Are you sure you don't have any idea where he might have gone? Or when he's coming back?"

Her eyes clouded over and her frail jaw set. "Brendan's a grown man. He'll come back when he's ready. He doesn't need me telling him what to do, and he doesn't need to waste his time taking care of me. I'm perfectly capable of taking care of myself. Now if you'll excuse me, it's time for my afternoon repose."

Mrs. Haggerty dismissed the children to the playroom and hobbled upstairs. Vero and I waited until we heard her bedroom door close before speaking again.

"You're right," Vero said. "She's definitely covering for him. Penny and Brendan must be in this together."

"If we can prove Penny knows Mrs. Haggerty, it won't be hard to prove she knows Brendan, too."

Vero stiffened. She sat up and cocked her head. "What's that?" she asked, pressing her palms against the table.

The glass panes in the kitchen windows began to vibrate. "I don't know," I said, holding on to the counter as a repetitive, low thump reverberated through the walls. We didn't get earthquakes in Virginia—at least not ones anyone could actually feel—so why were all the dishes in my cabinet starting to shake?

Vero ran to the window and pulled back the curtain. The

thumping grew louder, the vibrations rattling the wineglasses I still hadn't gotten around to washing from last night. A vehicle drove slowly toward my house, its windows open and stereo blaring. If it wasn't for the grinning face behind the wheel, I never would have recognized Mrs. Haggerty's Mark V.

The car's body had been painted a garish shade of purple. Flecks of glitter sparkled in the finish, and the new chrome grille glistened in the sun. *Eggplant Ecstasy* had been hand-lettered across the hood in fancy looping script. The tires were brand-new with wide, whitewalls, and a disco ball hung from the rearview mirror, spraying the interior of the car with rainbow-colored light.

Vero and I came bursting out of the house. Cam beamed at us through the windshield, his face mostly hidden behind an enormous pair of purple rhinestone sunglasses that could have belonged to Elton John. Arnold Schwarzenegger was riding shotgun, strapped in a tiny purple helmet, his front paws braced on the dashboard. There was a high-pitched whine as the entire front end of the car lifted on a pair of stilt-like hydraulics.

"I'm going to murder Javi," Vero said as the car began to bounce. The front tires dipped low, then ricocheted off the pavement, catching more air every time they hit the ground.

I covered my ears, the music almost deafening as Cam slung his arm over the door. His hand tapped out the rhythm, his head bobbing to the beat of the trembling bass that was blasting through the souped-up stereo.

"What did you do to Mrs. Haggerty's car?" I shouted over the music.

"I know, right?" he shouted back, his smile as bright and wide as the car's shiny new bumpers. "Vero's boyfriend's got some mad skills. This thing is sick! Mrs. H is gonna love it!"

The children came running out of the house, drawn by the noise. Mrs. Haggerty came out after them, scowling and covering her ears. Vero caught Zach as he zipped past her, demanding a ride.

"Turn it off!" I shouted.

Delia giggled maniacally as Cam attempted to lower the hydraulics. The car dipped and bobbed erratically as he fiddled with buttons on the dashboard. The car dropped with one final chassis-shaking bounce, then the stereo fell abruptly silent as the engine cut off.

My ears were still ringing when Cam opened his door and got out. He held Arnold in one arm and splayed the other wide, showcasing the car. "Gorgeous, am I right? Your boyfriend gave me a killer price on the paint job. But the mods cleaned me out. Cost me the last of my reward money, but it was totally worth it. Right, Mrs. H?" He took off his rhinestone sunglasses and placed them gently on her nose, positioning them over her own wire-rimmed spectacles as she came over to inspect the car.

"I like the color," she said, looking genuinely pleased.

Cam put a hand to his chest and let out a breath. "I wasn't sure about it at first—you know, if it would attract the ladies—but Javi really sold me on it. He said it projects the message that I'm confident in my masculinity."

"An eighteen-foot eggplant will do that," Vero said.

"How about we all take it out for a cruise and get some ice cream?" Cam asked. "The back seat is huge. We can all go! It'll be like a party on wheels."

The kids cheered. Cam looked at me expectantly. Delia pulled on my pant leg. "Can we please go for a ride in Cam's pretty purple car?"

"*I* think that's a lovely idea." Mrs. Haggerty's tone suggested she expected me to say no.

I was probably going to regret this. Cam's last party involved dead loan sharks and strippers. "Only to the drive-through at the end of the street," I said with a pointed look at Cam. "And they have to use their car seats."

Cam held up three fingers in a Scout Promise. The children clambered into the open door of the car. Delia gripped the enormous steering wheel and pretended to drive while Zach poked the disco ball, making the glittery lights swirl around the ceiling.

I pulled Cam aside, out of earshot of Mrs. Haggerty as she buckled herself into the passenger seat.

"What's up, Mrs. D?"

"I need to borrow Arnold Schwarzenegger for a few hours."

Cam tucked the dog snugly under his arm. "What for?"

I was afraid he was going to ask me that. "I'm going to visit an old friend. She's very fond of dogs. I thought she'd like to meet him." That middle part was true. Patricia Mickler was very fond of dogs. It was *me* she never wanted to see again. Cam chewed his lip as he stroked Arnold's head. "We'll only be gone a few hours," I assured him. "Vero and I will take very good care of him."

Cam looked over his shoulder at my children as Vero buckled each of them into their car seats. "I guess that'd be okay," he said, passing me the dog. "But Arnold needs to be walked every hour or he'll piss on the floor. And don't let him ride in the back seat. It makes him carsick. He starts drooling right before he—"

"Got it," I said, sparing myself the details. I'd endured far worse with Kevin Bacon.

I gave Cam a few twenties to buy everyone some ice cream and reminded him to keep his music at a reasonable volume as he got into the car. "And no explicit lyrics, or the kids will repeat them."

"Cool," he said, buckling himself in. I wasn't sure if he meant he was cool with the request or he thought it would be cool to test it. It was too late to ask him as I watched them drive off.

Vero disappeared inside the house. She came out a moment later, holding a baseball cap and a pair of dark sunglasses. "You sure about this?"

I handed the dog to Vero and passed her his leash. "Not at all."

Three hours had passed since we'd parked behind the animal shelter, and Vero and I had almost given up. "That's her," I said, ducking lower in the driver's seat.

We watched from my minivan as Patricia Mickler got out of a familiar brown station wagon and approached the employee door. Her head was down as she dug in her purse for her key card, but she wasn't hard to recognize. She hadn't changed much since the last time I'd seen her four months ago. She had the same mousy brown hair, pulled back in a casual ponytail, and wore the same jeans and sweatshirt matted in dog and cat hair. She had a bit more color in her cheeks after her long trip to the Caribbean with her boyfriend, and maybe a little more spring in her step, but she was still the same meek, unassuming woman who had propositioned me to murder her husband by slipping a note under my plate in a crowded Panera dining room last fall.

According to Patricia's social media, she had only returned to the country a few weeks ago. She probably figured it was safe to come home, now that the Russian mobster who had employed her husband was no longer a threat to her.

"Maybe we should just wait until she gets off work," Vero suggested, rolling up our empty fast-food bag and tossing it in the seat behind her. "We can follow her back to her place and talk to her there."

We'd been sitting here for hours waiting for her to show up. My fuel light was on empty, Cam's dog had eaten most of our french fries, and my bladder was full. Unlike Arnold, I couldn't take a leak in the narrow strip of grass beside the parking lot. That would definitely turn heads.

"Traffic is too heavy. We'd probably lose her. I'll go inside and see if she's willing to talk." I tucked my hair up into my baseball cap, put on my sunglasses, and put Arnold under my arm. I gave Vero my keys and got out of the van, following the sidewalk around the building to the main entrance at the front.

With my cap pulled low, I approached the check-in desk and signed in using a fake name. They handed me a form on a clipboard, inquiring about the purpose of my visit. "I'm surrendering a pet," I said, holding Arnold up to the counter. "He pees on the carpet. I can't keep him anymore."

I held my breath, hoping I had correctly predicted what might happen next. That they would want one of their volunteers to meet with me first, to talk about support and resources, to persuade me to keep the dog before allowing me to walk out.

The woman behind the counter offered me a polite but unconvincing smile. "Before you go and leave the little guy with us, we'll just ask you to meet with one of our staff. They'll have some questions about your dog that will help us rehome him."

"Does Patricia still work here?" I asked. "She helped us with his adoption several months ago. I'd prefer to meet with her if she's free."

The attendant checked her computer screen. "Looks like she just got in. Let me put you and Arnold in a room where you can wait for her."

The attendant buzzed us through a heavy steel door and escorted us into the room of cages behind the counter. Arnold and I were met by a cacophony of barking dogs, and his ears perked, alert and anxious as I tucked him inside my jacket to help him feel safe. Cam would murder me and Venmo my entire life savings to himself in revenge if I let anything happen to his beloved dog.

The attendant showed us into a tiny sterile meeting room with a small table and two chairs and a large plexiglass window. I had been hoping for something more private (and less like a police interrogation room), but it was better than having this conversation out in the open. She gave me a full-color glossy brochure to read about the shelter's services while we waited for Patricia.

I sat down with Arnold in my lap, studying the pamphlet: adoption, rehoming, vaccinations and emergency care, end-of-life assistance . . . My eye snagged on a photo of a pale blue gift bag with a paw print embossed on the side. *Your pet's cremains will be returned to you in decorative casket bag—*

"Who do we have here?" I dropped the brochure at the sound of Patricia's voice. She came in holding a clipboard. She gave my form a quick skim, then knelt in front of Arnold and scratched his tiny head. "Aren't you just a handsome little guy?"

I cleared my throat as she inspected his eyes and ears then moved on to his paws. "Hello, Patricia."

Startled, she looked up at my face. Her cheeks paled and she dropped her clipboard. She straightened slowly, taking a skittish step back from me as her eyes darted to the door. "What are you doing here? I thought we agreed never to see each other again."

"Believe me. I never wanted to see you again either." It felt like walking back into a nightmare, right back to the moment my unwitting life of crime had begun. I had that same sick feeling in the pit of my stomach. "I need to talk to you."

"It's over," she said, reaching clumsily for her clipboard. "Harris is dead, the case is closed, and you and I have nothing more to say to each other."

"I need to ask you about Elizabeth Chen."

She kept her eyes on the floor as she searched for her pen. "Birdie doesn't work here anymore."

"But you know her," I concluded, noting her use of a nickname.

Patricia gritted her teeth. "Not well," she said curtly.

"How about Margaret Haggerty?"

Patricia froze on one knee. Her gaze slowly lifted to mine. She glanced past me, through the plexiglass window into the kennels. Then she bolted.

Patricia strode fast toward the nearest exit. I scooped up Arnold and followed her, matching her brisk but cautious pace, neither one of us wanting to attract attention. She pushed open a fire exit. Arnold bounced and yapped in my arms as I picked up speed to catch up to her.

She cut through the grass, groping in her coat pocket for her car keys as she made a beeline toward the parking lot. I heard my van cough and rattle as Vero started the engine. The tires squealed, but I was too busy racing after Patricia to turn to see where Vero was going.

Dogs barked, chasing us along the fence and climbing up on the chain link to snap and growl at us. Patricia reached the employee lot on the far side of the building and stepped over the curb. She lost her balance when my van skidded suddenly into her path and jerked to a stop. Patricia whirled at the sound of my sneakers on the pavement behind her. She held up both arms in an effort to keep me and Arnold back.

"We only want to talk to you," I said, darting left then right, blocking her path. Arnold barked as Patricia tried to get past me.

"I have nothing to say to you!" she said, reaching for her phone.

Vero slid the van door open behind her. "I figured you might say that."

Vero grabbed Patricia around the shoulders and threw herself backward, using all her weight to leverage them both into the van. I slammed the door shut. Then I sprinted around the hood and climbed into the driver's seat. The whole van rocked as Patricia and Vero wrestled in the back.

I set Arnold in the passenger seat and put the van in gear. He barked, releasing a stream of urine as I peeled out of the parking lot. I didn't know where I was going, only that my plans for the day had not included kidnapping when I woke up that morning.

I jerked the wheel, taking the entrance into the parking garage of the mall. Vero and Patricia flew like pinballs across the floor in the back seat, thrown apart by the force of my turns as the van spiraled up the ramp. Vero sat up, her face triumphant in the rearview mirror as she brandished Patricia's cell phone. Patricia scrambled for an exit. Her face twisted as she attempted to wrench the sliding door open, only to find it locked.

"Childproof," Vero pointed out as she caught her breath.

Patricia smacked the door in frustration. She sat down hard with her back pressed to the door as she glared at me, red-faced in the rearview mirror. "What do you want?"

I skidded the van to a stop in an empty corner of the garage and turned in my seat to face her. "Who is Margaret Haggerty to you?"

"I told you, I've never heard of her."

"Then why did you run?"

"Why do you care?" Patricia twisted around to wrestle with the door again.

"Because my children's father is being held for murder right now, and I don't believe he killed the man they found buried in Margaret Haggerty's yard, but I think you know who did."

Patricia went still. "I can't help you!" she snapped. "I don't know anything about that man. Or who killed him."

"But you do know something." Her body language alone told me that much. She was hiding something, and I was determined to find out what it was.

"I don't owe you anything! Aaron and I are *finally* happy. And we don't need anyone rehashing what happened to Harris last fall."

"That's exactly what's going to happen if you don't tell us what you know," I warned her. "The police are pursuing a case against my ex-husband for the murder of Gilford Dupree. Their investigation has them looking very closely at Steven's business, and there's a very suspicious Loudoun County cop who's a little too curious about the bodies they found on his farm, including your husband's."

Patricia's jaw tensed.

"You can either help me figure out who really killed that man, or you can let the LCPD reopen the investigation into your husband's murder." We both knew that wasn't really a choice.

"If I tell you what I know, are you going to let me go?"

"That depends on the quality of your information," Vero said, as I said, "Of course." I glared at Vero sideways. "What's Birdie Chen's connection to Margaret Haggerty?" I asked.

Patricia pressed her mouth shut.

"A man doesn't turn up dead in an old woman's backyard for no good reason," Vero pointed out.

Patricia held up a finger, making her position clear to both of us. "I am not saying Birdie Chen had anything to do with this. But she knew people."

"What people?" I asked.

"You know," Patricia said, fumbling for words, "people who do what you do."

"People who write books?"

"People who handle problem husbands."

Vero's mouth formed a shocked O. No matter how many times or how many ways I had tried to explain to Patricia that her initial impression of me was based on a simple misunderstanding, she had stubbornly refused to believe I wasn't a killer for hire. Maybe because it made her feel less foolish for propositioning me to murder her husband in the first place.

Patricia lowered her voice. "One day, after a particularly bad argument with Harris, I came in for my shift at the shelter. Aaron noticed I was in a lot of pain. My wrist was swollen, and I couldn't hold any of the animals. I should have gone to the emergency room, but I had already been to the ER earlier that month, and I was worried someone at the hospital would report it. When I refused to let Aaron take me, he suggested I let one of the techs at the shelter look at my arm. Birdie was on duty that day. She took me back into the vet clinic, gave me some pain meds, and wrapped my wrist in a splint.

"When she asked me how I'd injured my arm, I made up some story about how I'd tripped over a curb. She told me she'd figured as much. That she'd 'tripped over the bad-boyfriend curb a few too many times, too,'" Patricia said, hooking her fingers into air quotes. "Birdie knew exactly how the injury had happened. For weeks after that, I avoided her at work, afraid she might report it to someone.

"I was relieved when she finally took a position somewhere else. That was the last I time I saw her. But a few days after Birdie left, a woman I'd never met before showed up at the shelter and asked to speak with me." Patricia bit her lip, as if she wasn't sure she should continue. "When I asked the woman who she was, she gave me a fake name, but it was definitely Margaret Haggerty. She was old and very sweet. She seemed harmless, so when she offered to take me to lunch, I went."

"Are you sure we're talking about the same Mrs. Haggerty?" Vero muttered. I jabbed her with an elbow as Patricia went on.

"Margaret wouldn't say *how* she knew, only that she knew Harris wasn't a good husband and she wanted to help me. I just assumed she was friends with Birdie—some kind of therapist or social worker or something. I figured Birdie had told her about my wrist. At first, I was upset, but then Margaret and I started talking. She asked me all kinds of questions about Harris—who he worked for, what he did for a living. It was such a relief to get it all off my chest—about the kind of person he really was. I told her more than I should have, about the horrible things he was involved in . . . you know, the stuff with the mob. She listened to it all, and I never felt like she was judging me. After I told her everything, she apologized. She said she was sorry she and her friends couldn't help me with my problem. That she wished they could. She seemed genuinely upset she couldn't do something more.

"As Margaret was leaving, she said she had heard rumors about a website." Patricia threw a pointed look at me. "She said she didn't know for sure, but she'd heard people talking about a place online where women could post anonymously about their problems. I told her I didn't see how gossiping with a bunch of strangers on the internet would help me get out of my marriage, but she kept insisting that I should try to find it. That I shouldn't feel guilty for asking for help. That I'd be better off without him. I asked her if she knew what the website was called or where to find it, but she said she had no idea. She said she had only heard whispers about it and she wasn't good with computers. Then she left, and I never heard from her again.

"It took me weeks of searching, but I finally found the women's forum she was talking about. I didn't have any luck there. I tried to look Margaret up to thank her anyway. That's when I realized the name she had given me was fake. I didn't know her real name until I saw her on the news a few weeks ago, when they found that man buried in her yard."

Vero's jaw fell open. "Definitely didn't see that one coming."

"Mrs. Haggerty was the one who told you about the women's forum?" I asked in an attempt to distill all this information into some digestible breadcrumb I could follow. The women's forum Patricia was referring to had only been a chat group on the surface. It had also been a thriving whisper network of disgruntled women searching for contract killers who were willing to dispose of problem husbands for a price. Before I'd met her, Patricia had been a frequent visitor to the site, desperate to find someone willing to murder Harris. But no one there had been willing to kill someone who had worked for the Russian mob. That's when Patricia had stumbled onto me, misconstrued the nature of my work, and offered me fifty grand to murder her horrible spouse.

"Look, I've told you everything I know. Can I have my phone back now?" Patricia held out a hand, but I was hardly listening. My thoughts had snagged on something Mrs. Haggerty had said to her. That Patricia would *be better off without him*.

Margaret Haggerty and Penelope Dupree had both given me that exact same advice.

And what had Mrs. Haggerty meant when she said *she was sorry she and her friends couldn't help*? Why had she sought Patricia out? What kind of help had her friends hoped to offer a woman who was desperate to get out of her relationship?

None of the members of Mrs. Haggerty's book club was married.

Except one—Sally.

Sally certainly wasn't happy in her marriage to Robert, and what had Mrs. Haggerty and her friends done for her? They had invited her to join their book club. A woman who worked for the Office of Vital Records had given her a certificate. They had given her a wooden box and a gift bag full of cremains . . .

Everyone has a job to do. Everyone contributes.

Suddenly, everything clicked into place. I could see all the characters and their roles in the story clearly. They all had a job. All made a contribution. Viola, the women's advocate and human resources professional, managed the group. Lola, the nurse, forged medical records at her hospital. Destiny printed death certificates at work. She provided custom engraving for the urns from her Etsy shop, and Birdie stole animal cremains from the shelter to fill them. Then there was Kathy, the cleaner who tidied up the evidence of their crimes and Gita, who used her flower delivery business to handle the memorial arrangements . . .

That tattoo over Mrs. Haggerty's heart—the one she claimed she got years ago—wasn't a three-leaf clover at all . . . it was a *club*.

Mrs. Haggerty wasn't protecting Brendan. She was covering for her friends. But what was Penny's role in all this? And how long until they initiated Sally?

I started the engine.

"Where are we going?" Vero asked.

"We're taking Patricia back to her car. Then we're going home."

"Why?"

"To get ready for book club."

CHAPTER 21

Vero and I raced home from the shelter. The van's tires screamed into the driveway just before dark. Cam greeted us at the door and plucked Arnold Schwarzenegger from my arms. "Where have you been? I was worried! And hungry." He planted a kiss on Arnold's head. "Man, I missed you, little buddy." Cam sniffed his ears. "Why does my dog smell like burgers and fries? He's not supposed to eat that shit. It gives him gas."

"Where are the kids?" I asked, trying not to look as frantic as I felt.

"Watching a movie on the couch."

"And Mrs. Haggerty?"

"Upstairs in her room. I think she's taking a nap."

I felt myself sag with relief. It had been one thing to have her puttering about in my house and homeschooling my children when I'd assumed she was innocent. It was entirely another after hearing Patricia's story. Until I knew for certain what Mrs. Haggerty and her friends were up to, I didn't plan to let that woman out of my sight.

"When's dinner? I'm starving," Cam asked.

"You work on dinner," Vero said to me. "I'll check on the kids."

Cam followed me into the kitchen, talking my ear off about their ride in the Lincoln—which he insisted on calling *The Eggplant*—while I boiled a pot of spaghetti and reheated a container of sauce.

"How was Arnold? Did he behave?" he asked.

"He was a very good boy." Minus the puddle of pee he'd left on the passenger seat of my minivan.

"He is, isn't he? I mean, we're still working on the pissing-on-the-floor thing. Mrs. Haggerty gave me some pointers. She's got a pretty good track record with the potty training and shit. Check it out, Mrs. D." Cam held up a finger to get my attention. "Arnold and I have been doing obedience training. Show her your trick, buddy." Cam sank to his haunches and held out a fist. Arnold lifted a paw and gave it a gentle bump. Cam's face was giddy with pride. "See? Arnold isn't dumb. He's just *extrinsically motivated*," Cam said, enunciating his newfound vocabulary word. "That means you should give him a treat. But if you don't have any, that's cool." He opened the refrigerator. "We'll settle for a beer."

"Nice try," I said, closing the fridge.

"Then how about some of those brownies Mrs. H was telling me about?"

"Not on your life. Our deal was spaghetti and chocolate cake." I served out a heap of spaghetti and passed him the plate.

Cam licked his lips as he carried it to the table. "You won't hear me complaining."

I set one hundred and forty dollars in cash in front of him as he shoveled spaghetti into his mouth. He tucked the money into his pocket as he chewed. "Can I get an extra twenty?" he asked. "I need to catch an Uber back home."

"I thought Mrs. Haggerty was letting you use her Lincoln."

He shrugged as I pried open the lid on the grocery-store bakery box and served him a slice of cake. "She said she needed the car to run an errand tonight, so I left The Eggplant in her garage."

I blinked, wishing he hadn't left me with that disturbing visual. "Any idea where she's going?"

"She didn't say." He cringed around a mouthful of cake. "I just hope she's careful. I used the last of my reward money on that paint job. I offered to help her with her errands before I go, but she said she was tired and needed to take a nap." Cam looked a little glum as he scraped the last of the frosting from his plate. "I guess I won't get to say goodbye."

"Where are you going?"

"My grandma's coming home from her cruise tomorrow, so I'll be heading back to her house. You won't have to worry about me starving at my uncle's anymore." Cam cleared his dishes and put them in the sink. "Tell Mrs. H I'll come back in a couple of days to visit with her and we'll take The Eggplant for a spin. I've got to get back to my grandma's place and clean it before she gets home. I want it to look nice when she gets there."

A car honked outside. "That's my ride. Thanks for dinner, Mrs. D." He kissed my cheek, picked up Arnold Schwarzenegger, and was out the front door before I could give him money for his Uber. Though I was betting he had already used my Venmo to pay himself, and he had probably included a generous tip.

"What was all that honking outside?" Vero asked, coming into the kitchen and peeking in the spaghetti pot.

"Cam's Uber. He said Mrs. Haggerty needed her car tonight." Vero and I exchanged a long look. I leaned against the counter, remembering Mrs. Haggerty's late-night visit to Sally's mailbox. "Hurry up and finish your spaghetti. I'll ask my mother to take the kids for a sleepover. You and I will be running errands with Mrs. Haggerty tonight."

Vero and I fed and bathed the children, packed their overnight bags, and drove them to my mother's house. She had been more than happy to babysit when I'd told her that Vero and Javi were going out on a date and I needed to meet with Sylvia over a late dinner to go over some contracts.

Vero and I had driven straight to Sally Mullen's house from there, parked the Charger down the street a few minutes before nine, and had been staking out her driveway ever since.

Sally's house was atypically dark for the early hour. Every porch light was off, even the coach lamps beside the garage, as if everyone inside was long asleep. Every few minutes a shadowy figure peeked out from behind the curtains.

It was just after midnight when we finally heard the rumble of The Eggplant's engine. We ducked low in our seats as Mrs. Haggerty's Lincoln rolled slowly to the red sign at the end of the block. The purple paint glittered as it passed under a streetlamp and came to a complete and dutiful stop before continuing on to Sally's house. The driver pulled alongside the curb and killed the headlights, then the engine.

I held the binoculars to my eyes and adjusted the focus. Mrs. Haggerty (thankfully) wasn't in the driver's seat. Kathy Sanderson, the cleaner, sat behind the wheel. Another figure was in the back seat. From the staff photos I'd seen on her hospital's website, I was pretty sure it was Lola de la Rosa.

"What do you think they're waiting for?" Vero asked.

"I don't know."

A few moments later, a white van rolled past The Eggplant with its headlights off. It braked before reversing into Sally's driveway, inching back slowly until it was nearly touching the garage. I watched through my binoculars as the driver killed the engine and the taillights cut off.

The vehicle was devoid of markings except for the flowers stenciled along the side. The interior lights remained off as Gita Chaudhary climbed down from the driver's seat. Vero and I ducked as Gita looked both ways up the street before signaling to the others. Elizabeth Chen got out of the passenger side and quietly shut her door.

The curtain in the house peeled back as the rest of the women filed out of The Eggplant and hurried up the driveway. A moment later, the garage door opened. No lights, no motor. Sally braced the door in both hands and gave it a final heave, locking it in place. The women walked past her into the house. Sally followed them inside, wringing her hands.

"What are they doing?" Vero asked, sitting up in her seat.

I adjusted the binoculars' focus. "I don't know. They're all inside the house. They closed the door. I can't see."

"I'm going to get a closer look." Vero plucked her keys from the ignition and got out of the car before I could stop her.

I followed her, careful not to slam the car door. "Don't get too close," I whispered as we shuffled to Sally's house and hid in the bushes. Vero crept out of the hedge and peered into the back of the open van.

"It's a reefer truck," she whispered.

"A what?"

"A refrigeration truck." Her voice became harder to hear as she hauled herself inside. Her phone light flooded the dark interior in a harsh, white glow. "There are insulated compartments in here. Big ones. They're filled with those fancy little potted spruce trees. The ones with white lights and cinnamon-scented pine cones glued all in them. This must be the truck Gita uses for her deliveries."

Muffled voices came from inside the house. "Someone's coming!" I hissed. Vero killed her phone light as the doorknob to Sally's kitchen began to turn. I ducked back into the bushes, pressing myself flat against the side of the house. There was a thump in the back of the truck. I waited for Vero to scurry into the bushes with me, but she must not have had enough time to get that far.

The door creaked open. I peeped out from the hedge as the women began to file out of the house. Lola appeared first. She staggered backward toward the van, her arms looped around something heavy. Destiny hobbled after her, both women bent low at the waist, grunting and breathing hard as they hauled a dark bundle between them. The long parcel was wrapped in something that looked suspiciously like tree netting.

Where the hell was Vero?

I peeked between the bushes, searching for her as the two women hauled their parcel into the back of the van.

"Open the lid," one of them whispered through a strained breath.

"I'm trying, but I can't see anything. It's too dark in here." A heavy thump rocked the frame, followed by a soft grunt.

"Did you hear that?" Destiny's small voice carried from inside the van.

"It's probably gas," Lola said. "That happens sometimes." Another soft thump, like a compartment lid closing. Then the two women jumped down from the back and dusted off their hands.

The rest of the women filed out of the house, stripped off their rubber gloves and hair nets, and deposited them into a trash bag.

Kathy came out last, holding a spray bottle and a wet rag. The chemical scent of bleach wafted from it as she shook it out. Sally tugged down the garage door, bracing its weight with both hands to soften the noise before it hit the ground.

"Let's go," Gita said, closing the van door.

My cell phone vibrated in my coat pocket, and I scrambled to turn it off.

"What's that?" Mrs. Haggerty snapped, eyeing each of the women in turn. "You all know the rules. No phones."

"Sorry!" Destiny reached into her coat pocket, the pale glow of her screen illuminating her face as she checked her notifications. "The kids are staying with a new sitter tonight and I promised her I would keep my phone on in case she needed anything." Several of the women gave her sympathetic nods as she typed a quick message back.

Mrs. Haggerty grabbed Destiny's phone before she could hit *Send*. With an admonishing look, Mrs. Haggerty powered it down and stuffed it in her pocket. "Sally will ride with us. Let's go, ladies. Vi's waiting."

Sally, Lola, Destiny, and Kathy retreated to The Eggplant with Mrs. Haggerty. Elizabeth and Gita climbed back into the van.

I waited until both sets of taillights had disappeared down the street before poking my head out of the bushes.

"Vero?" I whispered, afraid of drawing the attention of Sally's neighbors. I crept out of the hedge, but Vero was nowhere in sight. A sick feeling settled in my stomach as I remembered the quiet thump I'd heard in the van right before Lola and Destiny had hauled their bundle into the refrigerated compartment. It had made the same soft thumping sound when they'd closed the lid. Right before my cell phone had buzzed.

I rushed to turn it on.

"Oh, god. *No, no, no, no*!" I whispered as my notifications began to load.

One missed voice mail message from Vero.

"I'm locked inside the reefer truck, Finlay! Get me out of here. NOW!"

I dialed Vero's number as I ran to the Charger.

She picked up on the first ring, frantic and breathy. "I'm covered in tree sap, there's a pinecone jabbing my ass, and a dead dude in fishnets is lying on top of me. Please tell me you have a plan!"

"Don't panic!" I put my phone on speaker and tossed it in the passenger seat.

"Where are you?"

"Everything will be fine," I said with as much calm as I could muster. She was definitely panicking. My heart stuttered as I pushed the ignition and nothing happened. *Oh, god!* Vero had the key.

I got out of the Charger and sprinted down the street toward my house. "Just relax and stay where you are!"

"That's not funny! Tell me you're right behind me!"

"Not exactly," I said, starting to panic. Because *now* was the time to panic.

"Why not?"

"Because you have the car keys. But do *not* worry," I panted. "I'm running home to get the minivan."

"I'm going to die."

"You're not going to die!"

"A group of remorseless killers are going to cremate me and put my ashes in a jar on some old lady's mantel!"

"We don't know that! Just stay calm," I said, fumbling to retrieve the hidden key from under the downspout and unlock my front door. I hurried inside, grabbed my van keys off the kitchen counter, and ran to the garage.

I got in my minivan, put the key in the ignition, and gave it a hard twist. The van coughed and stalled. I smacked the steering wheel and pushed the gas pedal to the floor. The engine roared and then started to shudder. "Keep your phone on. I'll call you back."

Vero shouted my name as I disconnected and speed-dialed Cam.

He answered on the first ring. "About that last Venmo, I can explain—"

"Listen to me very carefully. I need you to track Vero's phone."

"Is that a trick question?"

"No, it's not a trick question!"

"I feel like it is, because you told me not to do that anymore."

"This is an emergency, Cameron! Vero's missing, and I need to know where she is *right now.*" I left rubber in the driveway as I tore down the street.

"Okay, okay. Don't get your undies in a bunch."

"Where is she?" I asked again, growing more impatient the closer I was to the entrance of the community. Should I go east or west? There was no time for wrong decisions.

"She's on the interstate."

"Which way!" I shouted when I reached the stoplight.

"West. Jeez. Calm down."

I hit the gas and wedged myself into oncoming traffic, then made an illegal U-turn to circumnavigate the light.

"Take the exit ramp coming up. You're about ten miles behind her."

"Do I want to know how you know where *I* am?"

"Probably not."

That was just one more thing I didn't have time to worry about. "Do not lose her, Cam! Text me every turn she makes."

"Fifty bucks and a steak dinner sounds fair. And maybe one of those fancy cheesecakes with the—"

"Just do it!" I disconnected and dialed Vero back. "I'm less than ten minutes behind you. Cam's tracking your phone. Whatever you do, don't turn it off."

"Where the hell am I?"

"I-66 in Prince William County, headed west."

"Fabulous. I can hear the banjos already."

"Don't be hyperbolic."

"If I die," Vero said through chattering teeth, "tell Delia and Zach I love them. And tell Zach I said to keep his pants on. On second thought, tell Javi that, too. And tell him I don't care how many girls he dated while we were apart. Unless one of them was Sophia Martinelli. If he slept with her, tell him I hope he gets gonorrhea in his next life and I'll haunt him from the grave. And tell my cousin— "

"I told you, Vero, I'm not going to let you die. You trust me, don't you?"

"Of course I trust you. Would I be in this situation if I didn't?"

"That's not helping my confidence."

"Just hurry up and get me out of here. It's freezing, I can't breathe, and I think Sally's husband and I just got to second base."

"I'm driving as fast as I can. Just keep your phone on. I'll call you back."

I heard her muffled protests as I disconnected again. Cam texted the number of an exit ramp eight miles ahead of me. I gripped the wheel, trying not to think about everything that could go wrong in the span of ten minutes. My gut said these women weren't going to drive too far tonight. Destiny had kids at home, and they all had jobs to report to in the morning. The women would have to handle their business quickly once they arrived at their destination.

I drove with one hand, my thumb hovering over Nick's name on my phone.

When are you going to start trusting me?

I tapped his number before I could talk myself out of it. He picked up quickly. Too quickly. I didn't have time to think about what to tell him or how to explain. "Hey," he said, sounding pleasantly surprised. "I was thinking about calling you but I didn't want to wake you. I was just leaving the station. Want me to come over?"

I tried and failed to control the tremor in my voice. "Do you remember when you said I could trust you with anything?"

I could feel his smile slip. "What's wrong?"

"Before I tell you, you have to promise me you'll come alone. No backup. Not even Georgia or Sam."

"I can't make that promise. Not until you tell me what's going on."

"You said we have to trust each other. That means you have to trust me, too."

The tension between us crackled through his pause. "Tell me where you are."

"I-66. Westbound. I just passed exit 18. I'll explain everything when you find me, I promise. But Vero is in trouble, and I don't know how much time we have."

Tires squealed through the phone. A siren began to wail. "Pull over and stay where you are. I'm on my way."

I checked a mile marker as it blurred past me. If Nick was just leaving the station in Fairfax, even with his lights and sirens blazing, he was still fifteen minutes behind me. "I can't pull over. I have to get to Vero. Cam is tracking her phone. He's texting me directions. I'm getting off at the exit for Linden. Just get here as soon as you can. I'll forward you my location as soon as I have it."

I disconnected, one hand on the wheel and one eye on the road as I veered off the interstate and began maneuvering the dark country roads, following the directions Cam had sent me.

I dialed Vero. "Are you okay?" I asked the second she answered.

Her teeth chattered. "I don't know. We slowed down. The van's bouncing all over the place. It feels like we might be on some kind of dirt road. Wait . . ." Vero's voice dropped to a whisper. "I think we've stopped. They turned off the engine. I think they're getting out." A car door slammed and Vero whimpered.

I mashed my foot down on the accelerator. "Just stay quiet! Turn off the notifications on your phone. They have no idea you're in the truck. As long as they don't see or hear you, you'll be—"

The line went dead.

"No! *No, no, no!*" My van skidded, nearly running off the pavement as I let my eyes drift from the road to reconnect the call. It went straight to voice mail.

Another text came from Cam with my next turn. Then a second text with a map pin embedded in it. I reduced my speed as the road began to wind and narrow. Ten torturous minutes passed before I reached the final turn onto a winding, gravel driveway. My headlights ghosted over the overgrown branches that formed a dense tunnel around it. I slowed, turning my lights off as I closed the distance to the red pin on the map.

Gita's flower truck appeared around the next bend. The Eggplant was parked beside it, along with two other cars. I recognized one as Viola Henry's Honda, but I had never seen the hatchback parked beside it.

I put the van in neutral and leaned forward in my seat, searching the woods around me for signs of the book club. A distant light burned in the window of a cabin through the trees.

My phone vibrated with an incoming text from Cam. *I like my steaks medium rare.*

I swiped the message away and sent the map pin to Nick before killing the engine.

Pine needles crackled under my feet as I slipped quietly out of my minivan and crept to Gita's flower truck. I pressed an ear to the door.

Not a peep came from inside it, and I tested the lock. My heart missed a beat when the handle didn't budge.

Oh, god. They must have found her. By the time Nick got here, it would be too late. Vero could be chopped up into little pieces. Her head could be stuffed behind a bag of broccoli in a freezer in that cabin before—

The back door of the truck flew open, bouncing off its hinge.

I shrieked, suddenly face-to-face with the barrel of a gun.

Vero sat up on her knees, her arms extended in front of her. She gripped an orange plastic pistol in both hands, swinging it wildly from side to side. Her lips were blue and her face was a sickly shade of car-sick green, her eyes wide and feral. Pine needles stuck in the strands of her hair, most of which had escaped her ponytail in a sunburst of static and snarls.

She collapsed back on her haunches and lowered the flare gun as I pressed a finger to my lips, hoping no one had heard us.

"You scared me to death!" I whispered. My heart was galloping so fast, it could probably run back to South Riding on its own.

"What took you so long? I could have suffocated in there!"

"Keep your voice down." I darted an anxious glance at the cabin, then at the woods all around us. Vero's legs were a little unsteady as I helped her to the ground. "Where did you get that?" I asked, pushing the nose of the flare gun away from me.

"The emergency kit in the spare tire compartment."

"That's a safety device, not a Smith & Wesson."

"And this isn't duct tape," she whispered, shoving a flimsy roll of first aid tape at me, "but a girl's gotta do what a girl's gotta do." She lifted the cover to the wheel well and removed the tire iron from the spare. "Take this," she said, passing it to me. My elbow buckled under its weight. She hooked a small pair of pruning shears into her belt loop and jumped down from the back of the van. "What now?"

"Nick's on his way," I whispered, handing her the tape.

"You called him? Why the hell did you do that? What did you tell him?"

"I told him I needed help and to get here fast. Come on. If we leave now, we can call him from the road and tell him not to come." I would worry about how to explain why once we were a safe distance away.

We started through the brush toward my minivan. A rifle cocked behind us. Vero and I froze.

"Drop everything in your hands and turn around slowly," a woman said.

Vero dropped her flare gun. I let my tire iron thump to the ground.

"Phones and keys, too," the woman demanded.

We dropped our phones and our car keys and slowly turned around. One by one, the members of Mrs. Haggerty's book club came into focus. Viola Henry aimed her rifle right at us. "You two had better come inside. We have a few things we need to discuss."

CHAPTER 22

Mrs. Haggerty and her friends directed us down a narrow path through the woods to a small, rustic cabin with a handful of tiny windows and wide front porch. It was nestled deeply in the trees, camouflaged by the thick landscape. If it hadn't been for the oil lamp burning in the window, I might not have spotted it at all.

"Watch your step," Kathy said, pointing out a fallen log beside the porch. On second look, it wasn't a log at all, but a long human-shaped bundle wrapped in green tree netting.

"Keep moving." Viola nudged me between the shoulder blades with her rifle. The warped wooden planks creaked under us as we climbed the porch steps. I paused at the top to steal a look at our surroundings. The cabin overlooked a pond at the bottom of a hill. Beyond its dark, rippling surface, it was all woods and shadows as far as the eye could see. I wasn't even sure I could find our way back to the minivan in the dark. And even if we could, these women had my keys.

The rusty hinges on the screen door whined, calling my attention back to the house. Lola held it open as we all filed inside. The air in the cabin was close and musty, as if the place hadn't been used for a while. A lantern burned on a table, casting a soft halo of light around a low-ceilinged room with warm wooden walls and butter-yellow curtains. It was sparsely furnished but cozy. Or maybe it was only staged to look that way.

"Sit down," Viola said, pointing out two wooden chairs beside a rickety table. Vero looked to me, but I didn't see how either of us had much of a choice. We both sat down. Gita and Lola came behind us with bundles of tree twine. It chafed against my skin as the women tied my wrists behind my back. Judging by Vero's wince, they were rough with her, too. I was beginning to regret making Nick promise to come alone. A little police backup suddenly didn't sound so bad. And the risk of going to prison seemed preferable to being murdered and wrapped up like a Christmas spruce.

Lola held Vero's cell phone in front of her face, using the facial recognition to access her home screen. Destiny held mine, and I turned away too late as she waved it in front of me.

Vero leaned toward me. "Is this karma?" she whispered out of the side of her mouth. "It feels like karma. All we're missing are donuts and bags over our faces."

Mrs. Haggerty sighed. "I wish you girls hadn't come here."

Birdie pulled out another chair and helped Mrs. Haggerty sit. She looked down her nose at us and shook her head. I felt like a student in her homeschool classroom, but I didn't imagine she'd be giving out stickers for good behavior.

"If you didn't want us crashing your book club meeting, maybe you shouldn't have framed my ex-husband for murder."

"I don't see what you're so upset about," Mrs. Haggerty said dismissively. "All you've wanted for months is to be free of that duplicitous, horrible man. What's wrong with letting him suffer a little? Besides, there's no death penalty in the state of Virginia, and a few years in prison won't kill him."

"She has a point," Vero whispered.

"Steven didn't murder anyone," I reminded them both. "He may have done some terrible things, but killing Penny's husband wasn't one of them."

"You're right. He didn't kill Penny's husband," Mrs. Haggerty conceded. "But you didn't know that when you went storming off to her house. You went because you believed the accusations against him *could* be true. You don't trust that man, you never have. Because he never earned it. And he's made you doubt the only people in your life you shouldn't. So tell me, whose good name are you so desperate to protect—Steven's or your own?" Mrs. Haggerty fixed me with a piercing stare. It was the first time I had looked at the woman and known with complete certainty she was seeing me clearly. That she knew I was hiding secrets, too.

"If I had known *you* murdered Gilford, I never would have let you move into my house!"

Mrs. Haggerty sighed and shook her head. "This is not how our book club meeting was supposed to go. Frankly, I'm not sure what we're going to do now."

"We have to take a vote," Lola said. "Those are the rules."

"I know the rules," Mrs. Haggerty fired back. "I was there when we wrote them. But before we vote on anything, we're supposed to *discuss* it. And it seems we all have some discussing to do." Mrs. Haggerty turned to us and planted her bony hands on her hips. "Why don't you two tell us how much you saw before you followed us here."

"Nothing!" Vero said, shaking her head emphatically. "We saw absolutely nothing. Right, Finlay? And we didn't follow you. Tell them we didn't follow them, Finlay."

Vero's phone buzzed in Lola's hand. She narrowed her eyes at the screen.

"What's wrong?" Birdie asked.

The buzzing continued with a relentless frequency. Lola grimaced as she read. "Someone named Cam is blowing up her phone. He says he knew all along she wanted the eggplant. He says his eggplant is too good for her. That it will never belong to her and he'll make her regret she ever touched it." Vero and I exchanged a look while the women's faces puckered with disgust. Cam must have put a tracer on the Lincoln. He must have realized that Vero's phone was in the same location as the car, and he assumed she took it.

"He sounds like a disgusting jerk," Birdie said.

"If we get rid of the eggplant guy for them, maybe they'll swear not to tell anyone what they saw tonight," Gita suggested. "We can make them part of the club."

"It's not a bad idea," Kathy agreed.

Destiny checked her watch. "Maybe my sitter can stay for a few more hours."

I tried to get up but I was tied to the chair. "No one's killing the eggplant guy! He's practically a child!"

The horrified women gawked at Vero.

"I didn't touch his eggplant!" she cried. "It belongs to Mrs. Haggerty!"

Mrs. Haggerty smacked the table. "Forget all that nonsense. We have far more pressing problems to deal with."

"Um . . . Guys?" Everyone turned to Destiny as she scrolled

frantically through my phone. "Finlay texted our location to someone named Nick. It looks like he'll be here any minute."

"Oh, dear," Mrs. Haggerty said. "That's a shame. I liked that one. He always did smell nice."

"Who's Nick?" Birdie asked.

"He's a detective," Mrs. Haggerty said, rising stiffly from her chair.

A wave of panic rippled through the room. Sally's lower lip began to tremble.

"What do we do?" Destiny asked.

Birdie peeped through the curtains toward the road. "I say we shoot him."

"No!" I wrenched my wrists and bounced in my chair. "That would be a very bad idea!"

"A very, *very* bad idea! He's a really good cop!" Vero called out over the women as they started to argue. "The best! He's like John McClane in *Die Hard,* but with better hair. And a lot more backup!"

I shook my head and whispered to Vero, "I made him promise to come alone."

"What were you thinking!" she cried.

"You were the one who said I was stupid for calling him!"

Viola grabbed her rifle and shoved Kathy and Birdie toward the door. "Put Robert under the porch. The rest of us will deal with the cop."

"Stop! Wait!" I shouted. Panic took hold of me as the women rushed out of the cabin, leaving Vero and me lashed to our chairs. I called after Mrs. Haggerty as the screen door slammed behind her.

We had to get out of here. We had to stop Nick before he made it to the cabin, or the three of us were going to end up in a grave with Sally's husband. All I'd wanted was to prove that Penny had lied about Steven—that she'd known Mrs. Haggerty all along—and Penny wasn't even here.

"What are you doing?" Vero asked me as I started bouncing in my chair. It thumped over the floor as I steered it toward the kitchen. "There must something sharp in here. Maybe we can cut the twine."

Vero bounced up and down in her chair and thumped into the kitchen beside me. "The knife block is empty"

"Help me look for something else."

She followed my lead, using her teeth to grab the knobs and open all the drawers. "There's nothing here!"

"What about the pruning scissors you took from the truck?"

Vero's eyes widened. "They're in my belt, under my coat. Maybe you can reach them."

Vero and I bounced in our chairs, rotating ourselves inch by inch until we were back-to-back.

"You're too far away," I said, stretching my fingers behind me. "Push yourself closer." There was a soft screech as Vero's chair slid backward into mine, close enough for my fingers to brush the hem of her coat. "I've got it," I said, prying the tool from her belt loop. "Hold still. I'm going to try to cut you free."

"If you accidentally kill me and join their creepy book club cult, I swear to god, Finlay, I will never forgive you."

"Shh! I'm concentrating." I gripped the scissors and felt around for the twine. "I really hope this isn't your finger," I said, wedging something long and thin between the blades.

"There's no dismemberment coverage on my cheap-ass HMO, Finlay! Please do not cut off my—"

I squeezed my eyes shut and snipped. When no one screamed, I opened one eye.

Vero leapt to her feet and shook off the last of her twine. She knelt and took the scissors from me. With two quick snips, I was out of my chair.

"What do we do?" she asked, peeking out the window. The women were huddled in a circle, their raised voices muted but clear as they argued with one another at the bottom of the porch.

"I vote we shoot him," Birdie said. Kathy raised her hand. So did Gita.

Sally wrung hers. "This wasn't in the bylaws of the membership agreement."

Lola crossed her arms and paced. "We don't have time to wait for a fucking quorum!"

Viola clutched her rifle. "Whatever we're doing, we need to decide quick. You heard Destiny. He could be here any minute."

Vero crouched under the window beside me. "We need to call Nick and warn him."

"We can't. Destiny and Lola have our phones."

"What about your keys?" she suggested. "If we can get to the van without being seen, maybe we can intercept Nick at the road."

I searched frantically around the room and found my keys hanging on a hook beside the door. I stuffed them in my pocket. "Maybe there's another way out," I said. "Come on."

Vero scurried after me down a short, dark hall. There were only two doors, both of them shut. I tried the knob on the first one, but it was locked. I could have sworn I heard rustling behind it. My heart skipped a beat as I wondered if one of the women might still be inside.

"Hurry!" Vero whispered. "Try the next one."

The next door opened easily. Vero and I slipped inside the bedroom and locked the door behind us. I ran to the window on the back wall.

"It's kind of small. Sure you can fit?" Vero asked. "What? I'm just saying."

"Go!" I wedged it open and gave her a boost. She shimmied through it, grunting when she hit the ground.

"Come on!" she whispered.

I put both arms through the opening, then my head. Vero grabbed my hands and pulled. The window scraped the sides of my coat. I wriggled as she tugged.

"This must be what a farmer feels like when he's delivering a cow."

"Shut up," I hissed as my hips got stuck. "Pull harder!"

Vero gave one final pull, and I came tumbling out. My body hit the ground, the force of it knocking the wind from my lungs. With a wince, I forced myself to my feet.

"I think the minivan is that way. If we cut through the trees, maybe they won't see us." Vero pulled me behind her as she broke into a run.

We rounded the corner of the house. I slammed into Vero's back as she skidded to a stop.

Viola leveled her rifle at us. The rest of the book club stood behind her.

They were all holding knives.

I grabbed on to Vero and started walking us backward. "That explains why the knife block was empty."

Vero put up her hands. "I saw those things in a TV commercial once. They cut through tin cans. And firewood. And blocks of frozen spinach. These ladies are not fucking around, Finlay."

"There's more tree netting in the truck," Gita told the others.

"Wait!" I held out a hand as Kathy and Birdie started toward us. "No one has to die tonight." Vero tugged my sleeve. She jutted her chin at a human-shaped imprint in the dirt where Robert had been a few minutes ago. The ground cover had been scraped away, leaving a trail that disappeared under the shadows of the porch. "No one except for *Robert* has to die tonight," I corrected.

"You have a better idea?" Destiny asked.

"Yes, she does!" Vero called out. "She has a much better idea! A brilliant idea! Tell them your awesome idea, Finlay."

"Right . . . " I said, struggling to come up with a plan that did not involve tree netting or chopped spinach. "Nick will be here in a few minutes. He'll be driving onto private property, outside of his jurisdiction, without cause and without a warrant. Which means all three of us are trespassers, and you are completely within your rights to point that gun at us and threaten to shoot us—"

"That's your brilliant plan?" Vero cried, taking another step backward as the women closed in on us.

"But if you let us go and give us our phones, we can call Nick right now and stop him before he gets here. Vero and I will get in my minivan and leave, and this can all be explained away. As far as anyone needs to know, the only crime you will have committed here is confronting two trespassers on Viola's property, and everyone makes it out of here safely. We can all go home to our families and pretend this never happened. But if you harm one of us—*any* of us," I said, making eye contact with each of them—"there is no going back."

The women cast uncertain glances at each other.

"How do we know you won't double-cross us?" Lola asked.

These women didn't trust me. And for good reason. If Vero and I were lucky enough to walk out of here with our lives, I was damn sure going straight to Nick to tell him what I'd seen tonight.

"We won't say anything. Right, Finlay?" Vero elbowed me in the ribs.

"They won't say a word," Mrs. Haggerty answered for me.

"How can you be sure?" Birdie asked.

"Because these two are as guilty as we are." She pointed a knobby finger at us. "I've been watching both of you for months. Don't think I haven't seen a few things."

Vero tensed beside me. I felt the blood drain from my face.

"Detective Tran was very interested in my neighborhood watch diaries," Mrs. Haggerty continued. "There's one in particular I'm sure he would be very eager to see right about now, considering how curious he is about the two of you. I've been keeping that notebook someplace safe. Didn't figure you'd want the police getting hold of it."

I couldn't be sure how much Mrs. Haggerty had seen the night Harris Mickler died in my garage, or what she knew of Vero's criminal charges in Maryland. But I wasn't willing to take any chances, and, judging by the calculating gleam in Mrs. Haggerty's eyes, she knew it.

"What will you do with it?" I asked as headlights swept across the cabin.

"I suppose that's up to you," she said. "But if you don't want to dig your own graves, you'll keep your mouths shut."

CHAPTER 23

There was a flurry of panic as Nick's headlights approached. Viola issued quiet orders. Knives were hidden, stuffed in pockets, or tossed into the trees. Sally scurried into the cabin to hide. Lola, Birdie, Kathy, and Gita sat on the porch steps, blocking the entry. Mrs. Haggerty stood beside Vero and me at the foot of the stairs. Viola positioned herself like a sentry in front of us.

A car door shut. Footsteps crunched cautiously along the path.

Viola cocked her rifle and stared down the barrel. "You're trespassing on private property," she called out as Nick came into view. "Announce yourself if you don't want to be shot."

Nick paused. He raised one hand and used the other to hold up his identification. His badge glinted in the moonlight. "I'm Detective Nicholas Anthony," he called out. "Fairfax County Police. I'm looking for two women, possibly in distress. I have reason to believe they might be on this property."

"Is anyone else with you?" Viola asked.

"No, ma'am."

"Keep your hands and ID where I can see them." She kept her gun trained on him as he slowly approached the cabin.

She gave his badge a performative glance before lowering her rifle. "I apologize, Detective. I don't get many visitors out here, especially at this time of night. My friends and I were enjoying our retreat, and we heard your car come up the driveway. Women have to be careful. I'm sure a man in your position understands. I hope you'll forgive our hostile greeting."

Nick nodded once, his posture tense and wary, his hand hovering close to his side as he put away his ID. His eyes made a quick pass over Vero and me. "You two okay?"

"We're fine," I said, thankful for the dark as I glanced at Mrs. Haggerty. "It was all a big misunderstanding."

Nick's eyes narrowed on us. "A misunderstanding?"

I cleared my throat. "More of an accident, really." It was, wasn't it? How else could I explain any of this without dumping more lies on the heaping pile that already existed between me and Nick? He stared at me, waiting for an answer. "You see, Vero and I were very concerned about Mrs. Haggerty," I explained. "We heard her leave the house after dark, and she isn't supposed to be driving—"

"Because she's a menace to the public," Vero said through her teeth.

"If we had known Mrs. Haggerty wanted to join her friends at their book club retreat so badly, we would have offered to drive her. But she left without telling anyone where she was going or who she was meeting here. So we followed her." That was all true, if not entirely complete.

"We thought maybe she was having one of those senior moments," Vero said flippantly. "You know, like wandering off and not remembering who she is or where she lives. I, for one, would have been satisfied to pretend she didn't exist and let her shrivel up and die like the big, fat pimple on my ass that she is, but Finlay was determined to go after her, just to make sure she wasn't getting into any trouble. Right, Finn?"

"In a manner of speaking." I was finding it hard to hold Nick's gaze. He wasn't buying a word of this. Any trust I had earned with that phone call, asking for his help, was slipping like cremains through my fingers.

"If you both followed her, why wasn't Vero with you when you called me? You said she was in danger."

Vero threw up her hands. "That was *totally* my fault. See, Mrs. Haggerty stopped to pick up a friend on the way here. They were all following each other," she explained, "and while they were stopped—"

"We were snooping," I admitted. Nick's eyes cut to me. "Vero was curious about what was in the refrigeration truck, and she accidentally locked herself in it. Mrs. Haggerty's friends started driving away before I could stop them. I was terrified Vero was going to freeze to death. But she's fine. See? We're all fine." I winced, remembering Sally's husband.

"What were you looking for?" Nick asked in his cool cop voice.

Vero's eyebrows shot up. "Who, me?"

"You said you were worried about Mrs. Haggerty. But that truck isn't hers." All of Nick's focus shifted to me. "What were you looking for in the truck, Finlay?" A chill tightened my skin, every one of his questions peeling back a layer, leaving me more exposed. He was about to catch me in a lie and he knew it in that way detectives always seem to know that something isn't what it seems.

The cabin door creaked open behind me. "They were looking for me," a voice said.

We all turned to stare at the figure on the porch. In the dim light from the window, I could just make out her short bob and the soft lines of her long sweater. Nick stiffened as Penny Dupree stepped out into the moonlight.

Mrs. Haggerty gasped. The others shot to their feet.

The bathroom. Penny must have been hiding in the bathroom the entire time we'd been here. Just as she had at Birdie's house, during the last book club meeting. When I'd tried to flush the brownies in the toilet, the downstairs bathroom had been occupied. It all made sense now, why Mrs. Haggerty never wanted me to join her club. Why Viola met us on the porch when I'd come to her house. Why Birdie had only cracked the door when I'd knocked, forcing me to barge my way into her home.

They'd been hiding Penny.

Penny had been a member of their book club all along, in cahoots with all of them. And now that Nick knew she had lied, what would these women do to us?

His eyes darted over her as she descended the stairs, as if he was trying to reconcile this modestly dressed, fresh-faced woman with the glamorous blonde he'd met five days ago.

She tucked back a lock of her chestnut hair and hugged her cardigan closed over her chest. "I don't know why you look so surprised, Detective. Finlay's been telling everyone who will listen that she suspected I was lying about her ex-husband. She's a damn sharp and determined young woman. I'm guessing she was looking for proof in that truck because no one was willing to believe her." She shook a reproving finger at him. I reached for Vero's hand as Viola tightened her grip on the gun. The women all tensed. Time stood still, suspended on a fulcrum as we waited for Penny to seal his fate.

Her sigh was heavy with remorse when she finally spoke. "Now that we're all clear on why we're here, would you please call Detective Tran and ask him to meet me at the station? I'm ready to offer him my full confession for the murder of my husband, Gilford Dupree."

The women in the book club cried out.

Mrs. Haggerty reached for her. "No, Penny! You mustn't!"

Penny took Mrs. Haggerty's frail hands in her own. "A man has been murdered, Maggie. The police won't stop looking until they identify the person who killed Gilford. *I* am that person. *I* murdered my husband, no one else. And once I come forward, that investigation will close and no one else has to suffer." Penny cast a meaningful look at her friends. The subtext was clear. As far as the police were concerned, there had only been one murder. Only one body.

One confession would put the investigation to rest.

She squeezed Mrs. Haggerty's hand. Mrs. Haggerty squeezed back.

Mrs. Haggerty sighed and turned to Nick. "I suppose I'm ready to confess, too." The women all gasped, including Penny. A few of them began to cry as Mrs. Haggerty confessed, "I was there the night Penny killed Gilford. I helped her cover up her crime, and I concealed the truth from the police. I have a responsibility in this, too. If Penny is willing to tell her story, then so am I."

"I'm listening," Nick said with an encouraging nod to both of them.

Penny drew a shuddering breath as she prepared to explain. "I fantasized about it all the time," she began. "I felt so trapped. I had never been so relieved as I was on the days when Gilford would pack up his bag after one of our fights and leave for our vacation home in Florida. I didn't care what he was doing there, only that he was gone and I could finally breathe. He always returned in a better mood, so apologetic, bringing me flowers and gifts, and I would have to put on a smiling face and pretend I was happy he was home.

"I had met Maggie at the library that spring. I was so glad to have a friend—Gilford never let me have any, and it was a relief to finally have someone to talk to—someone he didn't know about. I was so careful to keep our friendship a secret because I was terrified he wouldn't let me talk to her anymore if he knew. Things at home had gotten so bad, I cried to Maggie about it all that summer, imagining all the ways I could make my problems with Gilford disappear. To make *him* disappear. But I couldn't do it alone, and Maggie said she couldn't go through with it. It was too risky, she'd said. Too frightening. I was so desperate, I didn't care. My life with Gilford felt like a far worse punishment than the consequences of killing him, but Maggie was convinced we would both be caught, and I was more worried for her than for myself." Penny and Mrs. Haggerty exchanged a tearful smile. "The next time Gilford left for Florida, Maggie met me at the park. We went for a long walk, and I told her I couldn't live one more minute trapped in his house, walking on eggshells, waiting for him to snap. It was him or me, I told her. I had to *do* something.

"Maggie convinced me to run. To pack up and leave town while Gilford was gone. She said I should only take what I needed for a few days, that she would send me enough money to deal with the rest later. I packed a single suitcase. I was just getting ready to leave when Gilford came home and surprised me. He saw my hatch open in the garage with the suitcase inside it and he exploded. He demanded I unpack my car but I refused, so he reached inside to unpack it for me. I don't know what happened—I guess it was my turn to snap," Penny said through an anxious laugh and a sniffle. One of the women pulled a tissue from her pocket and passed it to Penny. She blew her nose before resuming her confession.

"While Gilford was turned away from me, I grabbed the garden shovel from its hook on the wall, and I struck him across the back of his head with it."

Nick listened, silent, every ounce of his focus on Penny, as if he was committing her confession to memory.

"Gilford fell over into the back of my car. His legs were just hanging out of the hatch. When he didn't move, I panicked. The only person I could think to ask for help was Maggie. I knew if I could just get to her house, she would know what to do. I lifted his feet and stuffed the rest of him inside the car. Next thing I knew, I was parked in Maggie's driveway. She told me her landscaper had just finished installing her new rose garden. She said the dirt was soft and the sod around it had only been there a few days. That it would be easy to pull up. We backed my vehicle into her garage, snuck Gilford through the back door into her garden, and had him in the ground just before sunup."

"Owen slept through the whole thing," Mrs. Haggerty recalled with a soft but bitter laugh. "He was a drinker. Had been for years. He had three glasses of scotch after dinner every night and passed out by ten like clockwork. When Penny and I were finished in the garden, I cleaned us both up, washed the shovels, and told her to drive straight to her vacation home in Florida. I told her to wait a full day after she got there before calling the police.

"When Owen woke up the next morning, I told him I needed to run some errands. I drove to the park near Penny's neighborhood, walked the rest of the way to her house, and snuck in through the back door. Then I took Gilford's keys and his phone and left the house in his fancy coupe, right around the same time he usually departed for work in the morning, to keep the neighbors from suspecting anything. I left his car at the park and took my own car home. I only knew Penny had made it to Florida when I saw that Gilford had been reported missing on the TV news."

"You didn't talk to her?" Nick asked.

Mrs. Haggerty shook her head. "Penny and I agreed we would only communicate by hand-delivered letters from then on out, and we would only meet when absolutely necessary."

"It was weeks before we spoke to each other," Penny said. "I thought it would be safer for Maggie if the police never figured out we knew each other. If Finlay hadn't been so determined to prove her ex-husband was innocent, I'm not sure anyone would have ever known."

"Now that we've confessed all our secrets, our only choice is to turn ourselves in." Mrs. Haggerty's eyes made a stern pass over their group, delivering an unspoken message to each of them. This was not up for a vote. Penny and Mrs. Haggerty had made their decision.

"But what will happen to you?" Gita asked them.

Penny and Mrs. Haggerty deferred to Viola. Considering her line of work, she was probably the only member of the book club who was capable of answering.

She frowned as she thought for a moment. "If Penny turns herself in and offers a full confession, she stands a much better chance of securing a plea deal. The prosecutor might consider a lesser charge that carries a shorter sentence. And given Mrs. Haggerty's age and limited involvement in the crime, I don't think the judge would expect her to serve for very long. Maybe six months in a minimum-security prison." Viola looked to Nick for confirmation.

He nodded, carefully wording his reply. "Assuming they can prove to the court she's not a danger to anyone."

Mrs. Haggerty frowned. "Do they have video games in those fancy white-collar joints?"

Nick almost cracked a smile. "I'm sure we can work something out."

"Then let's get this shit show on the road," she said. "The rest of you ladies, clean up this mess and get on home." She handed Vero the keys to The Eggplant. "I'd be grateful if one of you would deliver my car to Cameron's house. Tell him he can take care of it for me while I'm gone." Nick waited while Mrs. Haggerty and Penny exchanged tearful goodbyes with each of their friends. Then, arm in arm, the two women started down the footpath to the cars.

Vero followed them.

Nick took my hand and held me close to his side as we walked. "You're not off the hook yet. I'm assuming we're going to talk about this tonight when we . . ." He paused beside the porch. I turned to see him staring down at the moonlit ground beside it. He frowned at the track Robert's body had made through the pine needles and dead leaves.

Vero, Penny, and Mrs. Haggerty all turned to see why we'd stopped.

We all fell silent as Nick knelt, took his penlight from his pocket, and aimed it under the porch. He swept the beam slowly over the ground. The light sliced through the shadows across an empty stretch of dirt.

Slowly, he stood and clicked off the light. He pulled me close and lowered his voice. "Is there anything about this I need to know?" he asked. Not *What aren't you telling me?* Not *Are you hiding something?* Like every question Nick asked, this one, too, had been carefully worded.

I shook my head. Held his gaze. "There's nothing you need to know."

He glanced back at the remaining members of the book club where they stood huddled by the woods. He dipped his head in farewell as he returned his penlight to his pocket. "You ladies drive safely getting home tonight."

Then he tucked me under his arm and walked me to my van.

CHAPTER 24

It was nearly noon the next day when Penny and Mrs. Haggerty had finally finished meeting with their attorneys. Nick snuck us into a small adjacent room with an observation mirror, where we listened as the two women shared their confessions, one at a time, each of their stories perfectly aligning with the other's recollection of the night Gilford had been murdered. Both women had been careful to leave out any mention of the book club they'd created since and, more important, its intended purpose. According to Penny and Mrs. Haggerty, their story began when they met at the library five years ago and ended the night they buried Penny's husband. When Detective Tran asked if and how they had communicated with each other since, they admitted to a primitive system of hand-delivered letters and, later, a more modern approach using prepaid phones when the discovery of Gilford's body made it necessary for them to come up with a plan.

Penny admitted to having made the anonymous call to Riley

and Max in an effort to frame Steven. When Detective Tran asked her if she'd ever, in fact, had an affair with my ex-husband, she'd laughed outright, which had made me laugh as well. Even Nick had cracked a smile.

Mrs. Haggerty admitted that pinning the crime on Steven had been her idea, because "he was a horse's ass" and she'd "never really liked him anyway." The idea to frame him had come to her in a moment of panic after Gilford's body had been found in her yard. Since Steven had been the catalyst for their unlikely friendship five years ago, she said it seemed only fitting he become their solution to their mutual problem. When Mike Tran had scratched his head, looking befuddled, Mrs. Haggerty explained. It had been a Tuesday night in May five years ago when Penny and Mrs. Haggerty had been the only two people to show up to a book club meeting at the local library. They'd introduced themselves and made polite small talk, and that's when Mrs. Haggerty had mentioned her new landscaping project to Penny. Penny said the garden sounded delightful, and she'd asked who Mrs. Haggerty had contracted to do the work. When Steven's name had come up, Penny said that she was familiar with him already; she had met him once before, when he'd come to deliver a load of mulch to her home a few months prior. The two women had proceeded to gossip about Steven, including the promiscuous behavior Mrs. Haggerty had witnessed while living across the street from him. They had both felt sorry for me, and this small but fertile common ground had opened the first of many conversations between them about their own marital issues. As their friendship bloomed, so had Penny's resentment of her husband and Mrs. Haggerty's sympathy for Penny's situation.

It hadn't escaped my attention that Mrs. Haggerty made no

mention of her own deceased husband, who had coincidentally passed less than a month later. Apparently, it hadn't escaped Mike Tran's attention either.

"Where was Owen on the night you helped Mrs. Dupree bury her husband?" he asked, his pen poised over his notebook.

"Asleep," Mrs. Haggerty said with a dismissive wave.

"Asleep?" Detective Tran repeated, inviting her to elaborate. When she didn't, he asked, "Your husband was home at the time?"

"Yes," she said matter-of-factly.

"And was he in any way involved?"

"No."

"So . . . your husband was asleep upstairs in your bedroom when Mrs. Dupree arrived with the deceased in her trunk, and he remained asleep for the entire . . ." He consulted his notebook. ". . . three hours and thirty minutes it took you to remove the deceased from the vehicle, pull up the sod, dig the grave, bury the deceased, and replace the sod to conceal the location of the body, and he was unaware of those activities the entire time?" The detective's frown was understandably skeptical.

"Owen was a drunk and a heavy sleeper, Mr. Tran. A hurricane could have ripped through our bedroom and blown the roof off the house, and the man wouldn't have noticed. I never told him what Penny and I did that night, and he never seemed to have a reason to ask. As far as he was concerned, I had my new garden, and he was happy not to have to care for it. He never bothered to take much of an interest in it."

My heart ached a little at all the things I didn't hear her say. That her husband had never taken much of an interest in her garden because it was important to her. And he'd never noticed the quiet tempest brewing in their bedroom because he'd been too selfish to see it. I could have sworn Mrs. Haggerty's eyes lifted to the mirror for a second, or maybe it only felt that way. That she had seen herself in me. And maybe that, more than anything, was the reason she had chosen to punish Steven.

"And your husband passed when?" Mike asked.

"Oh, I'd say it was about three or four weeks later," Mrs. Haggerty said, doing the math in her head. "Heart attack. The doctor told Owen to cut back on the drinking and cigars on account of his blood pressure, but the man wouldn't listen. I've got the death certificate at home, if you'd like to see it." I was betting it was an official—if not truthful—certificate from the Virginia Office of Vital Records, probably a gift from Destiny. I was also guessing Mrs. Haggerty had a corroborating report from a physician's office, signed by a helpful nurse practitioner named Lola de la Rosa. The ashes in the cigar box on her mantel certainly looked convincing enough.

Mrs. Haggerty's attorney interrupted. "My client has been more than cooperative. She's had a very long night and I'm sure she could use some rest."

"I have one last question." Mike Tran put down his pen and steepled his fingers over his notepad. "What prompted you and Mrs. Dupree to confess? You'd both done a thorough job of incriminating Steven. Why show up here at the crack of dawn, in the custody of a detective from another jurisdiction, offering a full confession when you were already in the clear? Don't you think that seems a little suspicious?"

Mrs. Haggerty cocked her head. "Are you accusing me of something, Mr. Tran?"

He shrugged. "Let's just say, I'm curious about why you surrendered to Detective Anthony."

"Frankly, because I like him better. If someone's going to get the credit for *collaring* me, I'd prefer it be someone I'd enjoy seeing at my parole hearing. Why? What did Penny say when you asked her?"

Mike cleared his throat, humiliation coloring his cheeks. "That she felt guilty for lying to Ms. Donovan after she and Detective Anthony visited her home, and . . ." Mike Tran's flush deepened. "She said she specifically chose to surrender to Detective Anthony because he's easy on the eyes and he smells good."

I choked out a laugh behind the mirror. Nick put a finger to his lips, but it did little to hide his smirk.

Detective Tran signaled to the officer waiting in the hallway outside. "We're done here, for now. I'll have an officer take you to booking."

Mrs. Haggerty stood stiffly, holding her lower back as she rose from the hard metal chair. "Don't bother, I know the way. This ain't my first rodeo," she reminded the detective. She waved off her attorney's sharp sideways glance as he attempted to shush her, then shook a finger at the uniformed officer in the hall. "Don't even think about putting those handcuffs on me, young lady. I'm tougher than I look." The officer raised an eyebrow and tucked her cuffs back in her belt.

"Sit tight. I'll be right back." Nick left me in the observation room once Mrs. Haggerty and her attorney were gone. A moment later, he came into view on the other side of the mirror, cornering Mike Tran before the detective could follow them out.

"What do you want?" Mike asked, clearly annoyed.

Nick's voice was cold and clear through the small speaker in the wall. "I'm assuming you have everything you need to release Steven Donovan."

Mike gathered his files as he stood. "Those women's confessions don't change the fact that Donovan assaulted a police officer."

Nick put both hands on the table and leaned into Mike's space.

"Which he wouldn't have done if you hadn't goaded him into doing it to bolster your own investigation."

"Donovan's anger management issues aren't my problem."

"Admit it. You pulled the trigger before you actually had a case, and you needed a reason to hold him until you had enough dirt on the guy to make one up."

Mike's face hardened. "You want to talk about dirt? How about we start at Donovan's farm? Just because he wasn't guilty of *this* crime doesn't mean he isn't guilty of something."

"The same could be said of a lot of cops I know." Joey sauntered into the room and slipped a toothpick into his mouth. He leaned against the wall, making himself comfortable. "How are you, Mike?"

Mike stiffened, wary as he silently returned the greeting.

"I couldn't help but overhear all that talk about dirt," Joey said, his cool blue eyes making a slow pass over Mike. "You know, I worked with Internal Affairs for a long time. Even did some work for them while I was here in Loudoun County, but I'm guessing you already heard that. Things like that get around fast. Everybody's careful to warn their buddies, to make sure no one's saying too much around the snitch. But I do hear things, Mike. I hear all kinds of things. I don't bother looking into most of it, because a lot of those cops are good cops, and I don't really see much benefit to the department in recommending internal investigations and making more work for everyone. But sometimes someone rubs me wrong, and I start wondering . . . what if there's some dirt worth looking into?" Joey chewed on his toothpick as he studied Mike's face. A muscle in Mike's jaw tensed under Joey's close scrutiny. "I left IA in pretty good standing. We got rid of a lot of dirty cops when we took Zhirov's organization down. Nick's bust at the sod farm was a big part of that whole operation, and there are a lot of people in the FCPD—not to mention the FBI—who would hate to see all their hard work called into question because you botched a case and figured you'd do something stupid—like reopen someone else's—in some misguided, desperate attempt to save a little face."

Mike gritted his teeth. "I *solved* my investigation. Nick and I were just wrapping up here."

"That's good," Joey said. "I'm glad we understand each other." His eyes trailed Mike as he shouldered past them and out of the room.

"You think he'll push?" Nick asked.

Joey toyed with his toothpick. After a thoughtful pause, he shook his head. "He'd be a fool to try. His nose isn't as clean as he wants people to think it is."

Nick seemed to relax at that.

"You can come out now," Joey called over his shoulder, presumably to me. I poked my head out of the observation room, making sure no one was looking as I slipped into the hall, then into the interrogation room with them. "Why don't you two get out of here and try to get some sleep," Joey said. "You've both had a long night. I'll stick around and make sure Tran signs off on Steven's release."

I opened my mouth to protest, feeling guilty for leaving even though my eyes were so tired I felt like I needed two of his toothpicks to hold them open.

"And don't worry," he said before I could ask. "Cam made me promise to look after Mrs. Haggerty, too."

I nodded, grateful to be able to go home and get some rest. According to my phone, it had been more than six hours since Nick and I had arrived at the police station just before dawn, me in my minivan and Nick following with Penny and Mrs. Haggerty in his Impala. I'd sent Vero home in The Eggplant and promised her I'd text her updates from the station. At some point that morning, only after it had become clear that Mrs. Haggerty and Penny had stayed true to their word not to implicate either of us in their confession, Vero had stopped reading my texts, and I'd hoped that was because she had fallen asleep.

"Thanks, Joe," Nick said. The two men clapped each other on the shoulder, and Nick followed me out of the room.

We were both quiet until we reached the parking lot. I paused, unsure where to go. His Impala was to the left. My van was to the right. Nick paused as well, as if he also wasn't entirely sure where we stood. "You look too tired to drive. Want me to drop you off at home?"

"No, thank you," I said, forcing myself to look him square in the eyes. I didn't want him to drop me off. I wanted him to come home with me. But first, there was something I needed to do.

I took his hand and led him toward my minivan. He looked confused as I slid open the back door. I gestured for him to get in. His mouth quirked up and he almost laughed, until he registered the look on my face. This was not something I wanted to do.

He climbed inside, bending at the knees and the waist to fit as I climbed in after him. I slid the door shut and locked us in. Then I sat down on the floor of my van and gestured for him to sit, too. He eased himself to the floor, his worried frown deepening the longer I didn't speak.

I drew in a steadying breath and said, "Harris Mickler died right here, on the floor of this van, while it was parked in my garage."

Nick paled. I watched the knot in his throat bob. Saw the medical examiner's findings click in place in his mind. *Harris Mickler. Cause of death: carbon monoxide poisoning. Toxicology findings: traces of ketamine.*

"You told me once you wanted to hear my entire story, every

word. That you didn't want me to leave anything out. But there are parts of that story that don't belong to me," I explained. Vero's story, Patricia's, Irina's, the women in the book club, even Mrs. Haggerty's. "I can't—*won't*—share those with anyone, including you. Not because I don't trust you with them but because they're not my stories to tell. But I'm ready to tell you mine. Not because I need your help or your forgiveness. But because I want to. Because we'll never be able to have a future together if I'm not willing to be honest with you."

He was still—so still, I couldn't be sure he was breathing, as if he was afraid the slightest sound or movement would scare me off. He listened, silent and rapt, as I told him about the first time I'd met Harris Mickler. How I'd seen Harris drop a roofie into his date's drink. How I'd switched the glasses, drugging Harris instead, then lured him into my van, fully intending to return him to his home, until Patricia Mickler had told me not to because she was terrified of him.

I told Nick about the horrible things I'd discovered on Harris's phone, and how I had driven him to my house, not knowing what to do. I told him that even though I hadn't killed Harris, I'd been the one to bury him at the sod farm. And how by doing so, I'd accidentally put myself in Feliks Zhirov's path. I explained how Feliks, at every turn, had drawn me deeper into debt with the Russian mob.

I told him about the stolen Aston Martin. About Ike Grindley's accidental death. I told him about the close calls Vero and I had survived in Atlantic City and our brushes with one particularly dirty cop there.

When I was finished, I felt hollow, as if all my insides had just been poured out.

For a long moment, neither of us spoke.

"Why were you and Vero at the cabin last night?" His tone was hard to read. I couldn't be sure what he was thinking or feeling. All I knew was that he expected the truth, and Penny's answer last night had struck at the heart of it.

"Because I needed proof that Steven was innocent, and I didn't think anyone would believe me without it—including you."

He flinched. It was the first time I'd seen a reaction in his eyes since we'd climbed inside the van, as if, of all the horrible things I'd just told him, this was the confession that had hurt him most of all.

His next words sounded like gravel in his throat. "Tell me something that scares you."

I laughed, stunned. What I'd just told him hadn't been terrifying enough? Hadn't taken every ounce of reckless courage I could muster? I was terrified of being arrested. Of going to prison. Of losing my kids. And I had just put all of that on the line for him. "I'm scared of you!" I cried.

"Why do I scare you?" His voice was growing stronger, more demanding, like he needed to know the answer to this more than anything else.

"Because I'm more afraid of losing whatever we might have than the consequences of everything I just told you! Because I love the way you make me feel and the way you are with my children and how patient you are with my mom. Because I love that you read my stupid books and you know how I like my coffee. Because you look at me like I'm the most important person in the world and you answer the phone when I call you, even when you're busy. Because I think I'm in love with you. No . . ." I shut my eyes and shook my head. "Because I *know* I'm in love with you. And the fact that I can't seem to *stop* being in love with you scares me most of all!"

The intensity of his stare was searing. He swallowed hard. "You have nothing—*nothing*—to be afraid of with me."

"You can't make that promise."

"I *can* make that promise, because I'm in love with you, too."

He crossed the floor to me in the span of a heartbeat. His mouth was on mine, my hands were in his hair. The restraints holding us back had all snapped. Suddenly, we couldn't get close enough.

I pushed his jacket off his shoulders, and he unfastened my coat.

"Nick?" I panted as he lowered us both to the floor. "If you're not breaking up with me because I just confessed to manslaughter, grand theft auto, interfering with several criminal investigations, and concealing evidence from . . . well . . . you," I admitted as he unzipped my pants, "do you think we could maybe not do this here?"

He lifted his head, his chest heaving, his body hovering like a live wire over mine. He looked a little dazed as he searched my face. Then a light dawned as it occurred to him where *here* actually was. He glanced down at the apple juice–stained, crumb-crusted carpet where Harris Mickler had breathed his last breath.

"Bench seat?" he asked urgently, jerking his chin toward the third row.

I nodded emphatically. "Perfect."

He had said everything I needed to hear. I'd told him everything I needed to say. There was nothing more we needed to confess to each other as we tumbled into the back seat.

CHAPTER 25

It had taken me nearly two days to recover from the all-nighter I had pulled at the police station (and the hour Nick and I had spent in the back of my van before he'd finally driven me home). He'd fallen asleep curled around me in my bed. When his alarm went off before sunrise the next morning, we had both reached to turn it off and slept through the entire next day.

My mother, upon returning the children to my house on Sunday, had been delighted to find Nick standing barefoot in my kitchen, enjoying a cup of coffee and stirring a pan of eggs on my stove. His shirt was untucked, and a few extra buttons were open. To my surprise, Delia hadn't batted an eye. She'd called out a joyful, "Hi, Nick!," given each of us a vigorous hug, then skipped off to play with her Barbies.

Nick leaned down to let my mother give him a kiss on his cheek as he cooked. "Can I fix you some breakfast, Susan?"

My mother practically swooned. "Me? Oh, no, Nicholas! I already ate, but you're very sweet to offer." She leaned close to my ear and whispered, "I found a fantastic caterer who does very affordable receptions, and my friend Doris knows a wonderful florist who has her own truck—"

"Mom, we're not—"

She held up a finger. "He looks very good holding a spatula, Finlay. Do not screw this up. I have to go. Your father's waiting in the car. I told him we'd go to early Mass so he can get home in time to lay some mulch." She kissed my cheek, too, said goodbye to Vero, and was out the door, a whirlwind of grandma energy. I waved to my father through the window as Nick set two plates of eggs on the table, one for me and one for Vero. He came up behind me and wrapped his arms around my waist.

"I'm going upstairs to grab a shower before I head to the station. Can I convince you to join me?" He nuzzled my neck as his hands wandered to my hips. "Delia already thinks we're taking baths together."

"If we do, you might never make it to work."

He groaned into my shoulder.

I turned in his arms, tipping my face up for a proper kiss. "Can't I convince you to play hooky? It's a beautiful day. Vero and I thought we'd take the kids to the park. Javi's coming, too. You should join us."

"You're definitely making it hard to leave," he said as I looped my arms around his neck. "I promise, I'll be out the door at a reasonable hour tonight. How about I pick up dinner so you and Vero don't have to cook?"

"Throw in a bottle of wine, and I might agree to let you go."

"Done."

My mother was right. He was definitely a keeper.

He stole a bite of my eggs, washed it down with the last of his coffee, and double-timed it upstairs to get ready for work. I thought hard about his offer to join him in the shower, but my stomach growled and his cooking smelled far too good to pass up.

I called Vero to the table and our eyes rolled up in pleasure as we scarfed down our breakfast.

An engine rumbled outside. I peeled back the curtain to see Steven get out of a taxi. His jaw was dark with a few extra days of growth, and he was wearing the same clothes he'd had on the day Mike Tran took him into the station for questioning. He raked his hands through his unkempt hair as he walked to my door.

"Kids!" I called up the stairs. "Guess who's here!"

I opened the front door as the children thundered down the stairs. "Daddy!" they cried, leaping into his arms.

"Man, am I glad to see you two!" His eyes were a little wet as he held them and breathed them in.

"When did you get out?" I asked.

"About an hour ago. I came straight here. I would have called, but my battery was dead on my phone when they gave me my stuff back."

"Did you bring us a souvenir?" Delia asked. "Mrs. Haggerty said they do arts and crafts in jail, and she learned to make all kinds of things."

"I bet she did." He gave each of the kids another kiss, like he couldn't get enough of them. Maybe Mrs. Haggerty had been right, that a little time in the clink wouldn't be the worst thing for him. Sometimes, you don't realize how precious something is to you until you're faced with losing it.

He beamed at Zach. "Look at you, buddy, keeping your pants on like a big boy!"

"At least there's hope for one of you," Vero called out from the kitchen.

Steven's cheeks reddened, but, to my surprise, he didn't fire off a comeback.

He set Zach down, pulling back a little to look at Delia's face. "A little birdie told me you're going back to school tomorrow."

"Yep!" Delia said proudly. "After we went for ice cream, Mrs. Haggerty told Cam to drive us to my school in his giant eggplant. Arnold Schwarzenegger came, too! Then Mrs. Haggerty went inside to meet with the principal. Arnold didn't like her." Delia curled her fingers into claws. "He growled at her and peed on her floor. Mrs. Haggerty didn't like the principal either. She told her if they didn't let me come back to school, she was going to call her grandson and make a fuss. She said her grandson is a very important *polly-tippan*, and they'd better listen if they don't want to be on the TV, too. Mrs. Haggerty is famous, Daddy! All my teachers knew her!"

"That's . . . Wow," Steven said, looking at me. I shook my head. This was the first I was hearing about their field trip to the school, but that would explain the strained voice mail I'd received from Delia's principal yesterday, saying Delia was welcome to return to class on Monday.

Steven set Delia down and she tore off after her brother to play.

"Which little birdie told you?" I asked, wondering how he'd been getting his information while he was in lockup.

"Mrs. Haggerty wrote me a letter and asked one of the officers to deliver it to my cell. She apologized for letting the police arrest me before deciding to come forward. She told me all about homeschool and potty training and how well the kids were doing. And she said that if I screwed anything up for you, she'd make me disappear and it would look like an accident."

Vero snorted in the kitchen.

Steven smiled in spite of it. So did I.

"She also mentioned you bonded her out." He raised an eyebrow when I nodded.

"The judge set a very reasonable bail. I couldn't let her stay in that place, so Vero and I picked her up and brought her home with us."

His smile wavered. "She isn't here now, is she?" he asked, looking a little unnerved by the possibility.

"She's upstairs packing. Apparently, her grandson is coming to pick her up in an hour." I still had my doubts, but if and when he did show up, I had several questions I expected answers to, and I was sure Vero had a few choice words for him.

Nick came down the stairs, smelling like soap and shaving gel, his hair damp from the shower. He slowed on the bottom step when he spotted Steven.

Steven nodded and mustered a smile. "Hey, Nick. Good to see you."

Nick nodded back. "I'm glad to see you, too."

Steven bit his lip. "I guess I have the two of you to thank for that. So, thanks," he said, sincere in his gratitude. "You didn't have to help me. I wouldn't have blamed you if you didn't. But I'm grateful for everything you did to get me out of there. Joey, too. Tell him thanks for me."

"I will," Nick said. "I'll let you two talk. I have to get to work." He gave me a quick peck on the cheek and whispered, "I'll see you tonight."

Steven stepped aside to let Nick pass. I watched him go, already counting down the hours until he got back. "He seems like a really decent guy," Steven said with a strained smile.

"He is."

"That's good. You deserve to be happy."

"Thanks. I want that for you, too." Steven didn't deserve to be happy with *me*, but I hoped one day he'd be worthy of a chance at happiness with someone else.

"Speaking of that," he said, brightening a little, "you know that redhead attorney you sent to help me—Parker? You wouldn't happen to have her number, would you? Because I was thinking—"

"Goodbye, Steven," I said through a dry laugh. I handed him his truck keys and pushed him toward the door. The kids called out their goodbyes from the playroom as I closed it after him.

When I turned, Mrs. Haggerty was coming down the stairs, her footsteps a little uneven and heavier than usual. She looked tired and sore as she limped into the kitchen. The last few days had definitely taken their toll on her. She filled a kettle and put it on the stove, waiting for it to boil as she prepared her tea.

"Thank you for what you did for Delia," I said, leaning on my elbows beside her.

"Nonsense. I didn't do it for Delia. I did it for you," she said, her frankness surprising me. "Sometimes, you remind me of me," she admitted. "I always wanted to write a book of my own, but Owen used to say writing stories was frivolous. And I didn't have anyone like Vero to help me when my children were young. The closest thing I had to a friend was Penny, and she and I didn't find each other until much later on. Honestly, I envied you. Never more than the day your husband moved out," she said with a rueful smile. "Oh, how many times had I wished that for myself."

"Is that why you did it?" I asked quietly.

"Did what?"

"You know . . ." I dragged a finger across my neck.

She laughed, surprising me with a full-throated chuckle I'd never heard from her before. "I didn't kill Owen. Owen killed Owen, exactly like I explained to Detective Tran. I told my husband for years he was going to end up in an early grave if he didn't take better care of himself. That if his liver didn't kill him, his blood pressure would. In the end, it was both."

"But if Owen died of natural causes, why haven't you cashed his insurance policy?" I could have understood holding on to it if she was afraid she might get caught using a forged death certificate, but that was an awful lot of money to continue paying every month to insure a man who had a legitimate one. "Why not collect the balance of the policy and stop paying?"

She sighed and shook her head. "Guilt, I suppose. My marriage to that man was far from perfect. There were plenty of angry, lonely nights when I laid awake and thought about smothering him with a pillow. For all his flaws, I know I never could have done it, but we weren't happy together, and I wasn't all too *unhappy* about it when he died. I guess it didn't feel right to collect a reward for it. But," she said, holding up a finger, "that doesn't mean I can't understand how another woman might be driven to kill her husband and use that money to build herself a new life."

"Is that why you started the book club?"

"I guess you could say I started the book club out of guilt, too," she admitted. "It was gnawing at me. Not because I had helped put Gilford in the ground, but because I had convinced Penny to run away from her problem. If I had helped her deal with him, like we had talked about so many times, we could have been more careful. She wouldn't have been forced to handle that nasty business all by herself. I felt so awful about the whole thing. I just wanted to fix it," she said, pouring herself some hot water from the kettle. "I had been volunteering at the women's advocacy center with Viola for several months before I finally confided in her. I danced around the details, but something told me she understood the things I wasn't coming out and saying. She told me she had a family cabin in the woods, that if I had burdens I didn't feel I could hold on to anymore, for myself or anyone else, that she would take them and she would keep my secrets safe. She explained that she understood the guilt I felt. That she had guilt, too, over all of the women she wanted to help but couldn't. That's how I knew we understood each other.

"I thought about asking her to take Gilford, but moving him seemed like a reckless idea. Months had passed and no one had come looking for him. Better, we thought, to let sleeping dogs lie. But," Mrs. Haggerty said, tapping her temple, "Viola's offer had opened the door to other ideas.

"The club grew one by one after that. Inevitably every new member wanted to pay it forward and help someone else. Viola found Lola. Lola found Destiny. Destiny found Elizabeth. Elizabeth found Kathy. Kathy found Gita. And Gita found Sally." Mrs. Haggerty looked at me askance as she dropped a spoonful of sugar in her mug. "I stand by my opinion of your ex-husband, by the way. You know where to find me, if you ever change your mind."

I laughed. "Thanks for the offer, but I think we'll be fine."

"Why don't you go on upstairs and take a shower. You look like you need one," she said, resuming her usual judgmental tone, though now I sensed a glimmer of genuine affection in her teasing. "I'll watch the children for you," she offered.

I only hesitated a moment before relenting. In spite of her veiled threats to Steven and Delia's principal, Mrs. Haggerty wasn't a terrible person after all. Vero was just upstairs doing the laundry, the kids were playing peacefully, and Zach was fully dressed and potty trained. What could possibly go wrong?

EPILOGUE

My joy was cut short when Vero came bursting into my bedroom not ten minutes later. She banged on the bathroom door. "You might want to get dressed and get downstairs," she called through it.

I turned off the water and wrapped a towel around me. Vero tossed a pair of sweatpants in my arms when I came out dripping.

"What's wrong?" I asked. My clothes stuck to my damp skin as I quickly put them on. The last time Vero had dragged me out of the shower, Zach had covered the walls with poop. "Please tell me Zach's not finger painting again."

"Worse. Sylvia's here."

"She can't be here! She was supposed to be on a train back to New York two days ago!" I had already broken the news to her that Nick and I had no intention of signing the TV deal. I reached under my shirt to slap on some deodorant. "She must be holding out for a signature."

"I don't think it's your signature she's looking for," Vero said as she towed me down the stairs.

I froze at the sight that awaited me in my kitchen. Mrs. Haggerty and Sylvia sat at my kitchen table, their heads bent together, a pot of tea steaming between them. My stomach lurched as I recognized the spiral notebook in Sylvia's hands.

"Maggie, this is sensational," Sylvia said, holding it to her chest. "It's as riveting as *The Girl on the Train*. Or *The Woman in the Window*! We'll call it *The Killer Across the Street* and pitch you as the next Paula Hawkins." Sylvia practically swooned as she stroked the cover. "The diary format is so unique. It has such a raw, *brutally* honest quality to it. It's the literary equivalent of reality TV! The whole thing feels like one big dirty secret." She leaned closer to Mrs. Haggerty and placed a hand on her arm. "You said there are more of them. How many?"

Mrs. Haggerty looked at the ceiling, as if counting in her head. "Oh, they go back about five years or so."

"Five years!" Sylvia clapped her hands and rubbed them together. "I smell series potential. If you don't mind, I'd like to take this one with me. You know, feel out a few editors and see if anyone bites."

"Bites on what?" I asked, piercing Mrs. Haggerty with a hard stare. She looked up at me and smiled as if I hadn't just caught her breaking her word. She'd promised me she wouldn't show that diary to anyone so long as Vero and I kept our mouths shut about her friends, and here she was, delivering evidence of my crimes to someone who would love nothing better than to create a behind-the-scenes documentary-drama to follow my already problematic TV series.

Sylvia waved me to the table. "Finlay! You're just in time! How have you been hiding this extraordinary talent from me all these years? Have you seen Maggie's diaries? They're brilliant! I'm going to make this woman the next Gillian Flynn."

Wonderful. My overbearing agent and my tyrannical neighbor were already on a first-name basis.

"You can't do anything with that!" I argued. "It's not even a book, Sylvia!"

"Don't be so negative. Think of the possibilities!"

"Believe me, I have!" Including all the probable convictions that came with them.

"There could be something really special here," Sylvia said. "Your first manuscript was the most god-awful thing ever written, Finlay, but look what I made of you." I didn't have time to gasp over the insult before she stuffed the diary in her messenger bag.

"This notebook may not be anything yet, but it could be. All the content is already there," Sylvia said. "Except for those missing pages, of course. Are you sure you can't find them?" she asked Mrs. Haggerty. "I'm dying to know what happened in October and November. The entries over the summer were real doozies!"

Mrs. Haggerty smiled, catching my eye across the kitchen. "I think I must have spilled tea on those pages. I'm sorry. I don't really remember much of them." The look on her face said she knew exactly what she'd written on those missing pages and she knew exactly where they were hiding. But for now, it seemed, we'd both held up our ends of our bargain.

"I'm sure we can come up with something even better," Sylvia said. "I'm telling you, Finn, it has all the makings of a bestseller—the mystery, the intrigue, the sex! All it needs is the right ghostwriter. Have you two considered partnering? Maybe you could even bring your hot cop in on the deal. I still want both your signatures on that offer, by the way." She looked at her phone as she rose from her chair. "We have some extra time before my train leaves. Maybe we should stop by the police station and try to change his mind."

"It's Sunday. He's not at work," I blurted. Anything to keep her from showing up there again.

"That's even better," she said, undeterred. "I've been itching to see where Nick lives." She fanned herself as a hot flash came over her, and her décolletage started to sweat. "His bedding is probably very manly. I bet it smells good, too. Grab your keys, Finlay. You can drive me to his place on our way to the station. I can have everything I need in less than ten minutes. And I can get his signature, too." I felt a little sick as she winked.

The doorbell rang. I peeked through the front curtain. A white Volvo was parked in my driveway. Vero beat me to the front door, staring daggers at Brendan. "You have some explaining to do. Where the hell have you been?"

The weather in Florida had obviously been good. There was a fresh tan line across his forehead, and his nose and cheeks were peeling and pink. He looked at us, abashed. "Maggie didn't tell you? I took an impromptu vacation. It was her idea. I've been under so much stress between her arrest and the campaign announcement, she suggested a cruise might be just what the doctor ordered. It was! I feel like a new man."

Vero scorched him with a blistering look. I wasn't feeling so understanding myself.

His face fell. "I'm sorry," he said earnestly. "I assumed you knew. Maggie said she got the idea from the person who's been babysitting for you. She called me the night I dropped her off and said she had met the most wonderful young man who had booked a cruise for his grandmother. She said he taught her how to use the internet, and she used it to find a good deal on a last-minute reservation through a vacation company in Florida.

"I told her I didn't feel right leaving, that it wouldn't be fair to ask you to host her any longer than necessary, but she assured me she had discussed it with you and you had agreed she could stay through the rest of the week."

I cast a long, hard look at Mrs. Haggerty as she sipped her tea. "She did, did she?"

"What about the repairs to her house?" Vero asked, hands on her hips. "You were supposed to set all that up last week."

"I did!" he said, as if this was all news to him. "I had all the contractors booked to come out and give her estimates for the repairs. Maggie sent me a voice mail, saying everything was fine and the repairs were being handled. Grandma," he said, moving past me into the kitchen where his grandmother was avoiding his eyes. "I thought you said I didn't have any reason to worry."

"Because there was nothing you needed to be worried about. You've been working too hard, and you've been under too much stress. All that nonsense about solving the case yourself to prove my innocence . . . It wasn't good for you, losing sleep every night reading the news and talking to the police, looking for a way to get me out of jail." She waved off his concern. "You had enough to worry about without having to be a hero for me. I decided the house could wait until you got back—I had everything under control here. Besides," she said stubbornly, "if I did move back home, who would handle Zach's potty training and Delia's homeschooling? Finlay needed my help. And if I went home to that big old empty house on my own, who would keep my young friend, Cameron, company? I had very important things to do here."

"I see." Brendan turned to Vero and me and touched his heart, chagrined. "I'm deeply sorry for the misunderstanding. Thank you for letting her stay. I'm indebted to you both. I hope she wasn't any trouble."

"No trouble at all," I assured him.

"If I can ever return the favor—" he began.

"Actually," I said, recalling the location of his condo, "I can think of one thing you could do for us."

"Anything," he said.

"My friend Sylvia could use a ride to the train station. I know it's a few miles out of your way, but would you mind dropping her off?"

Brendan beamed. "It would be my pleasure."

Vero scurried upstairs, all too eager to gather Mrs. Haggerty's luggage.

"I don't suppose you were following the news while you were gone?" I asked Brendan cautiously, wondering what other information Mrs. Haggerty had withheld from him.

"Not at all," he said with a chuckle. "Internet was limited on the ship, and to be honest, I was just so relieved the charges against Maggie had been dropped, I did my best not to think about it. I did see that Gilford Dupree's wife confessed to the murder. Maybe now that they have the culprit in custody, we can all put this terrible situation behind us and move on with our lives."

I smiled, pressing my lips shut, letting him enjoy his few last moments of ignorant bliss.

Vero dumped Mrs. Haggerty's luggage at Brendan's feet.

"Ready to go, ladies?" he asked, offering his grandmother an arm. His eyes grew wide as she stood and stepped out from behind the table. He stared, openmouthed, at the glittering tracking bracelet around her ankle. Delia and Vero had bedazzled it with purple rhinestones to match the finish on her car, and it gleamed like a disco ball above her bright white orthopedic sneakers.

"This is Brendan, my grandson," Mrs. Haggerty said to Sylvia.

"He's a politician," she added proudly, making Brendan blush. "Brendan, this is Sylvia, my literary agent."

Brendan's eyes grew even wider. "Your . . . literary agent?"

"Sylvia is going to help me write a book," Mrs. Haggerty announced.

I patted Brendan on the shoulder when the cat stole his tongue. "It seems you and your grandma have a little catching up to do. Oh," I said as I handed him a business card. "I almost forgot. This is the phone number for your grandmother's bail enforcement officer. I posted bond, so don't let her miss her sentence hearing. The date is written on the back. I'll let her fill you in on the details of her plea bargain. But don't worry," I said, gesturing to Mrs. Haggerty's ankle monitor. "I was certain to let the court know she'd be staying with you for a while."

"Just make sure she stays within three hundred feet of your condo or her alarm will go off," Vero added.

Brendan's sun-kissed cheeks turned a little green. Mrs. Haggerty took the handle of her suitcase and nudged Brendan toward the door, gesturing for him to carry Sylvia's bag. Sylvia gave me a big, squishy hug. I suppose sharing her bra had graduated me from agent-client air-kisses to boob-mashing besties. Or maybe that title belonged to Mrs. Haggerty now. I wasn't sure.

"Give Nick a kiss goodbye from me," Sylvia said to me, "and tell him no hard feelings about the ride-along. We'll do it next time. I'll be back before you know it. Maggie agreed to draft her debut novel while she's stuck on house arrest. I told her if she goes to prison, it'll sell like hotcakes and she'll have plenty of time to work on her memoir." Brendan looked like he might be sick as he helped Sylvia into her faux fur stole. Sylvia wagged a finger at me on her way out the door. "Tell that hot cop of yours he'd better be good to you, or else."

When they had all gone, Vero and I sagged against the wall.

It was over. Mrs. Haggerty was out of my house. The charges against Steven had been dropped. Mike Tran was (for now) off our backs. Delia was going back to school on Monday. Zach was (for the most part) potty-trained. And even after confiding (almost) everything to Nick, I was pretty sure we were going to be okay.

"Got any more of those brownies?" I asked Vero, ready to celebrate. Or sleep.

"I thought you'd never ask." She shuffled to the freezer. Frowning, she moved the broccoli, then the peas. She turned and slammed the freezer door shut. "Someone stole my brownies!"

We both tipped our heads as the doorbell rang. I glanced back at the foyer, thinking maybe Mrs. Haggerty had forgotten something, but all the luggage was gone.

"Maybe it's Javi," I suggested.

"Or Nick."

Vero and I went to answer the door together.

Two uniformed police officers stood on the porch.

"Sorry," Vero said, "if you're looking for Margaret Haggerty, you just missed her. She went home with her—"

One of the officers held out an envelope. "Veronica Ramirez?"

Ramirez, he'd said. Not Ruiz.

Vero and I both stiffened. No one in Virginia knew her by that name. It was the name she'd abandoned when she'd fled her charges in Maryland—the one she had been so careful not to use here for fear of anyone finding her.

Her voice was brittle. "Who wants to know?"

"We have a warrant from the Virginia Governor's office. Would you please come with us?"

"A warrant for what?" I held an arm in front of her when the officer reached for his handcuffs. Vero hadn't committed any crimes in Virginia—at least any the state knew about.

"We received a report of a stolen vehicle on Thursday night—a purple 1979 Lincoln Mark V. The caller said he had reason to believe a Ms. Veronica Ruiz was in possession of the car."

"Oh," I laughed, "that was a very simple misunderstanding, Officer. See, the car belongs to my neighbor."

"We're aware of that. We were unable to reach her. I assume that's the vehicle?" he asked, pointing to The Eggplant in my driveway, which Vero hadn't yet gotten around to delivering to Cam.

"What gave it away?" My laugh fizzled when the officer didn't smile back. "I can explain. You see, my neighbor doesn't have a license, so she gave us the keys and asked us to hold on to it for her."

The officer looked skeptical. "I'm sorry, ma'am. But it will be up to the court to hear any extenuating circumstances." He reached past me and handed Vero the letter. "While we were conducting our search for the vehicle, we also found an outstanding warrant for Ms. Ramirez for theft charges in the state of Maryland."

Vero paled as she opened the letter. There were tears in her eyes when she looked at me and said, "They found me, Finn. I'm being extradited."

ACKNOWLEDGMENTS

This book, as with all the others, wouldn't have made it to the finish line without the support and encouragement of many wonderful people. My innumerable thanks to everyone who helped make this fifth Finlay adventure a success.

Steph Rostan, Courtney Paganelli, Melissa Rowland, Tim Wojcik, Miek Coccia, and the entire LGR team, you are the most wonderful found family I could ever ask for. Thank you for all you do for me and Finlay.

Team Finlay, how did I get so lucky to work with you? Kelley Ragland, Kelly Stone, Catherine Richards, Allison Ziegler, Sarah Melnyk, Lisa Davis, Isabella Narvaez, Claire Beyette, David Rotstein, Omar Chapa, Alisa Trager, John Morrone, Gail Friedman, Rowen Davis, you are the bee's knees. These books are so much fun to make because of the creativity, talent, and passion in this group.

Sanjana Seelam and Jordy Moblo, thank you for being my tireless champions.

Angela Dawe, narrator extraordinaire, I am your biggest fan! I can't begin to articulate what your contribution to this series means to me and my readers. You are a gift, and I am ever so grateful for you. Thank you for being my Finlay.

Catherine McKenzie, Kara Thomas, Mary Behre, and Hannah Morrissey, thank you for helping me brainstorm through the tough stuff. This book is better because you are all brilliant.

Ashley Elston and Megan Miranda, thank you for always being there. Thirteen years and three times that many books, and we're all still here.

Beyond the books and the writing, I'm grateful for the support of friends who help me keep my sense of humor, even on the darkest days. Jen Harrigan and Nicole Sullivan, thank you for the laughter and the shoulders to lean on. You make my world a brighter place.

My Virginia author squad (Katharine, Sara, Emily, Kate, Polly, Olivia, Rachel, Hannah, and Jo), I am so glad we found each other. Thank you, Flannery and Chelsea at Bluebird & Co, for bringing us all together.

Thank you to every reader who preordered a copy of this book! Preorders help extend the life of a series, and it's because of you that I get to keep doing this thing I love.

And finally, thank you to my family. My nest might be empty, but my heart is full. Tony, Connor, and Nicholas, I love you to the moon and back.

ABOUT THE AUTHOR

Holly Virginia Photography

Elle Cosimano is a *New York Times* and *USA Today* best-selling author, an International Thriller Writers Award winner, and an Edgar Award nominee. Elle's debut novel for adults, *Finlay Donovan Is Killing It,* kicked off a witty, fast-paced contemporary mystery series that was a *People* magazine pick and was named one of New York Public Library's Best Books of 2021. The third book in the series, *Finlay Donovan Jumps the Gun*, was an instant *New York Times* bestseller. In addition to writing novels for teens and adults, her essays have appeared in *HuffPost* and *Time*. Cosimano lives with her husband and two sons in Virginia.